Seasons of the Sword #4

紫

MURASAKI

A Kunoichi Tale

David Kudler

S

Stillpoint/Atalanta

Also by David Kudler

Seasons of the Sword
RISUKO · BRIGHT EYES · KANO · MURASAKI

Kunoichi Companion Tales
(Seasons of the Sword Prequels)

DEADLY BLOSSOMS:
White Robes, Silk & Service, Waiting for Kuniko, Wild Mushrooms, Ghost,
Schools for Gifted Youngsters: Headmistresses' Monthly Dinner

Shining Boy*, Blade*, Little Brother*, Old Wood*

* Coming soon

Find out more on **SeasonsoftheSword.com**

Follow on:
twitter.com/RisukoKunoichi • risuko-chan.tumblr.com
facebook.com/risuko.books • instagram.com/RisukoKunoichi
risuko.livejournal.com • tiktok.com/@kanomurasaki

MURASAKI

Murasaki: A Kunoichi Tale
Seasons of the Sword #4

Stillpoint Digital Press
Mill Valley, California, USA

Cover design by James T. Egan of Bookfly Design

Book design by David Kudler and Stillpoint Digital Press

ISBN: 978-1-938808-75-3 (hardcover)
ISBN: 978-1-938808-73-9 (pbk.)
ISBN: 978-1-938808-74-6 (e-book)

1. Japan—History—Period of civil wars, 1480–1603—Fiction. 2. Ninja—Fiction. 3. Conspiracies—Fiction. 4. Determination (Personality trait)—Fiction. 5. Young adult fiction.   I. Title.

First edition, September 2025
Version 1.0.1 (Rev 2)

Want to know what happens next in Seasons of the Sword?
Join thousands of readers getting exclusive stories, character secrets, and early access to new releases. Scan the QR code or visit **SeasonsoftheSword.com/sign-up**—your first bonus story unlocks immediately.

SeasonsoftheSword.com

To Manra
My companion, my guide,
my destination

—

春なのに
紅葉思う
初終

—

Contents

Characters

Note: *In Japan, as through most of East Asia, tradition places the family name before the given name. For example, in Kano Murasaki, Risuko's proper name, Kano is her family's name and Murasaki her given name—what English speakers would call her first name.*

Historical figures are marked either with an asterisk (*) or, if they do not appear in this book, with a dagger (†).

Kano Clan (Risuko's Family) and Neighbors:

Risuko—*kunoichi* bodyguard to Oda Hachihime; proper name Kano Murasaki; aka Squirrel, Bright Eyes, and Mouse

Okā-san—Risuko's mother; proper name Kano Chojo

Usako—Risuko's sister; proper name Kano Daini

Otō-san—Risuko's father; a disgraced samurai turned scribe; proper name Kano Kazuo (presumed dead)

Naru—Pig farmer

Miku—Naru's daughter

Irochi—Chicken farmer

Mochizuki Clan (Residents of the Full Moon):

Mochizuki Chiyome*—Mistress of the Full Moon; aka Spiderface

Yuri Mieko—Lady Chiyome's maid; *kunoichi* assassin; head teacher; *miko* dance master; currently impersonating Monogami Kuniko, rightful Lady of Wingtip (*Dewa*) Province

Tarugu Toumi—*kunoichi* spy; bodyguard to Oda Hachihime; aka Falcon

Hanichi Emi—*kunoichi* assassin; bodyguard to Oda Hachihime; aka Smiley and Sourpuss

Aimaru—servant, soldier, and a former initiate at Mount Wisdom; aka Moon-cake and Moon Face

Little Brothers—Lady Chiyome's carriers, bailiffs, and bodyguards;

Kee Sun—cook and herbalist (Korean)

Shino—*kunoichi* bodyguard; former senior initiate

Sachi—*kunoichi* spy; espionage teacher; miko music master; aka Flower

Hoshi—*kunoichi* bodyguard; armed combat teacher; miko calligraphy master; aka Horsey and Ho-*chan*

Mitsuke—*kunoichi* spy; strength and archery teacher; miko etiquette master

Rin—*kunoichi* assassin; garrote teacher; miko dance master

Chinatsu—novice; friend of Emi

Junko—novice; friend of Emi; aka Ju-*chan*

Yoshi—novice; friend of Emi

Monogami Kuniko—Lady Chiyome's maid; *kunoichi* bodyguard; combat teacher; miko ritual master; rightful Lady of Wingtip (*Dewa*) Province (dead)

Mai—former senior initiate; aka Foxy (dead)

Fuyudori—former senior initiate and spy for Lord Oda; aka Ghostie (dead)

Takeda Clan:

Takeda Shingen*—Lord of the Takeda clan of Worth (*Kai*) Province, allied with the Oda and the Matsudaira; aka The Mountain and The Tiger of Kai

Baba Nobufusa*—Takeda captain

Hara Masatane*—Takeda captain

Takeda Masugu—Takeda lieutenant; aka Gugu

Yamamoto Yaeko—Masugu's second older sister, Fūto's wife; chatelaine of the Takeda capital townhouse

Yamamoto Fūto—Masugu's brother-in-law, Yaeko's husband and chatelain of Takeda capital townhouse; aka Fufu

Takeda Himari—Masugu's youngest sister

Inuji—Takeda cavalryman; Masugu's second in command

Shirokage Akira—Takeda lieutenant

Takeda Jofū—Lord Takeda's late wife (dead)

da Clan (and guests):

Oda Nabunaga*—Most powerful lord (*daimyo*) of Japan, controlling the capital (*Kyōto*) and the military government headed by the warlord (shōgun); lord of the Oda clan of Rising Tail (*Owari*) Province, allied with the Takeda and the Matsudaira; aka Nobu

Azai Oichi†—Lord Oda's next younger sister; widow of Azai Nagamasa

Oda Hachihime—Lord Oda's youngest sister; aka Lady Bee, Brat, and Hime

Akita Chikasue—Lord of the Akita clan; usurping Lord of Wingtip (*Dewa*) Province

Harē—Oda lieutenant; nephew of Kano Chojo and Risuko's cousin

Kamenote—Oda admiral and commander of flagship, the Fukurukuju

Kuroi—Oda captain of the guard

Oda Nobukane*—Nobunaga's brother; monk, ordained name Rōtaisai

Oda Nobutada*—Nobunaga's son and heir; commander of Oda forces in Rising Tail (*Owari*) Province

Oda Kichō*—Nobunaga's wife, mother of Nobutada

Oda Washihime—Hachihime's mother; Oda Nobunaga's stepmother (dead)

Matsudaira Clan:

Matsudaira Motoyasu*—Lord of the Matsudaira clan of Three Rivers (*Mikawa*) Province; aka Tokugawa Ieyasu

Tokugawa Tokimatsu—Lord Matsudaira's nephew; friend of Masugu

Matsudaira Ietada*—Matsudaira captain

Hattori Hanzō*—Matsudaira captain

Sakai—Matsudaira lieutenant

Kobayashi—Matsudaira guard

Jesuit Missionaries:

Father Francisco—Jesuit priest (Portuguese)

João Afonso Alves de Sousa de Mandrágora—Jesuit novice; aka Jolalo (Portuguese)

Aodh Og O'Shea—Jesuit novice; aka Ēyogoshei (Irish; dead)

Other Major Historical Figures:

Imagawa Ujizane*—Head of the Imagawa clan; former lord of Serenity (*Tōtōmi*) Province, recently defeated by the Takeda and the Matsudaira

Hōjō Ujimasa†—Lord of the Hōjō clan of Armory (*Musashi*) Province

Uesugi Kenshin†— Lord of the Uesugi clan of Crossover (*Echigo*) Province

Ashikaga Yoshiaka†—Hereditary warlord (*shōgun*) of Japan; for all intents and purposes Oda Nobunaga's puppet since Oda-*sama* took control of the capital

Glossary

The straight line over some vowels (for example, ō or ā) is called a macron.
It indicates that the vowel should be given a longer sound.

-ane—older sister

-ani—older brother

-chan—child

-ko—ending meaning that the word is a girl's name or nickname

-kun—child, boy

-sama—my lord or lord (honorific)

-san—sir, miss, or ma'am (honorific)

-senpai—senior student (honorific)

Ai, minha cabeca! (Portuguese)—Oh, my head!

Amor é um fogo que arde sem se ver, é ferida que doi, e não se sente. (Portuguese)—"Love is a fire that burns unseen, a wound that aches yet isn't felt."—Luis de Camões

anata—A term of endearment and affection, usually used between spouses or lovers, or by a servant or retainer to a superior with whom they have a close, friendly relationship (literally, a formal form of the pronoun "you")

Ane-ue—Older Sister (formal, archaic)

baesinja (Korean)—traitor

baka, baka yarō—idiot, complete idiot (offensive)

baka ama—stupid woman (offensive)

bakufu—the military government headed by the *shōgun*

banzai/banzai no kotobuki—Ten thousand

Benten—Goddess of Beauty and Art (also known as Benzai-*ten*); one of the Seven Gods of Luck

Bishamon—God of Strength and War; one of the Seven Gods of Luck

biwa—a stringed instrument with a round body and a short neck, similar to a lute

busu—ugly person, usually used for women (offensive)

bushidō—The Way of the Warrior; the Zen Buddhist samurai code

byeong-shin (Korean)—idiot (offensive)

che—interjection (not particularly offensive)

daikon—a large, white, mild radish

daimyo—lord (roughly equivalent to an English duke or earl)

daruma—duty, fate; from the Sanskrit word *dharma*

Dōitashimashite—You're welcome (in answer to thanks)

dōmo arigatō—thank you very much

Fukurokuju—God of Wisdom; one of the Seven Gods of Luck

furisode—kimono with long, trailing sleeves, traditionally worn by unmarried women

genmaicha—green tea flavored with toasted rice

geta—sandals with high wooden soles

go—a Chinese game of strategy

gō—actions (in Buddhism, the spiritual weight of your actions—*karma*—determines your next life) *gomenasai*—I am sorry; also said in response to another's formal apology

hai—yes

hakama—wide, skirt-like trousers

hanyak (Korean)—herbal medicine

harai-gushi—a wand with strips of white paper attached at one end, used for purification (*harai*) in Shinō ceremonies

hiragana—phonetic script used for native Japanese words for which there are no *kanji*

Hotei—God of Laughter; one of the Seven Gods of Luck

ichi—the number one

Ikkō-ikki—During the Civil War era, groups of rebel peasants, frequently led by Buddhist monks

Imōto—Younger sister

jinmaku—circular, curtained enclosure used in military camps

Jizō-bosatsu—the Buddhist saint *(boddhisatva)* of lost children; he is often portrayed with a blank face and large sleeves in which he protects the children

ju—the number ten

kami—spirit or god; *Shintō* tradition says there are eight million, but that figure is meant simply to suggest "beyond number"

kanji—Chinese ideograms; over three thousand of these non-phonetic characters are widely used in Japanese writing

katakana—phonetic script used for most foreign words and for emphasis (similar to italics in English)

katana—a samurai's long, curved sword

kimchee (Korean)—pickled cabbage, often spicy

kitsune—a mischievous nine-tailed fox spirit

koshukin—gold coin, worth fifty silver *monme* or about 1000lbs (450 kg) of rice, enough to feed four people for a year

koto—a long, plucked stringed musical instrument, like a zither

ku or *kyu*—the number nine

kudzu—Arrowroot, a fast-growing vine

kumiho (Korean)—mischievous fox spirit (similar to a *kitsune*)

kunoichi—"nine in one"; a *special kind of woman* trained as an assassin, bodyguard, or spy

Kwan-um (Korean)—the Buddhist saint *(boddhisatva)* of mercy and beauty; called Kwan-yin in China and Kannon in Japan

Mãe de Deus (Portuguese)—interjection meaning "Mother of God"

matcha—powdered green tea

miko—shrine maidens; young women who assist at Shintō festivals and ceremonies

mizutaki—a hot-pot dish made with fish, chicken, or some other meat

Mochizuki—"full moon"; the clan of Lady Chiyome's late husband

mogusa—mugwort; formed into pellets and burned (with the lit end away from the flesh) as a stimulant and as a way to celebrate children's aging during the New Year festival

mon—the emblem of a noble house (like the European coat of arms)

monme—silver coin worth approximately twenty pounds (9 kg) of rice

mōshi wakē gozaimasen—"I am terribly sorry" (formal)

Mukashi, mukashi—"Long, long ago" (traditional beginning to Japanese folktales, similar to "Once upon a time")

musume-san—Daughter (formal)

nattō—fermented beans

não faz mal (Portuguese)—That's all right (literally, "It doesn't hurt") *no*—preposition meaning *of, in,* or *from*

no okā-san—mother of; used in the sense of "Mrs. [Family Name]"

obi—sash

ohayō-gozaimasu—Good morning

Okā-san—Mother

oni—ogre, monster

Onē-san—Oldest Sister

Onī-san—Oldest Brother

opa (Portuguese)—oops

Otōto-kun—Little Brother

Otō-san—Father

owari—The End (formal, said or written at the end of a story, book, or film)

oyasumi nasai—Good night

ronin—a disgraced, master-less samurai

Risuko—Squirrel (a girl's name or nickname)

sakaki—an evergreen, small-leafed tree used in many Shintō rituals

sakura—a cherry tree; by extension, cherry blossoms

samisen—a long-necked, five-stringed instrument, similar to a guitar or banjo

sarabada—farewell (archaic, formal)

sayōnara—farewell; said on taking one's leave for the last time or for a very long time (formal)

senhora (Portuguese)—my lord, ma'am

sensei or *-sensei*—teacher (honorific)

seppuku—ritual suicide (also called *hara-kiri*)

shi-de—offerings of zigzag or twisted paper

Shi-ne—Die!

Shintō—the native religion of Japan; Shintō believes that there are many gods or spirits (*kami*) inhabiting different parts of the natural world and is frequently practiced side by side with Buddhism

shakuhachi—a long flute carved from bamboo

shinigami—spirits of death; not ghosts, but *kami* that represent death and darkness

shōgun—the emperor's warlord

shoyu—soy sauce

soondae (Korean)—blood sausages

tatami—a straw mat that is traditionally used to cover floors in Japan

tengutake—a poisonous mushroom

torī—a large arch or gateway usually found at Shintō shrines or temples

uchikake—a heavy outer kimono worn by a bride on her wedding day

wakizashi—a samurai's short sword; traditionally used for defense and for committing ritual suicide (*hara-kiri* or *seppuku*)

Wihayeo (Korean)—Cheers!

yamabushi—a hermit; a holy man who lives in isolation in the mountains

yang (Chinese)—the male force

yin (Chinese)—the female force

Place Names

I have translated most of the place names in the book; after all, the names aren't exotic to a speaker of Japanese! The translations are my own, and sometimes aim more at a poetic than a literal translation of the name.

There is in fact a village called Mochizuki *in Nagano (what used to be* Shinano *or Dark Letter Province). It is not very far from* Midriver Island (Kawanakajima)*, the site of several of the greatest battles of Japan's Civil War era. I couldn't help but set the estate of the* Mochizuki *family there. The estate itself, however, is entirely of my own imagining.*

Armory Province—*Musashi no kuni*

   Estuary—*Edō* (later known as Tōkyo), *Musashi*

   Middlemanor—*Fuchū-shi, Musashi*

   Seaside—*Yokohama-shi, Musashi*

Crossover Province—*Echigo no kuni*

Dark Letter Province—*Shinano no kuni*

   Full Moon—*Mochizuki-machi, Shinano*

   Highfield—*Ueda-shi, Shinano*

   Longfield—*Nagano-shi, Shinano*

   Midriver Island—*Kawanaka-jima, Shinano*

   Tiptown—*Sakaki-machi, Shinano*

Fountain Province—*Izumi no kuni*

Full Pot Province—*Kaga no kuni*

Great Eastern Sea Road—*Tōkaidō*

Middle Pass Province—*Etchū no kuni*

    Morningsun—*Asahi-shi, Etchū*

Old Wood Road—*Kisodō/Nakasendō*

Pure Beauty Province—*Mino no kuni*

Rising Tail Province—*Owari no kuni*

    Harmony Castle—*Kisoyu-jō, Owari*

    Salutation River—*Ibi-gawa, Owari*

    Spirit Bay—*Ise-wan, Owari/Ise/Mikawa*

    Sunfield Shrine—*Atsuta-jingu, Nagoya-shi, Owari*

    Seabell Station—*Narumi-juku, Owari*

    Tranquility Town—*Nagoya-shi, Owari*

River Bend Province—*Kawachi no kuni*

    Bayhome—*Suminoe-ku, Kawachi* (now part of Osaka)

Serenity Province—*Tōtōmi no kuni*

    Pineshore—*Hamamatsu-shi, Tōtōmi*

    Redstone Mountains— *Akaishi-san myaku, Tōtōmi/Mikawa*

    Roughwell—*Arai-machi, Tōtōmi*

    Two Branches Castle—*Futamata-jō, Tōtōmi*

    Weatherbank River— *Tenrū-gawa, Tōtōmi*

Three Rivers Province—*Mikawa no kuni*

    Boundary River—*Sakai-gawa, Mikawa/Owari*

    Phoenix Temple—*Horai-ji, Mikawa*

Picnic Valley—*Shitara-chō, Mikawa*

Rock Ridge—*Okazaki, Mikawa*

Temple Castle—*Terabe-jō, Mikawa*

Swift River Province—*Suruga no kuni*

White Mountain Province—*Yamashiro no kuni*

Capital—*Kyōto-shi, Yamashiro*

Mt. Wisdom—*Hiei-zan, Yamashiro*

Winged Flight Province—*Hida no kuni*

Wild Heights Province—*Kōzuke no kuni*

Wingtip Province—*Dewa no kuni*

Worth Province—*Kai no kuni*

Worth City—*Kōfu-shi, Kai*

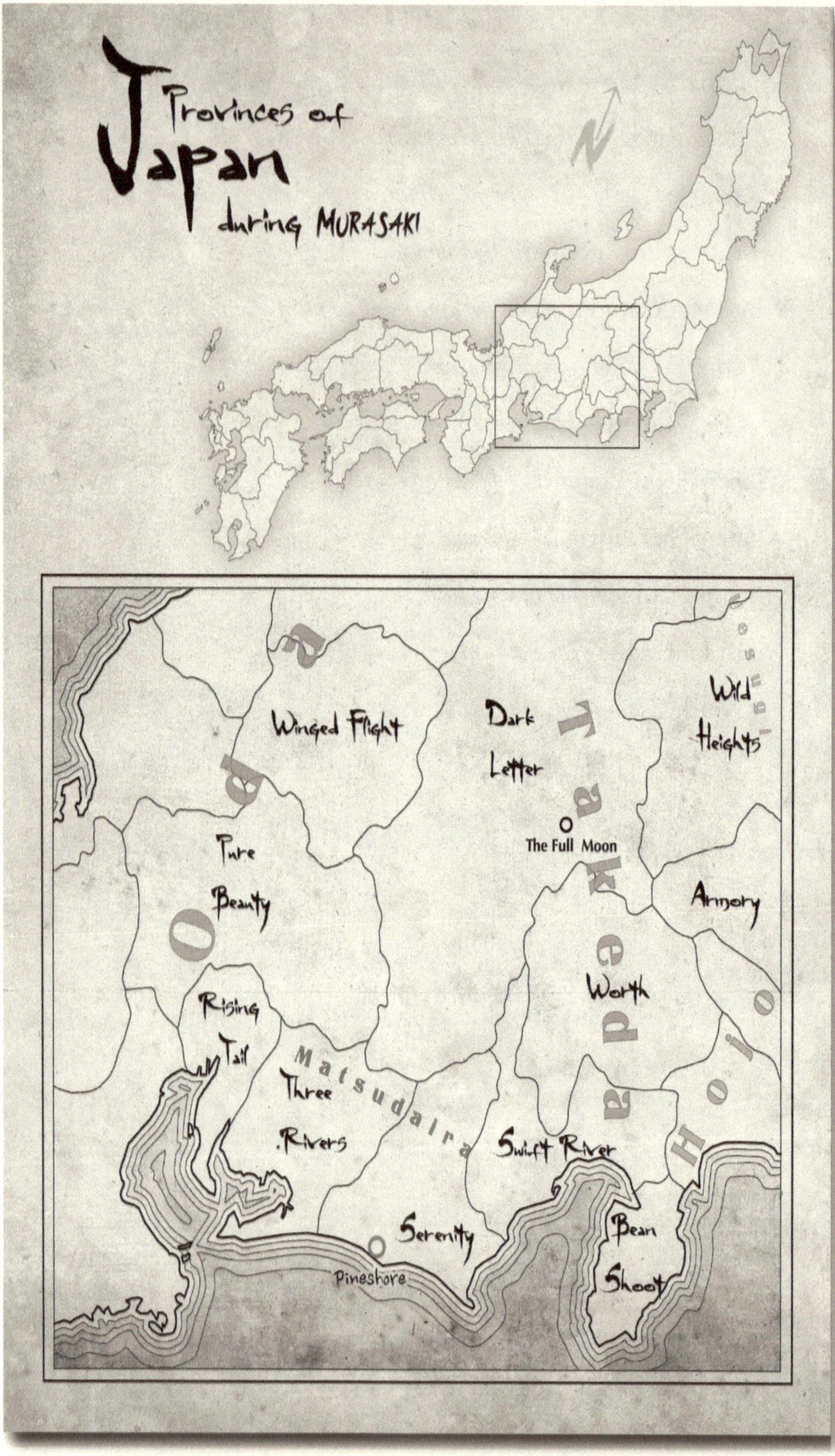

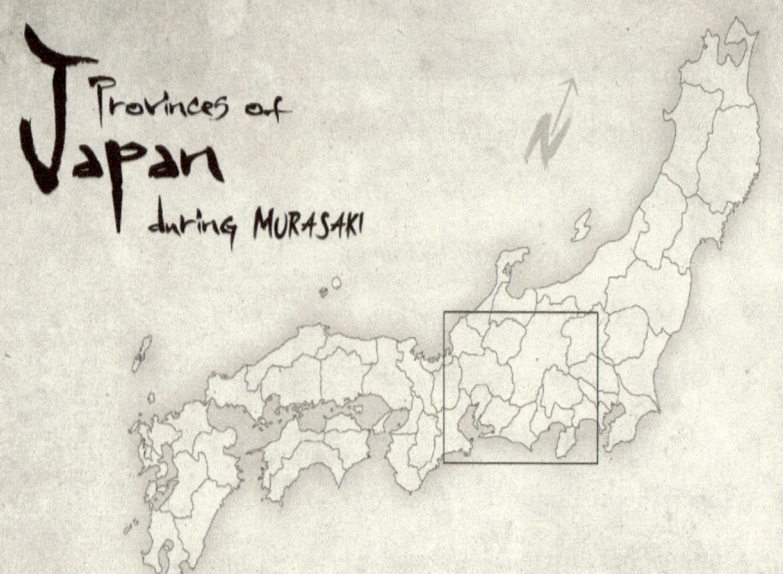

Provinces of
Japan
during MURASAKI
Oda
Takeda
Hojo
Matsudaira
Uesugi
Winged Flight
Dark
Letter
Wild
Heights
The Full Moon
Pure
Beauty
Armory
Worth
Rising
Tail
Three
Rivers
Swift River
Serenity
Pineshore
Bean
Shoot

Prologue – Destiny

My name is Kano Murasaki, but everyone calls me Risuko. Squirrel.

My whole childhood—or at least the part I remember—I was the daughter of a *ronin*, a disgraced samurai. After refusing to kill a group of children for his Lord, Oda Nobunaga, my father was banished and stripped of his rank, forced to live as a poor scribe in Serenity Province. Impoverished and dishonored we may have been, but we were together. Until Lord Imagawa summoned my father to his castle, and he never returned.

Even so, I was better off than my friends Hanichi Emi and Tarugu Toumi. Their fathers had also refused Lord Oda's order and committed *sepukku*, ritual suicide. My friends grew up on the streets of the capital, doing whatever they had to in order to survive. I got to do the thing I loved most, there in the shadow of Lord Imagawa's castle. Climbing trees and rocks, and even the walls of the castle.

That was before my mother was forced to sell me to Lady Chiyome, who brought me, Emi, Toumi, and our friend Aimaru to the Full Moon, her mountain school for shrine maidens. Chiyome-*sama*, Mieko-*sensei*, and the rest of our teachers didn't merely train us to be *miko*—dance and sing and serve the old gods.

They also taught us to be *kunoichi*. Assassins. Bodyguards. Spies.

My climbing found a new sense of purpose.

I don't want to be a killer. The last time I saw my father, on the way to answer Lord Imagawa's summons, he told me, '*Do no harm, Murasaki. No harm.*'

How can I do *no* harm?

Over the past year, I have defended myself and my friends. My actions have led to death. Deaths. Fuyudori, Lord Oda's spy at the Full Moon, who was trying to poison us all. The Torai brothers, who were spying for

Lord Hōjō. Kumo, who was trying to kill the Portuguese boy Jolalo. Three Uesugi soldiers. An assassin at the theater. An Irish boy who was paid to kill Lord Oda.

I didn't kill any of them, though my actions led to their deaths. But if they hadn't died, if I hadn't acted as I did, so many others would have suffered. They would have caused so much evil.

I'm unsure how to feel about that.

Now, Toumi, Emi, and I are riding with Lady Oda Hachihime, Lord Oda's half-sister. The half-sister of the man who destroyed our families. The lady we followed when we were little like a brood of ducklings.

We are on our way to her wedding with Lord Takeda, which I convinced them all would be the best chance at peace.

Serenity Province is where it all began. Where I grew up climbing trees.

That's what I wish I were doing right now.

The leaves are falling once again. The year is ending.

I have come full circle.

Where shall I go from here?

1 – Autumn Flame

Rising Tail Province, Land of the Rising Sun.
Month of Leaves in the Second Year of Genki.

(Owari, Japan, Autumn, 1571CE)

normous old ginkgoes and maples towered over the road on either side, burning with autumn flame. Red. Gold. Orange.

After four months in the capital, it felt so indescribably good to be among trees again—trees that paraded the change of seasons with vibrant colors.

On the horse next to mine, Hachihime looked around, eyes quick and wide. "Nobu hasn't let me out of the city in *years*. At least, no further than Millet Ferry or to see the cherry blossoms along the shores of the lake." She peered around. "This seems... nice. Very pretty."

I was going to say that it wasn't *nice*. It was glorious.

Emi spoke first, riding on Lady Oda's other side. "Why do you call him Nobu, Oda-*sama*?"

"Please, Emi-duckling. We're not in public."

"Yes, Hachihime. But..."

"I call him Nobu because that's who he is."

Toumi, who was riding behind Emi, jumped in. "But wasn't your dad Nobu-something?"

"Oda Nobuhide was our father, yes. And his sons, our brothers, were the bastard Nobuhiro—literally, I'm not being mean—and also the awful Nobuyuki. Nobukane, who's a monk, now. Nobuharu. I think I'm forgetting a couple. And then there's Nobu's sons! Nobutada, who we're going to meet at the castle later—he can't stand me, it's so funny. The twins, Nobukatsu and

Nobutaka…" She clicked her tongue, searching the brilliant leaves above for the names of more kin.

"Well, then," Emi asked, "Isn't it confusing that you call Oda-*sama* Nobu?"

"Is it? I call him that because…" Hachihime turned to my friends and then to me, her eyes half-lidded, the clever expression that always made me think of her brother. "Because, ducklings, he's the only one who matters."

"Ah," Emi granted. "I see."

In front of us, a furry parade scurried out of the road and into the woods.

Toumi sniffed. "What're those? Rats?"

"No!" I laughed. Fluffy black-and-white bodies, low to the ground—a mother *tanuki* and three kits, one draped across her back. "Raccoon dogs."

My surly friend's lip curled, predictably. She had no interest in wildlife, aside from the kinds that were edible or that might bite. "So big, furry rats."

Hachihime tittered, shifting on her red-and-gold saddle, but I felt I had to defend the creatures, now disappearing into the underbrush. "They're supposed to bring good luck. Prosperity. Fertility."

"Yeah, yeah," said Toumi, rolling her eyes. "Just what we want."

Emi clicked her teeth. "Actually, prosperity would be nice. And in some of the stories my mother used to tell, they're shapeshifters. Right, Murasaki?"

I agreed and began to share a story that my mother had told me and my sister about a *tanuki* that repaid a poor woodsman who had freed it from a trap by turning itself into a magical, ever-full teapot.

We were on the fifth day of leisurely travel out of the capital on the Great Ocean Highway toward Serenity for a wedding. A wedding I had brokered at sword-point. Though everyone saw the advantages for peace that I had. At least, they said they did.

A mounted honor guard of some fifty Oda cavalry accompanied us. A squadron of Takeda lancers brought up the rear, led by Lieutenant Masugu. Mieko-*sensei* rode with Masugu-*san* on his stallion, Inazuma. She held a parasol over both their heads.

We were just approaching the river bordering the Oda home province, Rising Tale.

The flaming foliage overhead thinned, revealing blue sky streaked with wisps of white.

At the front of the company, Lieutenant Harē led his white stallion down into a wide, slow-moving river. Harē-*san*, my mother's sister's son, the cousin I had only come to know that summer.

"This was where my mother died," said Hachihime, and I turned at the odd inflection of her voice. Her face, usually animated and full of mischief, was still and sad. She looked very, very young. "We were on our way to Harmony Castle, just like today. Because it was supposed to be *safe*."

I rode my mount closer to her until our knees touched and reached out, placing my hand on her arm. I assumed if she wanted to talk about it, she would.

She remained silent, lost in memory. Or grief.

Lord Oda had told me about that Imagawa attack. He had shared the tale on the night I had sneaked into his chambers, determined to assassinate him, to avenge the dishonor with which he had stained Emi, Toumi, and my fathers' names.

He had admitted to me that his actions had been far from rational—from sane. He had said, in fact, that he had been mad with grief at the death of his late father's wife, there at the ford of the Old Wood River. In his rage, Oda-*sama* had ordered our fathers to retaliate. To kill a group of Imagawa children, plus Takeda Masugu, whom the Takeda had sent to stay with Lord Imagawa in exchange for one of Lord Imagawa's sons. A hostage swap.

Our fathers had refused.

Endless retaliation. Endless, senseless bloodshed. Like the round of the seasons. Never-ending. Inescapable. A knot of sorrow that could only be cut through by the most subtle of blades.

I wasn't sure that my improvised solution—Oda Hachihime's marriage to Takeda Shingen—was actually that blade. But the opportunity to bind the two most powerful lords in Japan together seemed as if it offered the best chance to end over a century of killing, intrigue, and revenge.

And it would bring me back to Serenity, where my father had taken his family in exile. Where I had grown up happily climbing trees, far from scheming lords and rampaging armies.

Would I be able to see my mother, my sister? Had they survived the Matsudaira invasion?

I knew Lord Imagawa had survived. Oda-*sama* and Takeda-*sama* had agreed that it would be fittingly humiliating that the man who had once been the most powerful in all Japan be forced to host the wedding uniting their clans. A wedding at the castle in whose shadow I had played, all of those years.

If I met Imagawa-*sama*… could I get him to reveal to me, finally, what had happened to my father? Would I kill him?

'*Do no harm, Murasaki.*' Those had been *Otō-san*'s last words to me. And yet as I grew, as I became more enmeshed in the world of conniving *daimyo* and cold-blooded generals, *no harm* became an impossible goal.

Action caused harm. Inaction caused harm.

And so, I found myself constantly seeking the path that promised, if not *no harm*, then *the least*.

I had chosen not to kill Lord Oda, who had destroyed my father's life and ended those of Toumi and Emi's.

Could I kill Lord Imagawa, whose sneak attack at the very ford we were crossing had triggered so much tragedy? Who had ordered my father to come to his castle... Could I force Imagawa-*sama* to tell me *why*?

Could I kill?

I had agreed to serve as Hachihime's bodyguard. I had helped stop two assassination attempts. One on Lord Oda, the night I had sneaked into his chamber to assassinate him myself. Before that, at the theater, on Mieko-*sensei*, who had assumed the guise of the dead Lady Monogami Kuniko. Hachihime, of course, had thought the black-clad assassin at the theater was actually attacking *her*.

I had knocked men unconscious and two times slammed one boy to the ground. I had thrown spiked caltrops in a man's face and repeatedly drawn the short sword that I carried at my back. I had escaped up a tree in the midst of a blizzard, refusing to give another of Chiyome-*sama*'s student *kunoichi* the letter for which she had been willing to kill us all. And though I had not pushed her, she had nonetheless fallen. I knew that I was responsible for her death.

I could justify all of it. I had acted not only to protect myself, but others too. And yet could I say that I had done *no harm*?

As we approached the river, as I maintained my grip on grief-devoured Hachihime's arm, a question struck me. Why had the death of a stepmother devastated the crafty Lord of Rising Tail so?

Lord Oda had been young at the time, of course. He had admitted as much to me the night that I had stopped the Irish boy Eyogoshei from killing him. The night that Oda-*sama* had slit the would-be assassin's throat with the dagger that he had hidden in his bed, placed the bloody blade in my hand, and then proclaimed that I had saved his life.

When Lady Washihime had died, Oda Nobunaga would have been about her daughter Hachihime's current age—a few years older than me and my friends. He had just become head of the Oda clan.

Even so, it seemed like an extreme reaction to the murder of his late father's second wife.

I would have to ask Hachihime. But I would have to do it delicately. Not while the memory of her mother's death flooded her.

Flooded like the water swirling around our mounts' legs.

I glanced up at the trees overlooking the banks of the river—more ginkgo, stands of tall old oak and pine—and could only think that what I wanted to do more than anything was to jump off the horse, wade to the shore, and climb.

A buzzing sound by my ear, and then a splash behind me like a trout jumping for a bug. Strange.

It was late for bees, and why would they be out in the middle of a river?

Another buzz, from the other side. Looking up, I saw a small cloud of black shafts arching toward us from the woods on the near shore.

"Arrows!" I shrieked and pulled Hachihime down into the water between our horses.

2 – Steel on Steel

I grew up swimming and playing in the small river and ponds near our village. Though I preferred to be up in the air, I liked the water too.

The same could not be said for Hachihime.

As we fell into the flood between our horses, she jerked and bucked beneath me, arms and legs flailing, eyes wide.

Then two weights crashed down, pushing us both beneath the river's boiling surface.

I may have been comfortable in water, but as I slammed down onto Hachihime's thrashing body, horse legs churning the water and my breath driven out of me, I panicked.

I hope you won't think less of me.

I've spoken before about how time creeps for me in a crisis. Often, that slowing is a wonderful thing—I can see danger before it arrives and prepare to respond. Sometimes, however, underwater, under the weight of two other bodies, that slowed time tortures, as if I were being forced to gaze, unblinking, at my own death.

Actually, all that I could see was Hachihime's wide eyes.

No. I would not let her die. I would not let myself die.

I fought to get my feet onto the sandy riverbed. Grabbing Hachihime by the shoulders, I tried to lift us both back to the surface, but the burdens atop me were too heavy.

The river had seemed slow and placid from the surface. Now the flood whipped around and between us, scrubbing us with pebbles and gravel kicked up by the horses.

My feet scrabbled to find purchase against the sand. My lungs screamed for breath.

For the first time in my life, the thought bloomed, a fetid flower. *I'm going to die after all.*

That, of course, was the moment when the two leaden weights on my back shifted, hands grasping at me and Hachihime and pulling us back up.

"*Are you all right? Are you all right? Are you all right?*" Emi and Toumi coughed and spluttered at me. At Hachihime.

I was coughing myself, what felt like a whole river's worth of water streaming from my mouth, nose, and ears.

I held Hachihime close to me, having no other choice.

Her eyes remained wide, panic-white. "*Mama! Mama!*"

"Mouse?" Toumi shouted in my ear.

"Fine!" I spat out a piece of gravel and looked around for more arrows. The only marks in the blue sky were white clouds. Just upstream, one horse lay unmoving, three arrows piercing its chest. Two more were lodged in its red-and-gold saddle. Hachihime's mount.

Most of the soldiers were splashing toward the shore we'd just left—toward the attackers. "Let's get her to the far shore!"

A shadow blotted out the sun and we all looked up—Emi, Toumi, and I did, at least. Hachihime was still lost in the terror of another attack.

Harē had ridden between us and the shore upstream where the arrows had come from. "Injured?"

I was about to tell him we were fine, aside from almost drowning, when another horse splashed up.

"GO BACK!" screamed Mieko-*sensei*, grabbing at Inazuma's reins with one hand. Her other still held her parasol, which had sprouted a bouquet of arrows. "GO BACK!"

Masugu-*san* grasped the wrist of her free hand. His eyes were on me and Hachihime. He looked up at Harē.

Both soldiers nodded.

In a voice that managed to sound both calm and steely, Masugu-*san* said, "Koko, girls, we're going to get you to the other side."

Harē turned his horse around, and he and Masugu-*san* slowly walked us across the river, acting as shields against any further missile attacks.

Mieko-*sensei* growled in disapproval, trying to pull her hand free, but Masugu-*san* ignored her. Not something I'd ever seen him do.

Hachihime wept. Eventually, Toumi and Emi helped me carry her through the flood to the dry eastern shore.

In that moment, as the water streamed from our clothes and our hair onto the dusty road, I didn't think I'd ever want to swim again.

A small group of mounted guards formed up around us as my cousin and Masugu-*san* led us into a grove of gingkoes, their thin trunks providing some cover from any further enemy fire. Not that we had remained within easy range.

Muted sounds of battle erupted from across the wide river—steel on steel, cries of rage and pain. The silvery music of the water made it seem impossibly far away. Dreamlike.

"Why didn't we go back?" Mieko-*sensei* snarled. "We could have helped take them out! We need…"

"Koko," said Masugu-*san*, voice still deadly calm, "Think. Who were they shooting at?"

She huffed at him, but her eyes closed.

I looked at my friends. Toumi was wringing out her kimono, while Emi was checking her throwing knives. Then down at Hachihime, weeping wetly into my wet shoulder, and finally up at Mieko-*sensei*—at the dainty-looking parasol on her shoulder that I knew was actually a steel-ribbed leather shield. At the arrows that studded it. "They were aiming at us. At the women."

Harē nodded. "Yes, cousin. They were. The best thing to do was to remove you from the line of fire."

Mieko-*sensei* blinked. Emi scowled. For once, Toumi joined her.

Masugu-*san* drew Mieko-*sensei*'s now-limp hand to his lips. "Koko. My lady. Harē's troops and mine will deal with the assassins. We could not give them what they were clearly aiming for. Besides, you're still recovering from a serious wound."

Eyes still closed, Mieko-*sensei* let her forehead fall against Masugu-*san*'s armored back. "You are right, of course. Though the wound wasn't that serious. But I don't like being treated like a piece of baggage."

"Never that, Koko."

She smiled grimly. "Fine."

Masugu-*san* too smiled and looked down at us. "Ladies?"

"We're good," Toumi mumbled, now picking twigs and sand from her hair.

I tried to look at Hachihime, but she clung trembling to me like a baby *tanuki* to its mother's back. "I think Lady Oda is physically unharmed, but…"

Harē dismounted and peered at Hachihime. "My lady?" When she responded with a sustained whine like an over-boiled kettle, he looked to me. "Cousin?"

"She was telling me," I whispered, stroking her wet back, "this was where she and her mother were attacked. Where…"

Harē's eyes flew wide. "Where Oda Washihime died."

He removed his cloak and wrapped it around Hachihime, who was shivering uncontrollably. Then he looked up to Masugu-*san*. "Hachihime-*sama* needs care. At this point, I don't think we'll make it to the castle by nightfall, and it clearly isn't safe to travel in the dark. There's a monastery just up the road, renowned for its healers. Takeda-*san*, would you be willing to take command of the men here while this squadron and I—"

Masugu-*san* raised his hand, halting Harē. "I don't believe it's a good idea to split our force when there might be another ambush ahead. I think my uncle would be as unhappy as Lady Hachihime's brother if we were to allow anything to happen to her."

Mieko-*sensei* added, "And I think the fighting has ended. The riders are crossing toward us once more."

"Ah." Harē looked back at me and Hachihime. "Your points are well taken, Lieutenant. Lady Monogami." To me and my friends, he added, "Keep her warm. She's in shock. Understandably."

As Takeda and Oda's cavalrymen began to return, the three of us embraced Hachihime.

The soldiers returned in a good mood. Just two men had been hit by arrows as they charged the archers, and neither had been seriously wounded.

Three horses had died. One of them, I already knew, was Hachihime's.

The assassins, however, had provided five new mounts.

Inuji and the other Takeda lancers were teasing Aimaru for falling off his charger.

Our friend put up with the jokes with his usual good grace. He had, after all, been one of the ones who had defeated the men who'd attacked us.

The attackers had all been up in oaks overlooking the river, firing at us when the Takeda rode up beneath them. The Oda riders soon joined as well, cutting off the assassins' escape.

It hadn't been difficult to avoid their fire there among the trees, and once the attackers were out of arrows, a group of mounted Oda bowmen took down three of the enemy. The remaining two assassins had better cover, and so Masugu-*san*'s second-in-command, Inuji, had sent a group of limber volunteers up after them, Aimaru among them.

"You'd have enjoyed it," he told me as we rode away from the river.

"Enjoyed it?" I didn't think I'd have liked knowing there was a desperate killer waiting at the top of the tree.

"Well," he said with a shrug, "the climbing."

I couldn't disagree with that.

As we formed up, Harē ordered a pair of fast Oda scouts to ride ahead to inform the monastery of our arrival and request their aid with our wounded, and then to ride post haste to Harmony Castle to inform Lord Oda's wife and son that we had been attacked and so would be delayed.

Once they had galloped off, we got back on our way. Our pace was more leisurely, but there was nothing relaxed now about the guards. Our formation was much tighter, and we women were kept hemmed in on all sides.

We forded two more rivers without incident and then entered another forest.

Inuji reported to Masugu-*san*, Mieko-*sensei*, and Harē, informing them that the attackers had borne no insignia, nor any sign of their origin. The brands showed the horses had come from all over the provinces of the main island, Honshū. The men's hair had been recently shorn, as if they'd removed samurai topknots.

"*Ronin*," muttered Masugu-*san*.

"Like the assassin at the theater," Harē added with a sigh.

Mieko-*sensei* hummed in agreement and glanced over at me, riding with Hachihime wrapped around me from behind. "Risuko, well done getting Hachihime out of harm's way so quickly."

In front of her, Masugu smiled. "That offer of a job in the Takeda scouts still holds."

"No," Hachihime said firmly, though her teeth kept chattering. Her arms still pulled me close from behind. "She's staying with me. They all are."

I looked at my friends, their eyes wide, their hair wet and messy, their still-damp kimonos revealing the weapons hidden up their silken sleeves. "Yes, my lady."

———

We rode long enough for the sun to begin to lose its way among the trees. A monk stood in the middle of the road, his bright saffron robes perfectly matching the maple leaves above him and littering the path. "Brothers, sisters," he said, and bowed. "You are expected."

He led us uphill off the main road, along a narrow, brick-paved lane lined with stone lanterns and across a small, red-stained wooden bridge that crossed a stream. Amidst a cool stand of enormous, ancient cedars and hemlock stood a temple—a cluster of wooden buildings around a courtyard. A tall red pagoda reigned over one side of the space, and a large abbey the other. The abbey building brought very much in mind the great hall at the Full Moon.

A bell tolled, its deep tones rolling across the courtyard, over us, and out into the forest valley. From within the temple, we also heard a chant—not a prayer in praise of the Buddha or beseeching deliverance to the Western Paradise, but a repeated phrase in a foreign tongue I didn't recognize.

I looked over to Aimaru, who had grown up in a monastery. His eyes were wide in rare surprise.

Two men approached us from the abbey, the older with a staff and a white cloth around his neck, the other with a face that I would have placed anywhere. He was the sly-eyed spitting image of Hachihime's brother, Oda Nobunaga.

Behind me, the lady herself finally released me, slid from the horse, and ran, weeping, to the younger monk. "*Onī-san!*"

"Little sister," he answered, opening his arms to welcome her embrace.

3 - Dry Land

Hachihime wept into the monk's chest.

"That must be Nobukane," whispered Emi. "One of the Nobu-brothers she was telling us about."

Toumi muttered back, "How do you even remember that?"

"Well," Emi murmured, her face set in its deep memory frown. "Nobuhiro is the illegitimate one. And Nobuyuki is the one she said was awful, though she didn't say why. And then she said Nobukane was—"

"Whatever," snorted Toumi, rolling her eyes.

Masugu-*san* and Harē were presenting the two wounded soldiers to the abbot.

"Come, brothers," said the older monk. "Several of our number are quite gifted healers. Brother Rōtaisai, please lead these gentlemen to our infirmary."

The wily-eyed Oda monk bowed. "Of course, your reverence." Now he glanced down at Hachihime, who still clung to him. "May I show this lady and her attendants to the guest room? I believe that she is in need of healing as well, though of a more spiritual nature."

The abbot's placid smile flickered for a moment, but then he nodded. "Of course. Lady Kuniko," he said, turning back to Mieko-*sensei*, "would you like to join these ladies tonight? The guest room is small and spare, I am afraid, but comfortable."

Mieko-*sensei* bowed. "You honor me, Lord Abbot. However, I would not presume to impose on you or Lady Hachihime. I have my own tent. I can stay wherever my guards are housed."

"As you wish." He returned her bow and turned to the two lieutenants. "Gentlemen, I hope that you don't mind staying out here in the courtyard tonight with your men. I am afraid we have no stables and little unused space here."

Masugu-*san* and cousin Harē bowed. Harē said, "Your hospitality already honors us, your reverence. Thank you."

That settled, Hachihime's brother led us toward a set of small buildings between the abbey and the pagoda. A trio of monks met us at the first building and took charge of the two wounded men.

Then, his sister still clinging to him, he led us to an even smaller building, set back among a stand of enormous cedars.

Hachihime continued to sniffle, clinging to her brother, but as he slid open the door, he smiled at us. "Welcome to our guest house. I'm afraid it will be a bit cold, since it doesn't see much use. But we'll light the brazier and get my little bumblebee here settled."

We thanked him, but I felt I had to ask, "Pardon, your reverence. Are we to call you Nobukane-*san* or…"

He chuckled, leading us into the sparsely furnished room. "Ah, that is a name from another life, I am afraid. My ordained name is Rōtaisai. How did you know I was once an Oda?" He stopped and peered at me, then at Emi and Toumi, clever eyes widening. "Are you…?"

"Yes," sniffled Hachihime. "Kano, Hanichi, and Torugu."

"Ah." He blinked at us. "Well, do come in, ladies."

We finally got Hachihime to release him. Toumi and Emi prepared the one bed and helped her into it, and I assisted the monk in lighting the tiny brazier in the middle of the room.

"Do you know," he murmured as the charcoal began to catch, "I would have known you for Chojo's daughter anywhere."

"Thank you, Rōtaisai-*san*. It is very kind of you to say so." I had always thought my mother was one of the most beautiful women in the world. "That is how I knew who you were. You look just like Oda-*sama*, your brother."

Again, he chuckled and then winked. "Ah, don't ever tell Nobunaga that! He always said I was the ugly one."

One of the monks from the infirmary brought in a steaming pot of tea. "A calming draught for Lady Oda," he said. Emi and I sniffed at it, causing the new monk to frown, but Rōtaisai-*san* to grin.

The familiar scents of ginger, jujube, and of course corydalis wafted up from the pot. A calming draught indeed. We nodded and Emi poured a cup, gave it to Toumi, who sniffed it herself, then presented it to Hachihime.

The room began to warm slowly.

Hachihime's tears slowed and stopped. Her weeping was replaced by hiccups.

Her brother knelt beside her and stroked her head. "So, Lady Bee, I gather you have had a nasty experience?"

"Yes," she said, leaning into his hand, tears beginning to flow again. "It was like a nightmare coming back to life. Arrows flying. Men screaming." She blinked up at me. "Risuko saved me. She pulled me down off the horse before I even knew we were under attack. And then Emi and Toumi pulled us both out of the flood."

"Did they?" Rōtaisai-san gazed at us, then back at his sister. "Even so, it must have been terrible for you."

She nodded, weeping again, and buried herself in her brother's chest.

Rōtaisai-san rocked her as her deluge of sorrow poured out once more. His quick eyes shot to the teapot, then back to us. "Ladies, what I think Hime-chan most needs is rest. I can tend to her until she is able to sleep. Perhaps you might join Lady Kuniko and the guards for a meal?"

I shared a look with Emi, whose typical frown deepened. I turned back to the monk. "Your reverence…"

"Ah, I see you are your fathers' daughters as well." With a sly smile, he said, "I swear I will allow no harm to come to her. At the moment, I believe she needs an ugly older brother more than pretty bodyguards. Go."

"Not ugly," Hachihime managed to say between sobs.

———

As we stepped out into the gathering shadows, there beneath the enormous cedars, Emi murmured, "Is she safe, do you think?"

Toumi shrugged. "As safe here, with him, as anywhere."

Emi and I nodded, but I wasn't exactly reassured. "So, do you think the assassins were aiming for Hachihime? Or maybe for Lady Kuniko?" After all these months, we never used Mieko-sensei's real name. Not even in private. Too dangerous.

Emi just shrugged. "No way to know. Could be the Akita, after the heir of the Monogami. Or someone out to stop the alliance between the Oda and Takeda."

"Or maybe," said Toumi with a bark of a laugh, "they're just jealous of how pretty we are. Or they've heard how good you are with a knife, Sourpuss, or Mouse, how *deadly* you are with a sword. Like you said, no way to know."

That was certainly true.

As we stepped out from between the infirmary and the abbey into the courtyard, we saw Aimaru with a young man, his head shaved like a monk but in the white robes of a novice. "How can you work for a monster like Oda Nobunaga!"

Aimaru's usually open face was set in a scowl. "I serve Lady Mochizuki and Lord Takeda."

The novice leaned forward and growled, "And you're taking the monster's little sister to marry him! How many more monasteries do you think they'll burn together!"

Our friend held up his hands. "Koji—"

"They burned Mount Wisdom to the ground!"

"I know." Seeing us, Aimaru waved us over. "Emi, Toumi, Murasaki, let me introduce my friend Koji."

The young man turned, blinking at us. He was almost as tall as our friend, but much skinnier, and his sunken cheeks were red with anger beneath tears turned golden by the filtered light of the setting sun. "I... Ladies." He bowed, hands pressed together. "Pardon me. I must... speak to the prior. Good evening."

As he ran toward the abbey entrance, Aimaru sighed. "He hadn't heard about Mount Wisdom."

"Can't blame him for being upset," Toumi said, staring after the disappearing novice.

"No," Aimaru said. He shrugged an apology and walked toward the area under the trees where our mounts were tethered. "I need to watch the horses."

Not even a month before, Oda-*sama* had carried through on his threats and destroyed the thousand-year-old temple of warrior monks where Aimaru had grown up.

Emi started to go after Aimaru, but I stopped her. "I think he wants to be alone for a moment."

She sighed.

Toumi huffed. "Yeah. Probably wants a good cry."

Emi's shoulders bunched, and her habitual frown twisted.

I grabbed her fists. "She's joking, Emi."

"No. She's not."

Toumi goggled at our friend. "No, I'm not. Back off, Sourpuss!" She held up her hands. "I said, can't blame him. Bunch of people you know get killed, seems like a hells-damned good reason to cry. Take a breath or something."

Emi closed her eyes, then slid her clenched hands from mine. She stood, feet apart, and took a long breath.

The Two Fields.

"Emi," I whispered. "He'll be all right."

When she opened her eyes, tears gilding them. "Yes," she said. "He will be all right."

I fidgeted. "Are we doing the right thing?" The words found voice before I thought them.

"Right thing?" Toumi asked.

I tried to match Emi's balanced stance. "Maybe… maybe we shouldn't be helping Oda-*sama*." I looked at them and leaned closer. "Maybe it would have been better if I had killed him." When they just stared at me, I sighed. "He's not exactly a good person."

Now Toumi and Emi looked at each other. Emi murmured, "Perhaps not. But remember—"

I huffed. "…the *daimyo* are different, or they wouldn't need people like us."

"There you go," said Toumi. "Nobody ever won a war by being nice."

Emi nodded. "And Hachihime and—"

That was too much for Toumi. "If you try to tell us that Lord and Lady *Baka* are nice, you're crazier than they are, Sourpuss."

Emi held up her hands. "Not nice or good, definitely. But they at least…"

Toumi growled, "He destroyed our fathers. He destroyed our lives."

"And he regrets that," said Emi.

"Regret. I bet," she sneered.

My fidgeting settled into a sigh and a nod. I had seen Oda-*sama* the night that he admitted what he had done to our fathers. He might not be particularly truthful, but I don't think even the great actor Zenparu could have faked his deep sorrow and remorse. "Emi's right. I know that *honor* and *virtue* aren't Lord Oda's main concerns. But I know that he does regret what he did to our fathers. What he did to us."

Emi nodded thoughtfully.

Toumi answered with a snort. "But still, Mouse, you were right to begin with. Is helping him a good idea? If we hadn't saved Hachihime today…"

Now I felt more certain. "Her marriage to Lord Takeda is our best chance to finish this endless war."

"Yeah, yeah," Toumi said. "You keep telling us. Not that the Mountain seems like someone to trust in a dark alley either."

"No," I admitted. We had watched him plan to attack his ally, Lord Oda, after all. And then he had sent us to assassinate him. "But if we had let Hachihime die at the ford… What happens then? We're back to all-out war.

If we can unite the Oda and Takeda clans, then the other *daimyo* will support them."

Again, Emi gave a sad nod. "Or be crushed."

Now I was the one shrugging. "And if we don't, can either of you see a way out of the endless battles and betrayals?"

"No." Emi's expression took on the shadows of the trees.

"Nah," Toumi grunted, conceding the point. "If anyone could, we wouldn't be here, right?"

"Right." I looked at them. "So… dinner?"

———

We ate with Mieko-*sensei* and Masugu-*san* outside of her tent. I wanted to ask them about what we had been discussing but couldn't think of a way to raise the question without putting them in a difficult position. Masugu-*san* was, after all, Takeda-*sama*'s nephew. And Mieko-*sensei*. Well, she had a chance to regain the Monogami clan's former position with Oda-*sama*'s help.

Emi kept looking toward where the horses were tethered.

Gathering everyone's bowls, Masugu-*san* asked, "Something on your mind, Emi-*san*?"

My friend looked at the lieutenant, blinked, and shook her head. Then she turned to Mieko-*sensei*. "After this afternoon, I guess I wish there were more than four of us."

Mieko-*sensei* nodded. When Masugu-*san* quirked an eyebrow, she touched his hand. "Not that your troops don't make us feel much safer. "But…"

The lieutenant closed his eyes. "But the assassins targeted you."

"Yes," sighed Mieko-*sensei*. "Whether it was Hachihime, me, or all of us." She turned back to Emi. "Lady Chiyome wrote before we left the capital. She was worried that rival lords might find our party too tempting a target. And she was right. So, she has sent our fellow shrine maidens to scout the route ahead of us."

Toumi grunted. "Didn't do so great."

Shrugging, Emi said, "Yes. But it seems to me the route from the capital to Tranquility Town should have been pretty safe. These provinces are all firmly under Oda-*sama*'s control."

Mieko-*sensei* tipped her head in agreement. "Exactly. Lady Chiyome told me we could expect to see some of our friends on the road through the Three Rivers and Serenity."

"If this area is so safe, how did the assassins get through?" I asked.

"Harē-*san* and I were discussing that," said Masugu. "They were a very small group and may not have traveled together. They'd have been hard to spot."

Emi clicked her tongue. "And that crossing is pretty isolated. No villages or forts along the road. It was a good place to hide and wait."

As it had been a decade before when the Imagawa killed Hachihime's mother.

That thought had probably occurred to Masugu-*san*, who frowned down into the small campfire. "Fair point, Emi-*san*." He smiled up at Mieko-*sensei*. "Good thing Chiyome-*sama* has reinforcements scouting out the road ahead."

––––––

When we stepped quietly back into the guest house, Hachihime lay where we'd left her, in her brother's arms. She wasn't sobbing, though her eyes were still lined with red.

"Your bodyguards have returned, Hime-*chan*," the monk informed her.

She hummed. "What do you say, ladies, shall we head out for an evening at the theater?"

Emi and I looked at each other, but Toumi just laughed. "Maybe the frogs will be doing *Tomoe*. Or *Croaking Yamabushi*."

Hachihime tittered. "Or a squirrel warrior-poet doing a solo version of *Tadanori*."

I rolled my eyes. "Very funny, my lady."

Rōtaisai-*san* unwrapped himself from around Hachihime. "I will leave you to your entertainments."

I bowed to him. "Your reverence."

He put his palms together and bowed back. "Ladies. Do try to get some sleep, all of you. It is the best medicine, after all."

We said that we would and wished him good night.

Once we were alone, my friends and I sat around Hachihime.

As she burrowed down under her covers, I shared glances with Emi and Toumi. I could see that they too were thinking about our conversation outside.

Should we have let her die at the river?

Could we possibly have done that?

I had acted the only way I thought I could. Judging by Emi and Toumi's shadowed expressions, they too were doubting they could have let Hachihime die.

Hachihime's eyes drooped, half-closed, but not in the clever, tricksy way I always associated with her and her brother.

I asked, "Do you think you can sleep, Hachihime?"

"Hmm." She closed her eyes fully and nodded. Then she looked up at us. "Stay with me, ducklings. You must be exhausted."

"That's true," Toumi admitted.

She and Emi lay on either side of Hachihime. I sat at the foot of the bed.

Emi immediately began to snore. Toumi collapsed into slumber almost as fast.

I thought that Hachihime was asleep, but she peeked one eye over her covers. "Thank you, Murasaki. I owe you my life."

Then I was alone.

4 – The River of Heaven

I sat for a while, thinking at first that I might be able to slow my mind enough to join the others in slumber.

My mind, however, showed no signs of slowing.

Who had the assassins been trying to kill? Hachihime? Mieko-*sensei*? Someone else?

Would someone possibly want to kill me?

And was my plan—to unite the Oda and Takeda clans through marriage—actually a good idea? Or would it just lead to more disaster and destruction?

I stood and began to pace. But my movement began to wake the others, and so I stepped out into the inky night of the cedar grove. I thought perhaps I'd stand watch, but really, in the middle of a monastery—with a small army of Oda and Takeda guards nearby—who would I be watching for?

An owl hooted above. I looked up, seeing the spiderweb of stars shining between the soaring shadows of the huge trees.

Climb, I thought, *that'll calm you down*. I looked around to find the best tree to scamper up. But the shadow that called to me, that made my breath catch, wasn't a tree. To my right, the black outline of the pagoda seemed to challenge me, to beg me to try my luck.

I was already off the ground, scrabbling up the slanted eaves, before I could consider otherwise.

Seven levels.

I once asked *Otō-san* why many pagodas have seven levels, as he copied a drawing of one from an old scroll.

He said that the soul has seven stations through which it must travel to reach enlightenment, each a basic need to be understood and mastered: hunger, desire, ambition, love, truth, wisdom, and, finally, true understanding.

I asked him what level he had reached.

He put down the brush and looked at me with a smile— my father, who rarely smiled—and said that he woke every morning as a hungry animal. That through the day, he might feel as if, through discipline, he could almost glimpse enlightenment, true understanding, like the sun ready to peek over the horizon.

But then his stomach would growl, Okā-*san* would call us all in for supper, and he would realize how far away the dawn of enlightenment actually was.

The outside of the pagoda was not intended for climbing. Not at all. The curved roofs were slick and placed too far apart to clamber directly up the outer edges. However, this was not a tall pagoda—the distance from one story to the next was just a bit more than I could reach on my tiptoes. I had to make my way up the slanting surface toward the center, where I could climb onto the railing of the deck that ran around the central pillar, and then latch onto the beams supporting the next level. I looped my legs over and shimmied my way out to the edge.

There—the most terrifying, exhilarating part of the climb—I would grab onto the beam supporting the outermost edge, swing my legs like an apple swaying in the autumn breeze until I could flip myself over and onto the top of the roof I'd just clambered, monkey-like, along the bottom.

As I climbed, the trees opened up, revealing the stars of the River of Heaven, flowing brighter and brighter overhead. Their light and the exertion of the climb washed away thoughts of war and plans and harm and virtue.

By the time I flipped myself over onto the top level, I was breathing heavy and my heart was beating like a woodpecker searching for bugs. There was no deck, no central pillar at the center. Just a spire that thrust up into the stars. I had arrived at a place that couldn't be reached by stairs.

Yet a black silhouette leaned against the spire, staring upward.

"I see why Hachihime calls you Squirrel," said a voice that I soon recognized as Rōtaisai-*san*'s.

Ice shot through my veins. I felt as if I had been caught running naked through the middle of the street.

A cloud of steam revealed a huff of the monk's laughter. "How nice of you to join me. I come up here often when I wish to think; the meditation hall is well and good, but sometimes one needs the whole of the heavens to let one's thoughts roam freely."

"As you say, your reverence."

Again, a quiet laugh. "Come, Murasaki-*san*. You have nothing to fear from me. I am just as likely to get into trouble for being here as you."

Once my pulse had slowed to a drip and my blood once again ran warm, I walked up to his side. Together we looked up at the wheeling stars overhead.

In the city, it was easy to forget how many stars blazed in the night sky. It had been far too many months since I had seen them in all their glory. They may not have felt quite so close as they did in the mountains, where I always felt as if I could almost touch them, but they shone bright and clear. Stars beyond number like clouds of brilliant fireflies.

He pointed out constellations to me—the Seven Northern Stars, the bright Subaru. He pointed out Orihime and Hikoboshi, two brilliant stars separated by the River of Heaven, and told the story of how the lovers were separated by Orihime's angry father, but how a flock of magpies would create a bridge between them and allow the lovers to rejoin for a single night each year.

They were all stories I had heard before from my mother, who loved to show me and my sister the night sky and weave the legends behind the various constellations. And the monk recounted the tales with such pleasure that I could not help but be swept along.

After he had told a number of the stories, he fell silent. We both stared up for a while. Then he said, "When I was younger than you, your mother and I used to climb up onto the roof of the East Wing. The stars weren't as clear as they are here, but she used to love telling the stories."

Surprise gripped me. "My... mother?"

He nodded. "She was my best friend growing up. Your father, too, but Kazuo-*kun* was always so serious, even as a boy. He and the other boys were always playing at being soldiers. But Chojo..." He looked down at me. Starlight etched the corner of his mouth as it turned up. "Your mother was a wonderful storyteller."

"She still is," I whispered. "I hope she and Usako..."

He nodded and looked back up.

After some time, he said, "Seeing you and the other girls with Lady Bee brought back so many memories. Memories of you. Of your parents. And of course, memories of the attack that killed Washihime, Hachihime's mother." He grunted and looked down at me once again. "As well as everything that followed."

I nodded to let him know that I understood. Nobunaga's rage, his thirst for revenge, which led him to order the killing of a group of children. Our fathers' refusal. Dishonor. Death. Banishment. I nodded again.

He sighed. "It terrified me. If my brilliant, clever brother could lose his mind... If an attack on someone he loved could make him turn on others whom he cared for deeply, how long would it be before someone decided to use me to get at my brother? Or if, gods forbid, Nobunaga were to suffer another tragic loss, might he not turn on me? I know Nobunaga loves me, but he loved your father, Hanichi-*san*, and Torugu-*san* like brothers."

"Is that why you became a monk?"

He shrugged and smiled up at the stars. "The quiet, contemplative life suits me. And I am as far from the battles and court intrigue as possible."

"Yet your brother burned the monastery on Mt. Wisdom to the ground."

"Ah." He shrugged once more. "I came here precisely because this monastery is famed for turning inward, not outward. We are healers. We spend the largest part of our days meditating on the perfections of the True Word."

He gestured at the trees and the buildings below. "This monastery has stood since these mighty cedars were saplings. It has done so precisely because it has never meddled in the affairs of the empire. My brothers and I all mourned Nobunaga's attack on our brothers. But we could also see that the warrior monks had brought Nobunaga's wrath upon themselves. *I am the owner, the heir, and the child of my own actions. Whatever I do, good or bad, the consequences shall be mine, and mine alone.*' So we learn."

That was a lot to take in.

We both stared up.

A question I had been worrying at for months burst from my lips. "Is any action we take truly good?"

He looked down at me, head cocked like a crow's.

I sighed. "At the ford today. We saved Lady Hachihime. That's a good thing, right?"

The monk raised an eyebrow. "I certainly think so. *Dōmo arigatō*, Murasaki-*san*." He placed his palms together and bowed his head.

"*Dōitashimashite*, Rōtaisai-*san*." I nodded back. I'd have bowed more deeply, but didn't want to lose my balance on the slick rooftop. "But what I wanted to know... We killed those men. We've had to hurt and kill others who were trying to attack or steal from us. How can that be *good*?"

He stared at me for a moment, somber as an owl. Then he gave a huff of recognition. "Do no harm."

I blinked up at him. "What?"

"Your father always tried to follow the old Way of the Warrior. Tried to get my brother and the rest to follow it as diligently as he did. He'd tell us that a true samurai never acted out of anger or greed or spite. That a warrior, like his blade, should always be in balance."

I felt as if he'd punched me in the stomach. "My father... the last thing he said to me was *'Do no harm, Murasaki.'* And I've tried to follow what he said. But I'm not sure it's even possible."

Now the edge of his mouth turned downward, a frown carved into the shadows by starlight. "Is Kazuo-*san* gone, then?"

It was my turn to shrug. "I... don't know. But I'm afraid he must be." Seeing Rōtaisai-*san* sag under that thought, I continued. "But my mother is still alive. Or at least... She was when I left Serenity."

"Ah. Well, that is good." Rōtaisai-*san*'s face once again took on a wry smile. "Whenever Kazuo-*san* went on about *bushido* and *do no harm*, Chojo would tease him. *'Sounds like a terrific excuse to do nothing!'*"

My jaw dropped. "My mother said *that*? To *Otō-san*?"

He chuckled. "Well, I think your father liked the fact that she didn't take him as seriously as he did."

Could I ever remember Mother teasing my father? I could barely remember her smiling, let alone laughing.

The monk peered at me, then cocked his head to the other side. "As for your question, it sounds as if you've seen why *doing no harm* is both a worthy and an impossible goal—in this life at least. The Buddha's first teaching is that the very fabric of this world is woven with sorrow and suffering. He goes on to say that the way to release ourselves from suffering is to give up all attachment—to stop caring about the things of this world, including the people. And while that is an admirable path for a monk, a nun, a saint—or a true samurai, perhaps—it is an impractical lesson for anyone who must live in the world itself. Do no harm? Even a statue does harm, its weight pressing down on the boards and stones that support it."

I nodded, tears welling in my throat. "I understand."

"And remember what I said about being the owner of your own actions? Those men attacked you. They are the ones responsible, and so they're the ones who paid the price." He placed a hand on my shoulder. "And, if I knew your father at all, I think he would add that doing less harm is always better than doing more. And so, yes. I think what you did was far more good than bad. So it seems to me."

Yet again, I nodded.

The monk looked back up at the stars.

After a few breaths I joined him. We gazed up for some time, until the stars seemed as bright as distant bonfires.

Bonfires of blue ice.

My last question finally wriggled its way to the surface. "Speaking of doing less harm or doing more…"

When I paused, he looked down at me again. "Yes, Murasaki?"

"Emi, Toumi, and I were talking after we left you with your sister. We were trying to work out…" I didn't want to ask, '*Can we trust your brother? Should we be helping him and Lord Takeda take control of the whole empire?*' I chewed on my cheek. "We were trying to work out whether a great general, a great warrior, actually makes a great ruler."

"Ah." Now he smiled, a smile twisted with a bit of his family's wry amusement as well as a bit of Mieko-*sensei*'s sadness. "That's a very good question, Sister Squirrel. Unfortunately, I was never the finest political mind in our family. And while I have spent the past few years in contemplation, I'm afraid the matters we meditate on tend to be more questions of other worlds rather than this one." He added with a grunt, "It seems to me that the person who reunites the nation and ends the warring will have to be a great soldier, or he will never defeat the lords who will inevitably betray him, seeking their own advantage, however. We can only hope that he will also have the wisdom, once he has fought to victory, to rule justly and well."

Together, we nodded and looked up once again.

5 – Oak Leaf

When I awoke the next morning, golden sunlight streaming through the thin paper screens on the windows, Hachihime was already sitting up in bed. Her expression was set in a determined scowl, like a bear preparing to catch spawning salmon. "Teach me that *Sixty-four Changes* dance."

We all blinked at her.

"I know I've talked about wanting to learn it before. But after yesterday, I don't want to be tossed around like a sack of rice if there's trouble."

She had asked us about our training many times, saying that she'd love to join us. But whenever we'd tried to wake her at daybreak to do the exercise that prepared us for our work, she had pulled the covers over her head and begged us to leave her alone.

"Hachihime…" I began.

But her scowl didn't soften at all, and so we dressed her and then ourselves in light trousers and jackets. We went out to the courtyard.

Mieko-*sensei* was waiting for us.

She led us through the dance. The sequence of forms that moved us from balanced stances to defensive ones to attacking ones and back. I had watched my father do the same practice every morning with his *katana*. Emi, Toumi, and I had been doing the exercise daily for nearly a year, so it had become second nature to us.

Hachihime remained determined, but the movements weren't as familiar to her. She occasionally stumbled and complained. After the first four rounds, Mieko-*sensei* stood behind Hachihime and adjusted her placement, her balance, her movement.

I expected Hachihime to grow exasperated. She was generally about as patient as the bumble bees that decorated most of her kimono. But that morning, instead of barking or flouncing away, she bit her lip and persisted.

We all told her she was doing well for a beginner. Even Toumi.

Hachihime scowled as if we'd teased her and asked *Sensei* to start again.

By the time we had practised the entire sequence a dozen times, Hachihime was wilting, Toumi was whining, and Mieko-*sensei* was beginning to show signs of stiffness.

Even months later, she had not fully recovered from the wound the assassin had left in her side. Dr. Chan, Lord Oda's tiny Chinese surgeon, had been impressed that she was able to move at all, let alone with anything like the grace and strength she had owned before the attack at the theater.

Emi and I weren't complaining, but even we were beginning to tire.

The Sixty-four Changes may look simple, graceful, and easy, but it requires such precise placement and balance that doing it properly becomes, in fact, very hard.

———

We had finished and finally broken our fast when four dozen Oda warriors rode into the monastery courtyard. Heavy cavalry and horse bowmen.

At their head rode a young samurai and a lady who, despite her plain clothing, sat in the saddle with an air of elegant command.

Emi stepped in front of Hachihime. Toumi and I flanked her.

Cousin Harē ran smiling from where our horses were tied up and bowed to the newcomers. "Lord Nobutada. Lady Kichō. Your messenger reached us before dawn. Thank you for coming so quickly."

"You gave us no choice," grumbled the young warrior, who was apparently Lord Oda's eldest son.

"Nobutada," said his mother, face placid.

He closed his mouth but looked as if he had much more to say.

Whatever it might have been, Hachihime didn't want to hear it. "Your father left you to defend this province—our *home* province. And yet a band of *ronin* attacked us as we crossed the border! They tried to *kill* me and Lady Monogami!"

Nobutada's face darkened—in anger or in shame, I couldn't tell. Probably both.

Hachihime stood up to her not-very-considerable full height, glaring up at her nephew like a shrew at a badger that's disturbed its burrow. "Well? What are you going to *do* about it?"

When her son just ground his teeth, Kichō-*sama* said, "We understood that your guards had slain the assassins. What would you have Lord Nobutada do?"

"Do?" Hachihime's imperious gaze shot to me, Emi, and Toumi, then back up to the young Oda heir. He looked somewhat older than her, in fact. "Why isn't there a garrison at that crossing? That is the second time I have been ambushed where the Great Eastern Sea Road crosses the Salutation River. *My mother died there.* Why is that entrance to the province not more secure?"

Nobutada began to growl a response, but his mother laid a hand on the fist grasping his reins, stilling him. "That is a good point, Hachihime. The ford is not near any towns, and so the Odas have not in the past seen the need to expend the resources to defend that wilderness. However, we should clearly consider it now."

Nobutada grunted, nostrils flaring.

Hachihime gave her sister-in-law a curt nod, nose in the air.

Harē had been talking with the commander of the Oda cavalry. Now he jumped in, nervous as a rabbit in a dog pack, clearly eager to move the conversation in a less explosive direction. "My lady, my lord, may I introduce Takeda Masugu. He commands the honor guard accompanying Lady Hachihime to the wedding."

Masugu-*san* stepped forward and bowed. "My lord. My lady. And this is Lady Monogami Kuniko, Hachihime-*sama*'s chaperone on this journey."

Still glowing from the morning exercises, Mieko-*sensei* gave a deep, courtly bow. Unless you were next to her, as I was, you wouldn't have noticed the strain it took. "I am honored to meet you, Nobutada-*sama*. Kichō-*sama*."

Clearly seeing her for the first time, Nobutada gaped at our teacher, eyes and mouth suddenly wide. "Uh… Likewise. Lady Kuniko."

His mother glanced first at her son, then at Mieko-*sensei*. "It is a pleasure to meet you. We have heard so much about you from my husband." For the first time, her face took on an appraising, Oda-like expression.

Before the conversation could flow back into dangerous waters, Harē said, "My lord, my ladies, we had hoped to reach Harmony Castle by last night—I fear that not only are we behind schedule, but the delay may give whoever was behind the ambush more time to prepare their next attempt on the ladies' lives."

Nobutada frowned. "You believe this attack was aimed at the women?"

We all nodded.

Masugu-*san* said, "The archers were aiming at Lady Kuniko, at Lady Hachihime, and at Risuko, Emi, and Toumi here."

Harē agreed. "We're not sure of the actual target, but they were after one of the ladies, definitely."

"If not all of us," tutted Hachihime.

Nobutada continued to scowl.

His mother placed a hand on his, still clenching his horse's reins. "Since we cannot allow that to happen, and since my husband has asked his son and me to attend your wedding, Hachihime, I am sure that Nobutada and his troops will be happy to escort you across Rising Tail."

"Mother…" muttered Nobutada, but his mother's grip tightened, and he stopped. With a grimace that looked like an attempt at a polite smile, he nodded. "Of course. When were you scheduled to cross into the Three Rivers?"

Masugu-*san* and Harē shared glances. "This evening," said my cousin.

Nobutada's frown deepened. "Under ideal circumstances, that's a two-day ride. The rivers aren't flooding, but the roads are busy at harvest time. And my men have ridden all night."

Again, Masugu-*san* glanced at Harē, then at Mieko-*sensei*, Hachihime and us girls. He shrugged. "We completely understand, Oda-*sama*. It's amazing you got here so fast. But we do need to make up for the time the ambush cost us. There's no other way?"

Nobutada shook his head with a snap. "Any other route would take you further inland and further from where you're headed. We can make it as far as——"

Hachihime clicked her tongue. "We could take a ship."

"What?" scoffed her nephew.

"A ship across the bay." She smiled up at him. "It's a half-day trip at most. It's easy, Nobu-*kun*."

"Really, aunt?" Nobutada sneered. "With six cavalry squadrons?"

Mieko-*sensei* tilted her head demurely. "If it were possible, Nobutada-*sama*, it would certainly save us some time. And no assassins will expect such a detour."

Now Nobutada's frown softened to a scowl like a dog's that's eager to please, eager to bite, but not sure how to do both.

"And your troops would only have to escort us to the ship," mused Masugu-*san*. "They could return to Harmony Castle at their leisure. Do you have a large vessel nearby?"

Nobutada chewed on a lip and looked to Lady Kichō. His mother patted his hand and tipped her head. "The *Fukurukuju* is anchored at Oak Leaf. We could get there well before noon."

With a wince, Harē looked up at the young lord. "Admiral Kamenote won't like being pressed into ferry service."

"Oh, never mind that crusty old poop!" Hachihime chirped, "We're going for a sail."

———

We reached the tiny port town of Oak Leaf early enough that the light of the sun still left a trail of gold across Spirit Bay.

With the Oda heavy cavalry on guard around us and Harē and Masugu-san's squadrons dismounting and preparing to walk their mounts aboard, we stood on the dock, looking up at the floating castle that was the *Fukurukuju.*

Harē had been right. The ship's commander, Admiral Kamenote, didn't like it.

Face dark, he bellowed at Nobutada, "You want the pride of the Oda fleet, the most fearsome warship in these waters, to serve as a *pleasure barge* for a bunch of girls?"

Nobutada faced away from us, but his ears burned red. "As commander of Rising Tail—"

"Commander," sneered the scar-faced admiral, who was half a head taller than Nobutada and seemed twice as wide.

Hachihime strode up the gang plank to her nephew's side, a butterfly imposing herself between a falcon and a vulture. "Admiral Kamenote, you will speak to your commanding officer with respect, or he will place you in charge of a leaky rowboat, guarding a lonesome rock out in the bay. Do you understand?" When he gawked down at her, she barked, *"Do you understand?"*

Kamenote-*san* stood at attention and growled, "Yes, Oda-*sama.*"

"Good." She crossed her arms. "My brother, Oda Nobunaga, views this mission as a matter of the highest strategic importance. My marriage to Lord Takeda will cement an alliance that will bring with it over eighty thousand battle-hardened troops, a dozen warships that you *won't have to fight*, and control over the whole of the coast from here to the top of Swift River. We were ambushed by assassins yesterday and now require a ship." Hachihime lifted her chin. "So yes, Admiral, you will transport us *girls* across Spirit Bay to Tranquility with all possible speed. And you will treat orders from my nephew as orders from his father. Do you understand?"

"Yes, Oda-*sama.*" The man stared over her head, ready to bite.

"Good." She turned to Nobutada. "You're welcome, Nobu-*kun.*"

"Thank you. Hachihime-*san*," he said through gritted teeth.

Winking at us, she turned back to the ship's commander. "Oh, and some of these girls would take your ears off in a fight. So do treat them too with all due respect."

6 — Pelicans

Sailors with long poles pushed us away from the dock, out into the tiny harbor. Nobutada's cavalry were forming up, ready to return to base. On the pier, a flock of ungainly pelicans stood, wings outstretched as if saluting us—though they were probably drying their wings.

On a warehouse building behind them, a carved wooden sign caught my eye: an oak leaf, its stem wrapped around an acorn.

I felt as if one of the Little Brothers had punched me in the stomach.

Oars shot from the side of the ship and began to row it away from the small town I hadn't paid any attention to.

As I gripped the handrail on the top deck, far above the water, Emi put her hand on my shoulder. "Murasaki?"

Toumi came up on my other side. "Seasick already, Mouse?"

I pointed at the Kano *mon*.

"Oh," said Emi.

"Huh," said Toumi.

Harē and Hachihime came over to us. She burbled, "Told you this would be a good idea! What are you three gawking at?"

I pointed again.

"Oh. Yes. Oak Leaf. It's belonged to the Kano forever, not that your families have lived here as long as I can remember."

My jaw and stomach dropped. "*Belonged...*"

Harē clicked his tongue. "Belongs. To you, I suppose, with your father gone and your family name restored. The harvest, rents, income from the port, small as it is. They're what pay your families' expenses."

"Expenses?" Toumi coughed. "What expenses? We've been working for our rice and a roof over our head for the past year. Sourpuss and me lived on the streets before that, and Mouse was living off scavenged bird eggs!"

"Well…" Harē rubbed the back of his head.

Hachihime peered at us, incredulous. "Of course you have income. You're samurai. It's probably only a handful of *kushukin* a year, mind, it's not like it's a lot of money."

"Not a lot of money!" Toumi gasped.

"Murasaki?" Emi peered at my face.

"My… It was so bad last year… *Okā-san* sold me. To Lady Chiyome." A single gold *kushukin* would have been enough for her and my sister to live for more than a year—and still have plenty left some for new clothes, new brushes and inkstones, new paper…

Are they all right?

Are they alive?

"Oh." Hachihime actually looked as if she might apologize.

She didn't. But she seemed to consider it. Which shocked me, upset as I was.

"Your mother." Harē gazed out at the now-receding town that bore my clan's seal as its name. "She… *sold* you? Things were that desperate?"

I nodded, my lower lip trembling. The only thing keeping me from bursting into tears there on the command deck of the Oda flagship was that I didn't want to prove the admiral right about us *girls*.

Now it was Harē who looked as if he had been hit in the gut. "I… I am so sorry, Murasaki." I nodded again, incapable of any other response.

Emi put an arm around one shoulder and I was stunned when Toumi patted the other.

Emi said, "We will see them when we reach Serenity. You can tell them the good news."

"If they're still there."

"Come on, Mouse," said Toumi with a smile that you could have used to skin a goat. "They'll be there. Living it up on the two bronze pieces your little mousy tail was probably worth."

I forced a smile—one probably as lacking in actual humor as hers. "Two? You saw how scrawny I was when Chiyome-*sama* found me. I doubt I was worth *one*."

My friends all laughed, even Hachihime, though she looked as if she'd smelled something one of the seagulls wheeling overhead had deposited on the deck.

Harē didn't laugh. He just grunted and nodded.

———

Sailors raised a square sail bearing the melon-bud *mon*. It bellied out over our heads as it caught the breeze. On the deck below, Masugu-*san* stared up, mouth and eyes pinched.

"Something wrong, Masugu-*san*?"

He blinked, looked down at me, and shook his head. "No, Murasaki-*san*. Not… wrong. I was thinking about Yaeko."

"Ah." I looked up at the sail, which brought back my first impression of Yaeko-*san*, Masugu-*san*'s pregnant older sister. When we had departed the capitol, she had looked more as if she were carrying a full-grown *tanuki* in the front of her robes. "She seemed well when we left." The only thing she'd complained of when she and her husband Fūto saw us off the day we left the capital was difficulty sleeping. And Fūto's snores.

Masugu-*san* grunted, his face still upturned. He wasn't actually looking at the sail. "I worry."

Yaeko-*san* had told us that this was the first pregnancy she had carried past the fourth month. "The midwife said she and the baby were in good health. I'm sure she's fine." That hadn't stopped her or Masugu-*san* from crying when they hugged and said farewell.

He shrugged.

I had known women in the village who had had stillborn children, and even one young wife who had herself died giving birth. But they were poor women without the care Fūto-*san* could provide his wife. "She's got the best doctors, the midwife is supposed to be wonderful, and all those servants to look after her. I'm sure Yaeko-*san* and the baby will be fine."

He looked down again, smiling—but it was a smile that seemed to have much more Mieko-*sensei* than Masugu-*san* in it. "Even rich women die in childbirth, Murasaki-*san*."

"Ah." My own eyes pinched.

The billowing canvas overhead looked more decorative than practical. Men at banks of long oars in the lower decks of the ship did most of the work of moving the huge waterborne castle over the waves. The beat of a deep drum helped the oarsmen pull together.

Masugu-*san* and Harē's men offered to pitch in, but the Oda sailors laughed, saying rowing was work for real men. The cavalrymen laughed back, saying *real men* could ride a horse without falling off.

Back and forth. Back and forth.

As Masugu-*san* and I reached the front rail, Toumi turned to us and snorted. "Boys."

Emi and I giggled, though my eyes still stung with repressed tears.

Masugu-*san* and my cousin chuckled as well. Harē said, "If they weren't giving each other, um, a hard time, we'd probably have a lot more to worry about. So a little teasing is a good sign."

Aimaru stood at the side rail, looking back at the receding shore. His usually open face was clouded with thought.

I went to stand beside him.

The breeze was fresh, scrubbing our faces with the scent of the bay. Seagulls dodged a flight of pelicans that skimmed the surface of the choppy water.

I said, "I've never been on a boat before. You?"

He shook his head, but his attention still seemed to be elsewhere.

One of the pelicans plunged into the water, coming up with a mackerel in its huge beak.

Peering down at the line of oars, I continued, "When we first got on, I couldn't imagine how a huge thing like this could possibly move across the water. But it seems as agile as one of those pelicans." I nodded to where yet another of the comical-looking birds had caught a fish.

Aimaru turned to me. "Murasaki-*san*?"

I frowned. "Come on, Aimaru. Murasaki. Or Risuko. You don't have to..."

He shook his head and looked back out toward the shore. "You three... You're samurai women. You have a *town*."

"I guess." I shrugged, now frowning myself. "It's the first I've heard of it. And... I mean, you heard Hachihime. It's just a small one."

"And I'm a bastard born in a brothel."

"Aimaru—"

"She..." He sniffed and swiped at his eyes with his gauntleted hand. "She should marry a samurai. She's so... I bet she could marry a nobleman if she wanted."

"She..." I looked up at him, but he had turned away. "Aimaru. Emi doesn't want to marry a samurai. Or a nobleman." *Or anyone, yet,* I thought, and gripped his huge arm. Lady Chiyome's dry voice echoed in my head: *Kunoichi are married to their duty and to death.* "We might not make it to next year, Aimaru. We might not even make it back to Serenity. Please. She..." I didn't want to use words for my friend that I didn't think she'd used herself, yet, but I knew that Emi and Aimaru loved each other as much as anyone our age could understand love. "She would die for you, Aimaru."

He gave a half-shrug, half-nod. "And I'd die for her."

I gave his massive, armored shoulder a punch that Hoshi would have laughed at. "Then don't decide things for her, *baka*. Please."

We watched the seagulls and the pelicans play tag among the waves.

"Thank you, Murasaki," Aimaru said, voice low, and gave me a brief, manly hug.

Smooshed against his leather breastplate, I sighed. "Boys."

———

When I returned to the front rail of the command deck overlooking the ranks of oarsmen, Hachihime and Lady Kichō were chatting. Well, Hachihime was chatting, while Lady Kichō nodded politely. Nobutada was showing Mieko-*sensei* different aspects of the ship. Admiral Kamenote stood stock still, staring at our destination, apparently pretending we didn't exist.

Masugu-*san* looked more like himself, watching the others with a wry smile.

"Masugu-*san*."

"Murasaki-*san*." The smile broadened as he looked down at me. "This is quite a ship, isn't it?"

I nodded. "May I ask a question?"

"Of course."

"Is that part of being a samurai? Having a, um, town, or...?"

"An estate? Not usually. That's part of what distinguishes *daimyo* from samurai. But some samurai have them, sure. Just... smaller."

"Smaller." Oak Leaf had faded into the wash of gold and red along the coast, but the town still drew my gaze. "And there's money?"

He nodded again and shrugged. "Well, all samurai get paid by their lords. It's how we afford our arms, our supplies. How we feed and house and clothe our families."

"Do you have an estate?"

"Ah. Well, my father does. Part of my mother's dowry was a valley outside of Worth City. Her mother had been a Takeda."

I frowned. "Dowry."

"The property the bride brings into a marriage."

I shrugged. "I know what a dowry is, Masugu-*san*. My father wrote dozens of marriage contracts for merchants and samurai. I just..." Again, a shrug.

He shrugged back. "You never thought you would have one."

"No." *Oda*-sama *did promise*. I felt suddenly very, very young and small. "Or money."

He cocked his head at me.

"Even before father... left, we never had much money. More than anyone else in the village, but they all grew crops or animals. So we needed the coin to pay for our own supplies. And after, *Okā-san* tried to keep *Otō-san*'s clients, but no one wanted a woman scribe. And of course, Imagawa-*sama* stopped using us. There was nothing."

Masugu winced. "I'm so sorry, Murasaki."

Yet another shrug. "So… the money from Oak Leaf. Who has it?"

"Huh." He scratched the back of his head and glanced over at Hachihime. "I'd assume Lord Oda's bailiffs have been collecting the rents and tariffs and such since he banished your father. You'd have to talk with him."

"Ah." Not a conversation I was looking forward to. But if I was going to truly be the heir of the Kano, I needed to act like it. After all, it sounded as if my income would cover Emi and Toumi's expenses as well. And Mother's. And Usako's. I smiled up at him. "Thank you, Masugu-*san*."

He smiled back. "You know you're always welcome, Murasaki-*san*." His eyes returned where they so often did. To Mieko-*sensei*, who was listening politely to Nobutada talk, his chest puffed out, his gestures encompassing the whole horizon.

I whispered, "Masugu-*san*, does it, um, bother you that young Lord Oda is being quite so friendly with Kuniko-*sama*?"

He tilted his head, his smile broadening further. "No, Murasaki-*san*. I know where her loyalty lies. And her heart." He leaned closer and whispered. "And I know if he tried anything, he'd end up with the seagulls in the bay. And she'd make it look like an accident, too."

That actually made me titter, which got him chuckling as well.

Our laughter made Hachihime glance away from Lady Kichō to us, and then, following Masugu-*san*'s amused, adoring gaze, to Mieko-*sensei*, who continued to treat Nobutada's full-on flirtatious assault with polite indifference. "Nobu-*kun*!"

Her nephew flinched, anger flashing like autumn lightning across his face. He tried to school his expression and nodded to Mieko-*sensei*, then turned to his aunt. "Hachihime-*san*. I wish you wouldn't call me that. As I've told you before. I am three years your senior, after all." He attempted a smile but couldn't hide the wolfen fire in his eyes.

"Ah, but you'll always be my little nephew Nobu-*kun*," teased Hachihime, eyes half-closed. "Isn't that right, Kichō?"

"One can't change what one is, Hachihime." Lady Kichō's obsidian-black eyes took on a calculating edge.

Hachihime laughed. "No, very true. One can't!" She turned back to Nobutada. "Now I'm just going to save you from embarrassing yourself, silly boy."

Nobutada glowered. "Embarrassing myself?"

"Yes!" She laughed, morning lark-song at midday. "Lady Kuniko's intended is Masugu there—heavens know why, he's such a useless lump, but still, you're throwing yourself at another man's fiancée. Silly Nobu-*kun*!"

His face fell. Turning back to Mieko-*sensei*, he stammered, "Is... Is that so, my lady?"

She bowed her head slightly. "We have not announced it, since my own family name is scarcely alive again. But yes." She glanced back at Masugu-*san*. "When the time comes, it will be my pleasure and my honor to marry Takeda Masugu." Her tone was polite, her expression demure. But her eyes burned with a flame I had seen often over the previous months.

Though I had never had any doubt about how Mieko-*sensei* and Masugu-*san* felt about each other, I had never heard that they were engaged. For years, they had been estranged because she had refused to marry him. *Married to her duty and to death.*

I glanced up at Masugu-*san*, who looked both as if he'd been hit on the head and like a cat that's found a fisherman's catch.

Nobutada, on the other hand, looked like a dog that's been kicked when it was asleep. Embarrassed and bewildered. He bowed stiffly. "I beg your pardon, Masugu-*san*. Kuniko-*san*."

"Silly boy!" Hachihime laughed.

His face red as maple leaves, he turned and stalked past me to the stairs, muttering under his breath, "No aunt of mine!"

Lady Kichō glared at her sister-in-law, obsidian gaze now sharp as cut glass, and followed her son down the steps to the lower deck.

Hachihime clapped her hands together. "What fun!"

7 – Tranquility

As the sun descended halfway toward the horizon behind us, Hachihime was still tittering, Mieko-*sensei* and Masugu-*san* were still looking at each other as if no one else in the world existed, and Admiral Kamenote still stood in rigid fury, barking out occasional commands to the helmsman and the other sailors, but otherwise doing an impressive impression of an uninviting, looming island, there on the deck of the *Fukurukuju*.

Land approached ahead, and other ships. None were anywhere nearly the size of ours.

I told Emi and Toumi what Masugu-*san* and I had discussed. About the samurai and *daimyo*. About the money. About Oak Leaf.

"Your town," said Toumi with a smile that could cut glass.

"Our town."

She gave her best approximation of a dainty bow. "As it pleases you, Lady Mouse."

I frowned and stared at my feet, which only encouraged her.

Toumi finally got tired of teasing me about my newfound wealth and status—both of which I pointed out were completely not real. I glanced at Emi. She shrugged. Her frown had shifted to the one that let me know she was thinking something through. "Emi?"

"I was wondering about Masugu-*san* and, um, Kuniko-*sama*." She glanced over at them.

"What," Toumi snorted. "Wondering when they're going to find a dark corner to go—"

"Toumi!!" I groaned.

Emi clicked her tongue. "Did either of you know they were engaged?"

I shook my head, thinking back to overhearing them in the Retreat during a snowstorm. Masugu-*san* had said that Mieko-*sensei*'s refusal to marry him three years before had killed him.

Toumi laughed. "Not sure he knew they were getting hitched! He looked like someone'd smacked him in the face."

I couldn't help smiling. "Maybe, but it looked as if he enjoyed it."

Emi nodded.

Toumi chuckled. "Hey, anyone who'd want to marry her must be a glutton for punishment. Even if she is a lady."

That got me thinking of Aimaru, who was still staring toward the long-gone Oak Leaf at the back of the ship. "Emi," I whispered. "You need to talk to…"

"Ducklings!" Hachihime buzzed over from tittering with Mieko-*sensei* and Masugu-*san*. Hachihime had been doing all the tittering. Mieko had been smiling serenely, her eyes locked on the lieutenant's. "What are you three over here gossiping about?"

Toumi looked as if she were about to actually tell her, which seemed like a terrible idea, but Emi answered first. "You seem in a very good mood today, Hachihime."

"Mood?"

I nodded at Emi. "After yesterday."

"Ah." For the first time that day, her expression clouded over.

"I mean," said Toumi, "the way you talked to the admiral, and, you know, *Nobu-kun*…"

The noblewoman's demeanor cleared, a wicked smile breaking out like the rising sun. "It's such fun teasing him."

Fun it may have been, but I wasn't sure it was a good idea. "Perhaps, my lady, but neither he nor Lady Kichō seemed amused."

"Oh, they hate me!" Hachihime laughed. "They always have."

Emi cocked her head. "Why is that, my lady?"

Hachihime dismissed the question with a wave of her closed fan. "No idea. Nobu says they're just jealous of his affection for me, but really, what threat am I to them? I'm just the youngest of his siblings." She opened her eyes wide, all innocence, like a cat standing over a bowl that had once contained shrimp. *Wherever can* those *have gone?*

"Perhaps," I granted, since disagreeing with her was generally a waste of breath. "But it seems as if antagonizing them might not be the, um, wisest idea."

Emi nodded. "Especially when they're going to be escorting us the rest of the way to the wedding." With an armed guard.

Again, a dismissive flick of the fan. "They're Oda. And once I'm married off, I'm sure they'll be happy to be rid of me."

I shared a look with my friends.

Perhaps Nobutada and his mother wouldn't be willing to wait that long.

Perhaps they were behind the assassination attempts? We needed to discuss that. Not with Hachihime. Instead, I asked, "And are you looking forward to your wedding, Hachihime?"

She was silent for a moment, gazing down. Both rare acts for her. Then she squared her shoulders and looked me in the eye. "What girl hasn't dreamed of her wedding day? And to one of the most powerful men in the realm—aside from Nobu, of course." She flashed a fierce grin at Emi. "In any case, after yesterday, I decided to face my troubles like a dragon, not a flea."

As the *Fukurukuju* entered the port at Tranquility, much larger and busier than the one at Oak Leaf, Mieko-*sensei* finally broke away from Masugu-*san* and approached the four of us. "Ladies."

Hachihime nodded, while the rest of us bowed.

Still smiling, she came close and whispered, "Masugu has made a suggestion that I think is worth considering. We still don't know who is behind these attacks. Nor do we know which of us is the target of those attempts." We all nodded now. Emi frowned, and the rest of us joined her. "Masugu's thought was that we should make it as difficult for any potential assassins as possible."

"How?" I whispered back.

"By all dressing in nondescript clothing, by riding together."

Hachihime looked as if Mieko-*sensei* had fed her a raw egg. "You want *me* to dress like a servant?"

Toumi bumped her shoulder against Hachihime's. "Oh, come on. It's not dressing. It's a disguise."

The young noblewoman considered that for a moment, then broke into a foxish smile. "Ah. That sounds like *much* more fun!"

———

By the time the sailors tied the ship to the dock, the cavalrymen, offering loud and lewd commentary, the five of us had all changed into the plainest kimono we could find. Emi had suggested that we dress in soldiers' tunics and trousers, but Hachihime put her foot down. "Disguise is one thing, but I'm not putting on men's stinky clothes!"

"Not that we'd be able to find any small enough for you or Mouse-*sama* there anyhow," teased Toumi.

I would have objected, but she was probably right. Even the shortest of the soldiers was a full head taller than either me or Hachihime.

Emi and Toumi wore simple kimonos in yellow that Hachihime had given us for when we were attending her. Mieko-*sensei* wore mine. It was a bit tight on her but fit well enough that her blades remained well hidden by the sleeves.

I was in what had been intended as a dressing gown. A pale yellow linen robe with my family's oak-leaf *mon* in pink repeating down the sleeves. I would carry my *wakizashi*—Masugu-*san*'s *wakizashi*—across my horse's saddle.

Hachihime wore an even plainer kimono. It was silk, but also very pale yellow, to the point of looking white, with just one small oak leaf painted on the collar. It was another of mine, obviously. She had put it on with all the glee of a little girl playing dress-up. Of course, she informed us, she normally wouldn't be caught dead in such nondescript clothes.

Which was exactly the point.

Dock workers raised a huge gang plank up to the deck, one wide and thick enough to carry us and our horses. The *Fukurukuju* began to disgorge its passengers.

The commander of the Oda forces at Tranquility rode up to greet the unexpected arrival of the clan's flagship. Nobutada turned from supervising his horse being led down to the dock to inform the captain that our party required a cavalry escort to Serenity.

The captain frowned. "I can spare a squadron of light cavalry."

Nobutada responded that he would be commandeering six. Four heavy and two light.

They fell into a muted, bristly negotiation.

Mieko-*sensei*, Masugu-*san*, and Harē began to discuss where we women should ride, now that it was harder to tell us apart.

Masugu-*san* argued that we should ride in the center, with guards surrounding us, putting us as far from any attackers as possible.

Harē thought that having us separated, each escorted by our own guard, would keep any would-be assassins from going after more than one of us at a time.

Mieko-*sensei* weighed the options and turned to us. "Ladies, what do you think?"

Hachihime grumbled. "I want as many soldiers around me as we have." Not a dragon, now.

"Sure," said Toumi, "but won't that make us just one big target like Harē-*san* said?"

Emi clicked her tongue. "Both would have advantages. Mind, these clothes aren't exactly hard to see. If the point is to make us less likely to be attacked, putting us in the middle of all the soldiers seems like painting a target on us, doesn't it?"

The women all nodded. We saw what she meant. The men grimaced.

I stared down at the front of my golden robes. "And scattering us among them wouldn't be much better, would it? We'd stick out like mountain roses in a bank of briars."

Masugu-*san* sighed. "Good point, Murasaki-*san*."

Harē peered at me. "What do you suggest, cousin?"

Feeling everyone's gaze weighing on me, I looked at Emi.

She shrugged. "Well, these aren't meant to be inconspicuous so much as, um, *innocuous*."

Mieko-*sensei* raised an eyebrow. "What are you suggesting, Emi?"

Emi hummed, looking up at the seagulls wheeling overhead. "I was thinking that, perhaps, we'd look less interesting to any potential attackers if, instead of riding like a group of ladies protected by a company of cavalry, we ride behind the guards."

Toumi said, "So we look as if we're traveling with them, rather than them traveling to protect us."

Harē nodded slowly. "Security through obscurity." When Masugu-*san* cocked his head at him, my cousin continued. "Protecting yourself by making yourself unnoticeable."

Now Masugu-*san* and Mieko-*sensei* nodded, but Hachihime frowned. "That sounds risky."

"Maybe," Toumi said with a wink, "but remember, you'd be riding with the four of us."

That made Hachihime smile. "And what better bodyguards could I ask for?"

I expected more conversation, but everyone nodded. That was apparently that.

The two cavalry officers went to oversee getting all their troops and horses ashore.

We approached Lady Kichō and her son to discuss the plan.

Nobutada was smiling like a predator at the retreating Tranquility commander. "I let him talk me down to five squadrons—three light, two heavy," he said to Harē with a chuckle. "I expected him to hold out for four at the most. They'll meet us at the eastern gate."

His mother smiled. The most emotion I had seen on her face, aside from disgust at Hachihime.

"Nicely done, Nobu-*kun*!" Hachihime said, clapping as if he were a young boy who had just managed to read his first word.

Lady Kichō's smiled went brittle, like marsh grass in winter.

Nobutada maintained his wolfish grin. "Thank you., *imōto*."

I blinked, sharing a glance with Toumi. *Little sister?*

Whatever he meant by it, Hachihime didn't seem perturbed.

As Harē, Masugu-*san*, and their riders rejoined us, Mieko-*sensei* told the young Oda lord of our plan. I thought he might be upset that his aunt, the person he was escorting and protecting, would be following after the company with just a group of ladies to protect her. But he seemed ecstatic not to have to ride with her.

His mother informed us that she would *not* be riding with us either, and I have to say I felt as relieved as she seemed to be.

Harē and Masugu-*san* said that their squadrons would ride at the back of the Oda company, just in front of us. Even having suggested the separation, I was glad that they would be close by.

I could tell Aimaru wasn't happy that we weren't riding in the middle of the troop. But he mounted his horse and joined Masugu-*san*'s honor guard without looking back.

As we clambered into our own saddles, Toumi grunted. "Moon Face is acting weird."

"Yes," agreed Emi, scowling even more deeply than usual.

"You need to talk to him," I whispered.

Emi's frown now reflected more confusion than sadness. "He won't let me get near him."

I sighed. "I think he was even more surprised by the whole Oak Leaf thing than we were."

"Why…" she began, but then stopped, touching her two forefingers to her downturned mouth. "Oh."

"What?" Toumi asked. Then she gave a bray of amusement. "He's decided you're above him, or something? That's a laugh!"

"Yes," Emi said, pout deepening. "It is."

"Anyway," I continued. "You need to talk to him. Soon."

She shrugged, and we followed the soldiers into the town.

Tranquility wasn't as big as the capital, but it sprawled more than any other town that I'd been in. Between the port and the gate, we wandered through noisy markets, quiet neighborhoods, and an imposing gate that led, Hachihime told us, to a shrine that housed some holy sword or other.

"The Sunfield Shrine is one of the oldest, most important holy sites in the empire," said Mieko-*sensei*, her face managing to look both amused and respectful. Another of her abilities that I always wished I could emulate. She nodded back at the three of us. "Girls, do you know which sword Hachihime meant?"

Emi nodded. "The sword of the goddess Amaterasu. One of the goddess's three great treasures."

"Right!" I said, thinking of the stories *Okā-san* had told me and Usako. "The Grasscutter Blade!"

"Grasscutter?" Toumi snorted. "Amaterasu's blade was for mowing the lawn?"

"No!" Bouncing in my saddle, I recounted the story of the great warrior prince Yamato Takeru. How he had subdued the rebellious provinces to the south, once even dressing as a maid to sneak into an enemy leader's party. After his victory, the prince celebrated by going hunting on an open plain, when the defeated enemy set the whole grasslands ablaze, surrounding him with fire.

By the time we approached the eastern gate, I had reached the climax of the story. How Takeru slashed away at the grass around him, and the holy wind held in the blade swept the flames back toward his would-be assassins, killing them all.

Mieko-*sensei* continued. "And so every emperor has been enthroned while holding the blade, the mirror, and the jewel…" I burbled, "…representing the goddess's valor, wisdom, and generosity!"

Mieko-*sensei* smiled and nodded. "Precisely."

"Hey!" Toumi gasped. It wasn't at my story. "I see some old friends up there with the soldiers!"

By the gate, in the midst of the Oda cavalry, bright amongst the soldiers as poppies in a thorn bramble, four women in red and white sat astride black Takeda chargers. Sachi-*sensei*, Hoshi-*sensei*, plain-faced Mitsuke-*sensei*. And Shino.

Mieko-*sensei* had told us that the last of the Horseradish Sisters had won her *kunoichi* robes at the beginning of the summer and had been heading out on missions with the older women. Still, when I had last seen her, she had still worn the blue jacket of an initiate. She had been devastated by her sometime friend, sometime rival Mai's murder.

Her flat face was set in a neutral scowl. But when Toumi called out a greeting to her, she gave a smirk that looked more like the girl I'd known at the Full Moon. She nodded to us.

The five Tranquility squadrons formed up around Nobutada and Lady Kichō and flowed out the gate. Harē, Masugu-*san*, and their troops followed. Masugu-*san* and Aimaru rode at the very back of the company. They weren't looking our way, but I felt their attention very much on us. Or at least on Mieko-*sensei* and Emi.

As we passed under the gate, the four women in *miko* garb joined us.

"Fancy meeting you here!" Sachi-*sensei* said, smiling broadly.

"Yes," said Mieko-*sensei*, her smile less wide but looking no less pleased. "A remarkable coincidence."

Hoshi chuckled, "Well, we hear there's *quite* the wedding coming up in Serenity." She winked at Hachihime.

Mitsuke sighed, as if the older women's jokes were a burden. One she alone bore. "Lady Chiyome asked us to join you."

"Ah!" Hachihime said. "So, you *are* from the Full Moon. I thought you must be. Kuniko, you must introduce me to your friends."

"It would be my pleasure, Oda-*sama*," said Mieko-*sensei*, speaking formally since we were now in company. "These lovely servants of the gods are Sachi-*san*, Hoshi-*san*, Mitsuke-*san*. And young Shino-*san*, our newest graduate."

In their saddles, the four *kunoichi* bowed to Hachihime. "Oda-*sama*." Then they bowed to Mieko. "Monogami-*sama*."

For some reason, Hachihime tittered. "Oh, please! I see we shall all become great friends, riding to my wedding behind this army of dirt clods. No need to be so formal. These girls call me Hachihime in private. Feel free to do so." She leaned over in her saddle and whispered loudly, "After all, I feel much safer, now that my bodyguard has doubled!"

"Fine with me, Hachihime!" Sachi-*sensei* grinned.

Mitsuke bowed her head. "If you insist, my lady."

That made the rest of us laugh, Hachihime loudest of all.

8 – Seabell Station

As we rode behind the small army, the villagers and farmers along the highway very much ignored us. Nine girls on horseback—what could possibly be interesting about us? Compared to the combined Oda-Takeda cavalry, not much.

Never mind that I was carrying a sword in front of me, Emi and Toumi had bows and quivers of arrows in easy reach, and in addition to the armory of hidden weapons I knew they carried, the four women in *miko* robes had what looked like fine quarterstaves strapped to the sides of their mounts.

When I asked Sachi-*sensei* about the long poles, she tittered. "Aren't they pretty? They make such elegant walking sticks, don't you think?"

On her other side, Hoshi, who taught us calligraphy, and also armed self-defense, snorted. "Sure. But they also have some… surprises."

Toumi broke away from Shino, who'd been regaling us with tales of her missions. None of which involved killing assassins or saving the life of a *daimyo*. But we had let her burble on. It was good to see her happy. Or at least not angry or sad. "Surprises?" Toumi asked Hoshi.

Long face bright, Hoshi started to answer, but Mitsuke broke in. "Not here."

When our penmanship teacher started to argue, Mieko-*sensei* turned back from where she, Emi, and Hachihime were riding at the front of our party. "Patience, Hoshi. We'll be stopping for the night soon. If there's some privacy, you can show us your new toys."

Sachi-*sensei* and Hachihime both giggled, making the rest of us laugh. Even Hoshi, who agreed to be patient. Or try at least.

As we rode, we asked about the goings on back at the Full Moon. About Lady Chiyome, Kee Sun, and the Little Brothers, but especially about Emi's young friends Chinatsu, Junko, and Yoshi.

Shino complained that they were even more annoying than my friends and I, but Sachi-*sensei* laughed and said they weren't any more annoying than she had been. She and Hoshi went on to tell us the girls were doing well, young as they were. Mieko-*sensei* had given Emi an update when she'd rejoined us the month before, but it was good to hear that they were managing, and that, as Emi and I had hoped, they'd taken to the lives of novices.

"Of course," said Hoshi with a smirk. "They already knew all about *kunoichi* for some reason. But Chiyome-*sama* doesn't feel they can earn initiates' sashes until they're at least as big as this one here was when she showed up." She flicked her head at me, and all of the women laughed.

I laughed along. My size didn't embarrass me anymore. At least, not as much. It was part of who I was, and I was beginning to find that I felt all right about that.

We stopped at a small town called Seabell Station, which seemed to have more inns than inhabitants.

Shino sniffed, scowling. "What's a station?"

"A place where people stay on their way to somewhere else," I blurted. "Er. Sorry, Kuniko-*sama*." I only noticed that Mieko-*sensei* had been about to answer when I'd already opened my mouth.

"That's perfectly all right, Risuko," said our teacher with a tip of her head.

In my head, though, I could hear my sister sing-songing, *Just ask Risuko. She knows everything.'*

Apparently, I wasn't completely over feeling embarrassed. If I'm going to be honest—and I promised that I would—it has never gone away completely. But I've never felt quite as uncomfortable simply being myself as I did when I first joined the Full Moon.

Toumi snorted as if she'd heard Usako's tease and agreed with it, then asked, "And why is it called Seabell, when it's in the middle of a bunch of *baka* farms?"

It was a fair question. The only scenery breaking the monotonous plain we'd been riding across was a shadowy wall to the north. The mountains of Dark Letter Province.

Dismounting, Mieko-*sensei* said, "In fact, we're not that far from the shore. There are buoys along the coast to warn ships of rocks—we may be able to hear them tonight."

"We're close to the water, then?" I asked, sliding from my own saddle to the ground.

Mieko-*sensei* smiled. "Yes. If, instead of coming along the coast, we had come down the Salt Road from Dark Letter, you'd have been able to smell it, Risuko, just as you did when we reached the coast in Middle Pass."

I smiled too. It's funny how we stop noticing pleasant sights and sounds and sensations until they're gone. And when they return, they seem twice as wonderful as ever.

The soldiers all made camp in a dry rice paddy on the edge of town. Of course, there was an inn immediately beside the paddy—you couldn't throw a stone in Seabell Station without hitting a roadhouse or a hostel.

As we cared for our horses, Emi stared out the stable door to where Aimaru was doing the same. Removing his mount's saddle and staring back toward us.

I began, "Emi."

She held up her hand, and I let my question fall. But I knew they needed to talk, and soon.

Lady Kichō, Nobutada, Hachihime, and Mieko-*sensei* all took rooms in the inn. The innkeeper was delighted to have such distinguished guests under his humble roof.

Mieko-*sensei* said that she would share Lady Hachihime's small room, as the autumn night was likely to get cold.

We knew, of course, that she was staying with Hachihime as part of our mission. My friends and I had guarded the lady the previous night; she would play the bodyguard tonight.

Mieko-*sensei* alone was almost certainly more effective than the three of us combined. Even still recovering from her injury, she remained more than a match for any would-be intruder.

We ate a bland meal of boiled salmon that Kee Sun would have scoffed at—how do you make salmon bland? The Oda lord, his mother, his aunt, and our teacher all went off to their tiny private rooms.

The rest of us riffraff had to stay in the common room, along with several merchants and a small group of pilgrims headed to Sunfield Shrine.

The merchants had opened an enormous bottle of sake and were loudly arguing over falling rice crop yields, rising silk prices, and which towns had the prettiest girls. Several of the pilgrims joined them, and soon a raucous party broke out, making it impossible to sleep.

There would be no demonstrations of the *kunoichis'* new toys.

Sachi-*sensei* took Toumi and Mitsuke to play some drinking games with the travelers, trying to get them to fall asleep.

Emi and I spoke with Hoshi and Shino. "Were you sent to help us?" Emi asked quietly. "Or were you here on another mission?"

"Not happy to see us, Emi-*chan*?" Shino said with a sneer.

When Emi blushed and blinked, I answered, "Of course we are. Very happy. Lady Chiyome sent Kuniko-*sama* a letter saying we might see you, that the women of the Full Moon would be scouting the roads between Tranquility and Serenity. But we've been ambushed once already and—"

Hoshi gasped. "Ambushed?"

And so, Emi and I told her about the attack.

Even Shino seemed shocked. "So we still don't know which *baka* lord's behind this mess?"

Emi and I shook our heads. Hoshi sucked air in through her long front teeth. Leaning in, she whispered, "Has it occurred to you that Lord Oda's wife and his heir might want to bump off their lord's charming sister?"

We both nodded. I said, "They absolutely hate her. Hachihime thinks it's funny, but..."

Shino sniffed. "I can't decide if she's smarter than she looks, or even dumber. Does she ever stop yapping?"

"Not really," Emi said with a sigh. "But she's not stupid. Just... a, um..." Frowning deeply, she scowled at me.

"A brat," I said with a shrug.

Emi nodded, and Hoshi gave a snicker. "Sounds about right."

Falling asleep as the sounds of the party finally died down, I could almost have sworn I heard the sounds of bells, warning ships of hidden rocks.

9 – Boundary

The next morning, Sachi-*sensei* and Hoshi woke us to do the Sixty-four Changes there in the common room. Mieko-*sensei* dragged in Hachihime.

Unlike the previous morning, young Lady Oda didn't look at all eager to join the exercises. But Hoshi and Sachi-*sensei* teased her and cajoled her until she finally joined in, still grumpy as a bear stuffed into a kimono, but with the rest of us.

The hungover pilgrims and merchants grumbled, though we didn't feel at all sorry for them. Usually, we did the dance silently, but that morning Sachi-*sensei* and Hoshi-*sensei* seemed to delight in chattering and singing and generally making as much noise as possible.

Eventually, the sleepers awoke, and a couple even attempted to join us.

Hachihime still whined about not quite being able to keep up but she was pleased to be able to do much better than the two pilgrims struggling at her side.

Once we had finished the twelfth round of the forms, one of the merchants from the previous night sidled up to Sachi-*sensei*. "So, where're you pretty ladies going?"

The *kunoichi* tittered. "Oh, sir, we're headed from our village to the shrine, to perform the proper rites, you know."

The merchant nodded knowledgeably and went back to packing himself up.

One of the great things about traveling as *miko* was that there were shrines everywhere—holy days and festivals almost every day of the year. If you told people you were headed to *the shrine* or were participating in *the festival*, they would fill in the details themselves and leave you alone.

Sachi-*sensei* winked at me.

We bathed and dressed for the day. I helped Hachihime into her plain kimono. I didn't ask why she needed help putting on such simple clothes. It wasn't worth the trouble.

As we began the process of saddling our horses, a shout came from the soldiers out in the field.

A squadron of horses galloped from the road, bearing down on the camp, evoking panic among the Oda soldiers, who were all unmounted and unarmed. One of the horsemen rode with a blue banner, a ginger-leaf *mon* snapping above him. The Matsudaira.

In the midst of our enormous guard, two figures waved their hands and called out. Masugu-*san* and Harē did their best to keep the hundred or so cavalrymen from drawing their weapons on the newcomers.

The foremost rider leapt from his charger and ran toward Masugu-*san*, his arms open wide. The Takeda lieutenant grinned back and embraced his friend, lifting him off his feet and swinging him around.

As the two men spun, I recognized the laughing face of Tokugawa Tokimatsu. Of course.

Behind me, Sachi-*sensei* chuckled. "So, Kuniko-*sama*, it looks like you might have cause to be jealous!"

"No, Sachi," answered Mieko-*sensei*, her voice warm. "The captain may be my intended's oldest friend, but I know he will never take my place in Masugu's heart."

I was about to say that Masugu-*san* had said something similar about her on the ship the day before, but Hoshi brayed, *"Intended?"*

Mieko-*sensei*'s news naturally caused much laughter and much talk among the older women. Sachi-*sensei* actually began to cry, something I'd never seen her do, and embraced Mieko-*sensei*, congratulating her.

Masugu-*san* and his friend Toki rode toward us, along with my cousin. Nobutada and Lady Kichō, whom we hadn't seen that morning, strode out from the inn to the front of our group. When they reached us, all three officers dismounted and bowed to the Oda lord and lady.

Harē introduced Tokugawa Tokimatsu, who bowed again. "My lord Commander of Rising Tale, I bear greetings on behalf of my uncle Matsudaira Motoyasu, Lord Governor of the Three Rivers. He sent me and my troops to serve as an honor guard for Lady Hachihime on her way to marry the Lord Governor of Worth."

"Good idea," muttered Emi at my shoulder. "We wouldn't want the Matsudaira to think we were part of an invasion."

Toumi grunted. "Yeah. Wouldn't want that."

Nobutada welcomed Tokimatsu and his troops and proceeded to introduce the high-born ladies, starting with his mother, naturally. His aunt he introduced simply by name. He didn't mention their family relationship. I didn't find that surprising.

Then he nodded to Mieko-*sensei*, and Tokimatsu gave the grin we had grown so familiar with the previous spring during his visit to the Full Moon. But when Nobutada introduced her as Lady Monogami Kuniko, Toki's brows shot up. "Mono…?"

Mieko tipped her head. "My apologies, Captain Tokugawa, for having given you an assumed name when we met. Since the fall of Wingtip Castle, I have gone by that alias—Yuri Mieko. She was one of my ladies in waiting before the Akita betrayed my family. To pursue my claim to my heritage and my legacy, I decided it was time, once more, to take up my own name."

"I… see." His brows bunched like angry caterpillars, but then his smirk returned and he gave a cocky bow. "Lady Monogami. Pleasure to see you again."

"And you, Tokugawa-*san*," she replied, bowing more respectfully.

Toki glanced at me. "And it is a pleasure to see you as well, Kano-*san*."

I bowed deeply. "Likewise, Tokugawa-*san*."

"Oh, please," he said, and winked. "Call me Toki. Any friend of Masugu's is a friend of mine." He nodded to Emi and Toumi. "And I seem to remember you two from the Full Moon as well."

My own grin bubbled up. As my friends bowed, I introduced them. "May I introduce Tarugu Toumi and Hanichi Emi?"

Toki began to bow once again—but then stood back up, blinking. "Tarugu and…?"

Toumi huffed. "I hate that everyone reacts to our names that way."

Mieko-*sensei* answered, "Like the Monogami and Kano family names, Toumi, yours are phantoms. Revenants. Tokugawa-*san* didn't expect to hear them again."

"Please, my lady," Toki said, "I hope you too will condescend to call me Toki. After all, we have known each other since that lovely evening at the Imagawa Castle, all these years ago." The Matsudaira officer smiled again, once more as if he knew the punchline to a joke we hadn't yet heard. Masugu-*san* raised his eyebrow at his friend.

Mieko-*sensei* knew the joke, however, as did I. Toki had told her the previous spring that he recognized her from one of her first missions as a *kunoichi*. That he knew her abilities and our school's true purpose. He had promised that he wouldn't betray our secrets unless we threatened his uncle, but… "It would be my pleasure, Toki-*san*." She bowed her head politely, lips curved in a polite smile, but her eyes narrowed like a fox's when it's about to spring.

Toki smiled back, and Masugu-*san* began to laugh, though his eyes flitted back and forth between them.

He seemed about to say something when Nobutada cleared his throat. "If we are to reach Carp Pond today, we should get underway. Harē, get your men and the Tranquility riders mounted and ready to go."

"Yes, my lord!"

———

Once again, we trailed the soldiers, and the people in the town who looked up at all were turning away by the time we nine girls rode by.

Sachi-*sensei* clucked, "I can't say that I enjoy being ignored." Hoshi-*sensei* agreed, of course, as did Hachihime.

"Being ignored means freedom," said quiet Mitsuke. She said it with more force than I'd ever seen her use for anything other than a glaive thrust. "When no one pays any attention to you, you can do anything you want."

We all looked at her.

After a moment, Mieko-*sensei* nodded. "Very true."

Freedom. What did that mean, anyway? Duty, that my father and the teachers at the Full Moon had talked about a lot. Honor, too. *'Avenge your fathers' disgrace.' 'Do no harm.' 'Doing what our duty, our daruma, requires is always the right thing.'*

Where was freedom in any of that?

Emi seemed just as lost in her thoughts as I was, but it was clear those thoughts were directed outward rather than in. As she rode beside me, she stared at the back of Aimaru's head.

I turned to Mieko-*sensei* and Hachihime, who was riding with Toumi behind her. "My ladies, I have a question for my cousin. May Emi and I ride up for a moment?"

"Thought we were supposed to stay away from them," grumbled Toumi.

"It will only be for a bit."

Mieko-*sensei* peered at me, and then at Emi. "So long as you rejoin us before we cross the bridge over the Boundary River. We should be as *ignorable* as possible when we enter Three Rivers Province."

I nodded. "My lady."

As we trotted forward, Emi glanced at me, lips pursed. "What do you want to ask Harē-*san* about?"

"I don't."

Her eyes narrowed.

Looking forward, I continued, "If you and Aimaru don't talk, I'm going to push you both off the bridge."

"But!"

"He wants to talk to you, *baka*. You want to talk to him. *Do it!*"

She huffed, looked away, and shrugged. "As you wish, Kano-*sama*."

"Oh, come on!" I growled. "Not you too!"

She turned back toward me, still frowning but with a glint in her eye. "Serves you right, Murasaki."

Now I gave a huff. "Fine."

My cousin and the other commanders were riding behind their squadrons in the middle of the road. As we closed with them, I lifted my foot and pushed Emi's mount to the right, where Aimaru was riding with Masugu-*san*'s troops. "Go."

"*Hai*, Kano-*sama*." When I snorted, she lifted her gaze to mine. "Thank you, Murasaki."

Not wanting to distract her, I just nodded.

She trotted off in our friend's direction.

Toki was telling a joke as I came up beside him. Harē was laughing with his head thrown back like a rooster crowing. Masugu-*san* was chuckling, but his ears were red.

"What's so funny, Toki-*san*?"

"Kano-*san*! Lovely to have you join us. I was telling the story of when Masugu and I first met Lady Kuniko." His eyes sparkled.

Alarmed that he might have told the *whole* story, I glanced at Masugu-*san*, who smiled, the pink spreading over his whole face. Laughing, he asked, "So, Murasaki-*san*, what brings you to join us? Nice as it always is to see you, weren't you the one who came up with the idea of you and the other ladies hanging back?"

"It was Emi's idea." I looked over my shoulder to where Emi had separated Aimaru from his squadron. They were now back between us and the *kunoichi*. For a change, they both looked glum—but they were talking. "I wanted to give her and Aimaru a chance to, um, discuss some things."

"Things?" Toki teased.

Fortunately, neither my cousin nor Masugu-*san* joined him. Harē nodded seriously. "I've noticed Aimaru has been subdued."

"Lovers' tiff?" Toki speculated, eyebrow raised.

"Something like that." I looked back at him and Emi again. Their eyes were fixed on their horses' manes, but I didn't think that was where they wanted to look. I turned back to my cousin. "How would Lord Oda feel about one of us, you know, *being* with someone like Aimaru?"

Harē rolled his shoulders, glancing at the other officers. "I suppose... What is Aimaru's clan?"

"He doesn't have one." He didn't even know who his father was, as far as he'd told us.

"Ah." His eyes returned to mine. "Well, as you know, Oda-*sama* isn't as interested in tradition as in worth. His most trusted general, Toyotomi-*san*, comes from a low-born family, his father a common soldier. From what I have seen of young Aimaru, I imagine he will bring honor on himself."

I nodded.

Masugu-*san* asked, "Is Emi-*san* worried that Aimaru is beneath her?"

Now I shook my head. "No. The other way around. Since the whole conversation about Oak Leaf, he won't talk to her."

"Ah. That must be difficult. For them both."

"Yes," I said, and my cousin echoed me.

Toki chuckled. "It doesn't seem like it's difficult for you with *your lady.*"

Masugu-*san* laughed along, smiling like... well, smiling like a man who's just gotten something he always wanted, but never thought he could have. "When I first asked my lady to marry me, I didn't know she was heir to a title. She was a *miko* and a teacher at the Full Moon."

And one of the deadliest assassins in Japan.

I glanced at my cousin and Toki. I knew the Matsudaira officer was aware of Mieko-*sensei*'s capabilities. And mine. But his expression stayed in a foxy smirk. Harē looked lost in thought.

Masugu-*san* glanced back a hundred paces or so to where Mieko-*sensei* was riding next to Sachi-*sensei*. The music teacher was laughing about something, and Mieko-*sensei* was smiling, but her gaze was locked on Masugu-*san*.

"To be honest," he continued. "I would have married her if she'd been a kitchen drudge or a rag picker."

Toki crowed, "Well, lucky for you, it turns out she's the one marrying beneath her!"

"Lucky for me," Masugu-*san* agreed cheerfully.

Harē clicked his tongue. "He could take her name."

"He—? Who?"

"If Emi and Aimaru were to marry, he could take the Hanichi name as his own."

I turned to Masugu-*san*. "Can you do that?"

He shrugged, but Toki broke in. "I don't see why not. My uncle wants to change the clan name, says the Matsudaira name's too tied with the Imagawa. My branch of the family is the older one, and he wants to take that the Tokugawa name again for the clan."

"But it's still his family name," Masugu-*san* pointed out.

"It wouldn't have to be." He flicked his head back toward Aimaru and Emi, who were still staring straight ahead, but now both seemed to be *smiling*. "And since Hanichi-*san* has the higher rank, even if the young soldier had a name, there's nothing to stop him taking it for his own."

I looked to Masugu-*san*, but he seemed lost in thought.

Toki went on, the teasing edge back in his voice. "So, Kano-*san*, what about you? Do you have some boy swooning for you back in the capital?"

"No." The image that unfolded in my mind was of the two foreign boys, Jolalo and Eyogoshei. Both knocked unconscious. By me. "No, Toki-*san*."

He chuckled, but his tone softened—not teasing any more, just laughing. "I know the feeling, Kano-*san*."

"Oh?"

"Not all of us are as lucky as our friend Masugu, here."

Masugu-*san*'s smile widened even further. "True."

Not wanting to continue talking about marriage, boys, or any of the rest of it, I asked, "Did you have any trouble finding us, Toki-*san*?"

Again, he laughed. "Not many camps flying the Takeda diamonds in Rising Tail!"

"True!" Masugu-*san* laughed again. "And did you have any trouble crossing into the province?"

My cousin added, "I hope the guards at the border didn't hold you up too long."

"No! They waved us right through. Strange, actually. Expected at least to have to leave a man behind for assurance."

"Strange, definitely," mused Harē. "The guards should at least have stopped you."

"We're almost there," said Masugu-*san*. "You can ask as we pass through. Though I'm not sure Nobutada-*sama* seems in a mood to wait."

A small garrison straddled the road ahead, with a wooden palisade wall, a guard tower, and an open gate, through which I could see the high arch of the bridge.

"I should head back," I said. "Kuniko-*sama* asked us to rejoin the ladies before we crossed into the Three Rivers."

"It's been a pleasure, Kano-*san*," said Tokimatsu. "And I don't think you should disturb the young lovers. It looks like they still have some talking to do."

Aimaru and Emi rode close together, expressions serious, deep in conversation. Her hand clasped his.

A cataract of feelings spilled up into my throat, as hard to name as the colors in a rainbow over a waterfall. I nodded to the three men and began to slow my horse.

I was happy for my friends. Very happy. Their affection had been obvious from the first day I had met them. Through all the traveling, through the long months at the Full Moon and the capital, they had found every opportunity to spend time together, even when Toumi teased them both mercilessly.

But what I was feeling wasn't just happiness that they were finally talking about that affection. Was I jealous? Not really. I loved them both as much as I loved anyone outside my family. But would their growing closer distance them from me? They were my best friends. If they became more than friends, would they have time for me?

Looking back, I saw Toumi listening to Hoshi-*sensei* and Sachi-*sensei*, laughing at some joke as they so often did—often a joke that only they understood—and a pang of sympathy squeezed my chest. Toumi, who had so often been the odd man out in our group. Our team.

I shook my head and forced a smile.

Most of our small army was already through the gate and onto the arched bridge. It seemed Masugu-*san* was right. Lord Oda's son wasn't in the mood to dally.

The garrison did seem sleepy. Guards slouched on either side of the gate, with a couple more up in the tower overlooking the river.

A score of pilgrim monks, heads shaven, saffron-robed, sat in the shade of the wall, sharing a couple of bowls of rice.

As I passed through the gate, one of the monks began playing 'Cherry Blossoms' on a flute. He wasn't as good as Sachi-*sensei*. He wasn't even as good as Emi.

Why was I feeling sorry for myself? I wanted Aimaru and Emi to be together. To be happy. There was a reason I had threatened to push them off the bridge.

They were just behind me as my horse's hooves began to echo from the bridge's wooden planks. I pulled to the left to give my friends room. Ahead of me, Masugu-*san*, Tokimatsu, and my cousin were about to disappear over the peak of the wooden span.

I looked over the side of the bridge. A few small boats were rowing up the river, but one small, dark shape was swimming across it. A *tanuki*. Strange. Raccoon dogs usually came out at night, especially outside of the woods.

Ahead of it, a heavily laden boat floated downstream, a man in monk's robes at the tiller. A knot of rope in his hand trailed a dragon's tail of smoke behind him.

The *tanuki* swam upstream, its sharp snout pointing at the boat, up at me, and then back to the monk, as if to say, *Watch!*

As I rose up the bridge, I did watch him, though I couldn't say why.

I was approaching the bridge's center when the boat reached it below. But instead of passing beneath the bridge, it banged with a *thunk* I could feel, colliding with one of the piers supporting the span.

The monk threw back a tarp, revealing his cargo. A pile of canisters I thought I recognized. He reached down and touched the burning rope to a cord, which caught flame.

Then he dove off his boat and began swimming madly for the shore.

"BOMB!" I shouted. "GET OFF THE BRIDGE!"

I could just see Masugu-*san* and the others ahead of me, just on the downslope side of the bridge. Emi and Aimaru rode just behind me on be far side, still deep in their conversation. Mieko-*sensei*, Hachihime, and the others were through the gate and beginning to climb from the shore onto the wood.

None of them had heard my warning.

Holding my hands to my mouth, I gave three loud, completely unrealistic owl hoots toward the men in front of me, and then three more to the women behind.

I was going to repeat the Takeda scout call when I heard Masugu-*san* shout, "*Attack! We're under attack! Get off the bridge!*"

Mieko-*sensei* too had gotten my warning and was turning everyone around toward the now-shut gate. I began to gallop my charger back down the slope. Aimaru and Emi raced just ahead of me.

And the whole world seemed to come to an end.

10 – A Flower Opening

Toumi liked the idea of using gunpowder to kill people. *Boom*. Her fingers and hands flowing up and out like a flower opening.

Boom.

The explosion at the bridge wasn't anything like that.

It wasn't a single sound. First, there was a *crack* like a rock breaking against a wall, then a rumble like a big cedar falling in the forest, taking down other trees with it, and finally a roar so loud it was almost silent.

The bridge itself bucked and rocked like an angry bear, and my mount panicked, rearing on its hind legs. I was far from in command of myself, and I've never been the best with horses—they can tell I don't trust them—and so rather than taking a firm grip on the reins and bringing it back under command, I let go and tumbled to the wooden deck.

The horse bolted back toward the shore. Smart horse.

My ears ringing, I clambered to my feet and ran unsteadily after it. Waves rippled along the length of the bridge's curved surface.

If you've ever heard a rusty nail being pulled out of old wood, you'll know why hearing that sound from beneath me made the hair stand up on my arms, on the back of my neck. That sound, multiplied by a thousand, with the addition of snapping pillars and beams, pushed me forward on unsteady legs over the undulating river of wood that lay between me and safety.

The bridge had two sections. Well, three. A high arch over the deepest part of the river connected to either shore by relatively flat piers. I had been close to the center of the arch when the canisters of gunpowder in the boat exploded below. The downward slope wasn't terribly steep, but it was shaking like a drunken dancer, and that made my legs move even faster.

The center of the bridge was collapsing. And, if I didn't move fast enough, it would fall out from beneath me.

I've talked about how time slows for me when I'm in danger. It can be a wonderful thing, being able to see what's coming at me and reacting before a butterfly can flap its wings. It can also be terrifying, knowing something terrible is rushing at me, and knowing too that there won't be anything I can do to escape it.

I was almost to the level part of the bridge, which I hoped would be spared from the collapse, when I felt the wood under me begin to fall. With all of my fear-fueled strength, I dove toward the flat portion of the bridge, which seemed to be holding steady.

The bridge disappeared from beneath me.

I flew through a cloud of splinters and paint chips, reaching desperately for the still solid decking ahead. I strained to extend my hands, though I could see to my horror that I wasn't going to make it. In terror-slowed time, I fell below the surface of the bridge. My arms stretched. Fingers reached. And latched onto a thick crossbeam.

The weight of my falling body pulled me down, and lightning bolts of pain shot through my shoulders, wrenching the sinews of my desperate, clutching hands.

I swung beneath the beam like a wooden ball on the string of a child's toy. My arms howled at the sudden strain, but I held on.

A waterfall of wood rained down into the river below.

And behind that loud whisper, shouts and screams.

"Murasaki!" I heard above me. "Murasaki! Can you hear me?"

"Right here, Emi! I'm on one of the beams below you!" Ignoring my shoulders' protests and my kimono's imprisonment, I kicked my legs up and clambered to sit on the beam.

"All right?" Aimaru asked, his voice gruff and tense as I hadn't heard it since the Mt. Fuji Inn.

"Fine." That may have been an exaggeration, but I was much better than if I'd fallen five or six times my height to the churning river below.

An arrow whizzed over the edge of what had been a bridge—just a pier now.

Aimaru grunted above me. "They're finding their range."

I called, "We're under attack?"

"Aren't we always?" Emi grumbled, sounding more like Toumi than herself. "Can you get yourself up here?"

"Sure, but…" Sitting in the beam, my head almost reached the joists supporting the deck. "Why don't you come down here? It's safer!"

"We need to get back to the shore!" Aimaru groaned. "Toumi, Mieko-*san*, and the rest are holding their own, but there are over a dozen swordsmen, and some archers up in the tower. We need to get back!"

I gazed down the spider's web of beams beneath the bridge. "We can do that down here, out of sight of the bowmen!"

He started to argue, but the distinctive sound of a bolt hitting the wood above made my friends gasp.

"Let's go!" Emi commanded. "How far down are you?"

"Not far. Look over. You'll see me."

Their heads appeared over the edge, eyes wide, and if we hadn't been in the middle of a battle, I might have laughed. "Come on!"

Aimaru nodded and began to swing a leg over, but Emi's got even wider. "I… I…"

Aimaru grasped her hand. "I'll help you down, *anata*."

I blinked. When had any of us used that intimate form of address with one another, close as we all were?

Emi's legs slid over the edge. I guided them down onto the beam. She had tucked the tail of her kimono up between her legs and into her sash like the village women used to do at rice planting time, which I thought was a great idea.

I forgot about that when her face cleared the decking. Her eyes were squeezed closed, her face as white as when she wore makeup, before she put on the rouge. "I've got you, Emi."

I took one of her hands from Aimaru, then the other, and sat my friend on the solid wood next to me. Her eyes were still shut tight. She whimpered. "You do this for *fun*?"

"Oh, sure!" I forced a chuckle. "The whole blowing up thing aside, this is an easy climb!" I'd loved climbing under the bridge near my village, which was much lower than this one.

I looked down for the first time. No *tanuki*. I hoped it had gotten away.

Shattered pilings stuck out of the water like broken teeth, the water swirling around them to make them look even more menacing. Debris still tumbled into the roiling flood.

Aimaru slid onto the beam on Emi's other side.

Tucking the back of my own kimono into the front of my sash so that I could move freely, I gazed across the river. Some of the central span on the other side had survived, though it looked ready to collapse. "Did everyone make it off the bridge all right?"

Emi grunted, lids still closed but no longer squeezed. "The women behind us all did. And your warning saved Masugu-*san*, your cousin, and Toki. We saw them on the other side."

"Under attack," added Aimaru. "The ambushers closed the gates on both sides to keep us in."

"Yes," Emi agreed, finally opening her eyes, though pointedly *not* looking down. "But the cavalry on that side outnumber the attackers, so the gate being locked is more help to our troops than theirs." She stood on boneless legs, using me and Aimaru for support. "You lead the way, Murasaki. We need to get back to the others.

And so we did, ducking the joists that held up the deck of the bridge as we made our way along the net of beams that kept the bridge stable. At least, that's what they did. So long as no one blew up a bomb beneath them.

As we approached where the bridge met the shore, the sounds of battle grew louder. The *tsing* of steel sliding against steel. The screams of horses, and men. Shouts, many of them from familiar throats.

"GET AWAY FROM US, YOU POOPY POOPS!"

"I DO NOT WISH TO HARM YOU, BUT AS YOUR FRIENDS HAVE FOUND, I WILL CERTAINLY DO SO!"

"Kuniko and Hachihime?" I asked. I whispered it, though there was no need with all the noise.

Emi nodded. "I think the others are over on the upstream side. Do you think you could take a peek and see if we can get out there safely to help?"

I nodded back and scurried my way over to the crease where the bank rose to embrace the bridge. My friends crawled along behind me. Aimaru said, "Watch out for the archers up in the tower!"

I nodded again, and fought down a shudder. Sliding up as close as I could to where the bridge met the land, I poked my head out.

Three men dressed as monks were attacking Mieko-*sensei*. She stood beneath the guard tower in front of Hachihime, defending with the sword in her left hand and counterattacking with a *wakizashi* in her right. Masugu-*san*'s short sword, the red Takeda diamonds on the hilt below her hand. At her feet lay two unmoving figures. From behind her, Hachihime was throwing rocks. Not terribly hard, but with enough accuracy to distract and annoy the attackers.

At the top of the tower, three archers were aiming their bows, not at the ladies beneath them, but across the road to where another crowd of men—half in monks' robes, half in armor, lined up in front of a low shack. Arrows sprouted from the roof.

Behind a half-wall, the other *kunoichi* defended themselves with the staves they had shown us the day before. The *surprise* Sachi-*sensei* had hinted at was long, straight steel blades projecting from the end of each staff. What they'd called walking sticks were in fact glaives, and deadly ones, judging by the red dripping from several of the blades.

Toumi stood behind Mitsuke and Hoshi, firing between their shoulders at the massed attackers.

I ducked back under the bridge and told Emi and Aimaru what I'd seen.

"We need to help!" Aimaru said.

"Yes," agreed Emi, "but it sounds as if we'd be sitting ducks for the archers if we tried to go after the men attacking the guard shack."

I nodded. "And it looked like Toumi and the rest were holding their own. So we'll help on this side?"

"Yes," she said. "We'll need to hit them as quickly and as hard as possible." She pulled out two throwing knives from her sleeves and pulled the dagger strapped to her thigh as well. Aimaru drew his sword. They both looked at me.

I shrugged. "I've got some caltrops, but that's it. My sword was on my horse. Kuniko-*sama* seems to have it now."

Emi sighed. "Well, if you throw the caltrops and yell, it will distract them, at least." She looked at Aimaru and then at me. "Ready?"

We nodded.

Charging into battle sounds like it should be an exciting experience. Something out of a heroic story.

Mostly, in that moment, I felt as if I wanted to pass water, and my legs were arguing against my head, not wanting to leave the safety of the bridge.

But as my friends charged out of our hiding place, I told my legs to stop being cowards and ran out behind them, spiked metal balls in my hands.

Emi's knives exploded from the back of the closest man. I threw one caltrop and then another at the head of the man next to him, making him turn just as Aimaru brought his sword down through the man's arm. Blood sprayed from the stump and the man screamed, his sword dropping to the ground.

The third man's head bounced onto the road, followed by his body. Mieko-*sensei* returned to a guarded stance, but now her *wakizashi*—Masugu-san's *wakizashi*, my *wakizashi*—dripped gore.

An arrow thudded into the dirt by my feet.

"Get under here!" Hachihime screamed, and for once, none of us questioned her. As we dove beneath the guard tower, a volley of arrows rained straight down from the archers above.

"Good to see you, ladies," Mieko-*sensei* said. "Aimaru."

We bowed quickly.

Hachihime tutted, "What took you so long? Where were you?"

My mouth fell open as I tried to think of how to start answering her.

Aimaru beat me to it. "Murasaki-*san* warned everyone off the span before the bomb went off and the center of the bridge fell. She didn't make it off though, so Emi and I went to try to rescue her."

Emi continued, cleaning off her knives on one of the dead men's robes. "She was fine. She'd landed on a beam under the bridge. That's how we made our way back without being spotted by the archers."

Hachihime gave a pout but nodded. "Oh."

I peered over at the backs of the men attacking the women in the guard shed. "We should help on the other side!"

"But those poops up above with the bows will kill us if we leave here!" Hachihime said.

"Then we must make sure that they can't do that," Mieko-*sensei* answered, clearing the blood from the short sword with a rust-colored cloth she carried for the purpose. Aside from the blood splattered on her cheek, nothing about her suggested that she was in the middle of a pitched battle. "Risuko, do you think you could climb up there?"

I squinted upward. There wasn't a ladder. Access to the tower came across a walkway from the palisade wall. But the crossbeams keeping the legs of the tower stable were only a little more than my height apart. "Easily."

"Do you think you could take out their bows?"

"Uh..."

"Take this," she said, offering my sword back to me, eyes sympathetic but uncompromising. "You won't need to kill them, Risuko. Just make sure they can't shoot."

"I..." I stared down at the sword. Though its surface gleamed, I knew it had killed just moments before. Slipping it into the back of my sash, I bowed, murmured a strangled *Hai* and, before I could have second thoughts, began to climb up the post closest to the wall, but away from the fighting on the other side of the road. I figured it was the place the archers were least likely to look. I climbed up the inside—not the most convenient path, but it was still an easy climb, as I had said.

Unfortunately, that gave me time to think.

How could I *take out* the bows without getting myself killed? We were outnumbered by the attackers, and while we *kunoichi* were deadly, part of our weaponry was surprise. We weren't meant to fight pitched battles, clad in silk and linen as we were.

As I reached the level just below the platform where the archers continued to take pot shots, mostly hitting the roof of the shed or the palisade or skittering down into the reeds on the riverbank, I took a moment to look back across the river.

The battle there was almost over. Only a few of the enemy remained on that side. As Emi had said, closing the gate had been more of a danger than a help to those opposing the eight squadrons of cavalrymen—the Oda, Takeda, and Matsudaira. Most of them were dismounted, since there was so little room, but the riders' swords were just as sharp.

I hoped Masugu-*san*, Tokimatsu, and my cousin were all safe.

Downriver, two squadrons swam their horses across the river, through the debris of the still-disintegrating bridge. One banner was red with four diamonds, the other white with a melon bud.

Good. But if the archers spotted them while they were still in the water, the horsemen would be easy to hit.

A quick breath, a silent prayer to any *kami* that might be listening, and I edged up to peer over the walkway.

The three archers wore light armor, and they were facing away, arrows nocked, bows half-drawn. Against the low wall lay stacks of arrows and a couple of quivers.

The one on the right loosed a shot with a *thrum*.

The one next to him squawked, lowering his bow. "We're trying *not* to hit the men on our side, *baka!*"

The third grumbled, "No clean line of sight."

The first one shrugged, voice rebellious. "All we can hit from here's our guys or the roof."

The middle archer sighed. "Then hold your *baka* fire 'till you've got a *baka* clear shot."

The first one growled, but drew another arrow from the stack against the wall in front of them, and all three went back to aiming their bows down at my friends, waiting for one of them to show too much of herself.

They were completely focused, staring away from me, their long bows drawn, not fully, but enough to be able to get off a shot quickly. The bow strings sang as the men waited for the perfect shot.

I drew my sword. Licking my lips, I lifted myself up onto the walkway. As I began to pull my leg up, the wood creaked.

I froze.

The men continued to scan across the road for a good shot. Fighting down the quail of panic that wanted to jump from my throat, I pulled my feet beneath me and stood.

"On the right!" The middle one crowed. "The girl with the bow."

Aiming down at Toumi, all three of them strained, drawing their bows taut.

My sword sliced through all three bow strings. With *twangs* like an out-of-tune *koto*, the weapons exploded.

Two of the archers hit themselves in the face with the hands that had been straining to pull back their arrows. One, the impatient one on the right, knocked himself unconscious, while the one on the left broke his own nose and fell to the floor, holding his face. Shards of wood cut the face of the middle one as his bow disintegrated in his hand. He whirled around, gripping the arrow in his hand like a dagger, blinking blood out of his eyes.

I stood in the Eight Phases, blade tip pointed at the sky, stance balanced. "I do not wish to harm you, sir." He growled and thrust the arrow at me. I slapped it away with my sword and touched the tip to his throat. "Please. Don't make me."

11 – Quiver & Quaver

I encouraged the three archers to retreat across the walkway. Actually, the two awake wanted to leave the unconscious one, saying he was a *baka* who didn't deserve any better, but my sword convinced them otherwise.

As soon as they'd disappeared behind the palisade wall, I gave two loud loon calls—the Takeda scout signal for *all clear* and a crow's caw followed by a warbler whistle for *friendly riders approaching.*

As soon as they heard that, Mieko-*sensei*, Aimaru, and Emi charged from beneath me at the backs of the unsuspecting soldiers attacking the shed. Horses bellowed behind me. Masugu-*san* and Harē's riders clambered onto the riverbank. My cousin and the Takeda lieutenant gathered their forces and prepared for a charge.

Panicked, realizing that they were surrounded and outnumbered, the attackers ran, dropping their swords, sprinting upriver and around the corner of the palisade.

I slumped to the floor, my own panic draining from me like water from a broken dam. My back and side ached from where the horse had thrown me. My shoulders burned from the strain of catching the beam beneath the bridge. Sweat stung my eyes. My palms were raw.

But I felt an enormous sense of relief. I had survived another attack.

Could I survive the next?

Could my friends?

Legs protesting, I pushed myself back up to look over the railing.

Where moments before there had been a battle, my friends milled around as if it were the end of a training session.

Harē was listening to Hachihime, who waved her arms around so energetically that she seemed to be painting a picture the size of the sky.

Mieko-*sensei* and Masugu-*san* were staring into each other's eyes. Blood streaked both their clothes. Whether it was theirs or from the men they'd fought, I couldn't tell. I also couldn't make out their expressions from above, but they looked to be in the middle of a long conversation. One continuing from many earlier battlefields.

Hoshi and Sachi-*sensei* tended to a cut on Mitsuke's shoulder—Hoshi holding the wound tight, Sachi-*sensei* using a fine needle and silk thread to close it. The quiet *kunoichi* stood, heron-still and stoic. Behind them, Shino leaned against the battered half-wall of the guard shed, cleaning the blades of their glaives.

Toumi wandered around picking up arrows, discarding the broken ones. *Arrows.*

Grabbing two of the empty quivers the men had left, I filled them with the arrows stacked against the wall and slipped them over each protesting shoulder. Slowly and gingerly, I made my way back to the ground.

My cousin greeted me with a nod. Hachihime crossed her arms. "Lovely to see you back, Risuko. Have a nice climb?"

"Indeed, my lady." I bowed as gracefully as I could manage with my bruised back. "The three archers were no trouble at all."

"Oh." She blinked. "Good. Did you kill them?"

"No, my lady."

She scowled. "Shame."

"Thank you for the warning," Harē said. "Tokugawa-*san* and I were confused by you hooting like that, but Masugu-*san* understood it immediately. That bomb could have killed us all."

"Glad I helped."

"More than helped. We owe you our lives." He took my hands in his.

My cousin and I had grown close since our reunion. He'd told me stories about our mothers, about myself as a baby. Never having had anyone beyond my mother, father, and sister, I was thrilled to have someone else I could call family. But we had never touched. And so I did my best to hold in the grimace of pain as his gauntleted fingers squeezed mine.

He let go as if my hands were on fire. "Are you all right?"

"Fine," I lied, shaking the buzz out of my fingers. "Just a little sore."

Hachihime's eyes narrowed, this time in concern. "Sore? What did those poops do to you?"

"Nothing," I answered truthfully. Then I blushed. "I... um... got thrown from my horse."

She and Harē both flinched in sympathy, which at least made me a bit less embarrassed.

One of my cousin's riders walked up to them and said that perhaps a few of the men should cross the river again and inform the commanders on the other side of the outcome of the battle.

They fell into conversation.

I looked around.

"Hey, Mouse-*chan*!" Toumi called, sauntering toward me. "What are you doing with all those arrows?"

I smiled and lifted one of the quivers off my shoulder and held it out. "Giving them to you and Emi."

"Thanks." She peered dubiously at the cloth-covered sack but took it from me anyway.

Aimaru and Emi wandered over, side by side, backs of their hands not quite touching. I handed the other quiver to her.

"Thanks," Emi said. She, Aimaru, and Toumi all seemed uninjured. "And thanks for taking care of the archers. What did you do?"

"Cut their bowstrings."

Emi and Toumi's eyes shot wide, and Harē whistled in surprise. Hachihime asked, "What's so surprising about that? It sounds reasonable."

My cousin tried to explain to her just how much force goes into drawing a bow, and what would happen if you cut the string while it was fully drawn.

Toumi pulled at the cloth covering her new quiver, revealing leather and lacquered wood. "Huh. Nicer than it looked. Thanks, Mouse."

"You are most heartily welcome, Torugu-*san*." I bowed as deeply as my sore back would allow. "*Dōitashimashite*."

She rolled her eyes, but continued removing the cloth covering.

"So," mused Aimaru. "Who do we think these men were? Half of them were Oda soldiers."

Emi scowled at the bodies of the soldiers lying at the base of the tower. "Well, they were dressed that way, but I'm not sure they actually were. Toki-*san* said he and his troops weren't stopped when they rode through here. I can't imagine actual guards would have just waved Matsudaira soldiers through like that. And half of the attackers on this side were monks."

Aimaru grumbled. "Or just dressed as monks."

I pondered that. "True. And just because these soldiers weren't acting like guards doesn't mean that one of the other Odas mightn't have replaced the usual company with a bunch of killers."

Emi and Aimaru nodded, clearly understanding my reference to Hachihime's sister-in-law and nephew. Though would Lady Kichō and young Lord Oda have planned an attack on themselves?

Toumi, still fussing with the quiver, muttered, "Or it could have been the Matsudaira, couldn't it?"

I shrugged. "They did close both gates." We all peered over to where the gate on the far side of the river was now open.

Emi shook her head. "Would they have attacked a group with Lord Matsudaira's nephew in it, though?"

"Probably not," I admitted.

Aimaru gave what was for him a grim smile. "And of course there's always the Uesugi or the Hōjō."

Emi sighed. "Or Lord Akita. Or dozens of others."

"Um… guys…" Toumi was staring down at her quiver.

"What?" I asked.

Eyes wide, she held up the lovely quiver, now free of its covering. At the base, a familiar *mon* was painted in bright red—four diamonds.

When we all gaped at the Takeda crest, Toumi grabbed Emi's quiver and stork-walked over the five corpses and under the guard tower, away from the others. She dropped her quiver, probably scratching the lovely lacquer-work, and began tearing the cover off of Emi's.

Emi, Aimaru, and I stumbled after her.

I tried to think. Could the assassin have been a former soldier of Lord Takeda's? If so, hired by whom?

We circled around Toumi, trying to see if the second quiver bore the same crest as the first. I whispered, "Maybe he was a *ronin*? A disgraced samurai kicked out of the clan?"

"Maybe," granted Aimaru.

Emi clicked her tongue against her teeth. "Are *ronin* that common, though? Disgraced because of what they or their lord did? Or because their lord died and left them without a master?"

Aimaru and I both shrugged. I admitted, "Everyone seems to know about our fathers. So it can't be that common."

Emi gave her most thoughtful frown. "But our fathers' case was unusual. They refused Oda-*sama*'s order."

"With reason," I said.

"Sure. But they were his most trusted servants. That was what made it such a big story. I suppose that if a samurai has been caught stealing or running away… Or…" She looked up. "Everyone of the *daimyo* whose territory has been swallowed up—Imagawa-*sama*'s say—wouldn't a lot of his samurai have been let loose?"

"If they were still alive," Toumi muttered.

"Sure," I granted. "But I guess I'd assumed a lot of them would have been taken on by Lord Takeda and Lord Matsudaira."

Emi's eyes rounded. "But what if…?"

"Look!" Toumi growled softly.

This quiver bore a different *mon*—a decorative comb, painted on the black lacquer in the bright green of spring pine needles.

Imagawa.

I looked at my friends. "So, what does this mean?"

Emi and Aimaru shrugged.

"*Che!*" Toumi spat and leaned into us, speaking with deadly intensity. "Don't know who sent these *bakas*. Don't know how we'll ever find out. But I'll tell you this: Don't trust *any* of 'em. The lords are playing games. And they don't care about us. Not Oda-*baka*, not Matsudaira-*baka*, sure as all the hells not Uesugi-*baka* or any of them."

That hit hard and sank in slowly, like a rock in a mud puddle.

"Takeda-*sama*?"

"Nope." Toumi bared her teeth, but it definitely wasn't a smile. "Don't trust any of 'em."

Aimaru looked over her shoulder toward the others and gave a rare frown. "But can't we trust Chiyome-*sama?* Masugu and Kuniko? Hachihime?"

"NO. *Not one.* Full of secrets, all of 'em." Toumi was breathing hard, her cheeks bright red and her eyes cold. "Tell you who I trust. Me." Then she flicked her chin at me. "And you." Then Emi. "And you."

Her knifelike grin softened to a smirk as she nodded at Aimaru. "And even you, Moon Face, when you're not getting all gooey-eyed on Sourpuss, here." She tipped her head at Emi.

Our friends both blushed and glanced at each other.

"I don't like it, but I can't disagree, not completely," I admitted. I wanted to trust Masugu-*san*, Mieko-*sensei*, and my cousin, at the very least.

But I had to admit, each of them had loyalties and priorities that had nothing to do with mine. I looked at my three friends. "So… What are we going to do? Do we stay with Hachihime, protect her the rest of the way to the wedding?"

"We don't even know if she's the target of all these attacks," Emi said, tongue clicking once again. "If it's a…" She nodded at the first quiver, the one with the Takeda emblem lying at Toumi's feet. "…then it might be the

Mountain, or it could be one of his sons or his brothers. Someone who doesn't want the wedding to happen."

I nodded. "Or it could be someone like Lord Uesugi or Lord Hōjō who doesn't care who's killed, as long as it drives a wedge between Takeda-*sama* and Oda-*sama*."

We all looked over at Hachihime, who was still talking animatedly with Harē. Masugu-*san* and Mieko-*sensei* had joined them, and the other *kunoichi* were wandering over as well.

A groan bubbled up my throat. "I think we have to keep going, don't we? I mean, I guess we could all disappear, go back to living in the woods or on the streets..."

"Nah," sighed Toumi. "Turns out I like eating too much."

We all nodded at that. I added, "And we have a chance to revive our families' honor. We can rewrite the story of our fathers' disgrace."

Now Toumi shrugged. "I mean, we already kind of did. But yeah. And you've got a town and all." She elbowed me.

"Whatever," I grumbled. "Mostly, I just want to save my sister and my mother. I think I'd want to go to Serenity anyway."

"That makes sense," Aimaru said with a nod, though his expression remained uncharacteristically somber. "And it makes sense to stay with Hachihime."

Toumi and I nodded back. She said, "I mean, I guess the brat isn't all bad. Even if I would still like to push her out a window sometimes."

Emi blew out a breath. "I think we should split off from the rest of the group."

"What?" Now I was the one frowning.

Though we were already all standing close, she leaned in so that our heads were almost touching. "I'm not sure that traveling with this entourage isn't just painting a target on our backs. We're traveling slowly, we're easy to spot, we're easy to ambush, and, as you said, Toumi, we can't even be sure of who's in league with the assassins, though it seems as if there's probably someone. So it should just be the four of us traveling with Hachihime."

Aimaru leaned back. "No."

"Aimaru?" Emi and I asked together.

"You should go without me." Saying it hurt, I could tell. Before we could ask what he was talking about, he took Emi's hand. "Think about it. You want to look like four girls. Even one guard and anyone with a brain will know you're not what you look like. I have to stay with the honor guard."

"But—" Emi looked ready to cry.

I could see his point, though. "There'd still be a wedding procession, just like everyone expects. One of the *kunoichi* would have to take on the role of Hachihime."

"But—"

Toumi bobbed her head. "And while these idiots—" She kicked one of the corpses. "—keep going after a freaking army, we travel fast and light, and no one notices."

"Security through obscurity," I agreed.

"But!"

Aimaru took Emi's other hand in his. "*Anata*. I couldn't live if you got hurt. This is the best way to keep you safe." He looked at me and Toumi. "All of you. I'll be one of a hundred soldiers guarding Lady Kuniko and the fake Lady Hachihime. I'll be fine. But if you can sneak into the castle in Serenity, I promise I'll meet you there."

Emi's mouth and eyes spread wide open. She was leaning forward. To kiss Aimaru? To throttle him?

Hachihime sashayed up behind her. "What are you four talking about?"

Before any of us could come up with a reasonable answer, Toumi chuckled. "How nice it would be to cross a river without getting attacked."

Hachihime too kicked one of the dead men. The one whose arm Aimaru had cut off. "Yes. That would be nice." She narrowed her eyes though her lips bowed upward. "It would also have been nice if our bodyguards hadn't wandered away from me and Lady Mieko."

"We're sorry, Hachihime," I said, and Emi echoed me, though she was still looking at Aimaru.

Harē, Mieko-*sensei*, and Masugu-*san* approached us, along with Shino and our other teachers. Hachihime turned to the two cavalry officers. "We were all discussing how underwhelming the entertainment has been these past few days. What are we going to do about this?"

Before anyone could apologize, Emi piped up. "Actually, my lady, we have an idea about that."

Hachihime quirked an eyebrow at us. "Oh?"

"Yes," Emi continued. She finally tore her gaze from Aimaru's and turned to Masugu-*san* and Mieko-*sensei*. "Aside from this highway, is there another route from here to the castle in Serenity?"

12 – Squiggles in the Dirt

It turned out that yes, indeed, there were several. Sachi-*sensei* and Mitsuke-*sensei* drew maps with the ends of their walking sticks. The blades were once again retracted, naturally.

The Old Salt Road led up into the southern valleys of Dark Letter, where it met with the mountain roads that passed by the Full Moon, then down into Worth Province, Swift River, and finally into Serenity. Essentially, it would take us on the reverse of the trip we'd taken the previous autumn with Lady Chiyome.

Emi and I were both excited about the idea of returning to the Full Moon. Toumi tried to pretend she wasn't, but a smile ruined the attempt.

Unfortunately, even riding fast, that route would get us to the Imagawa castle much later than the wedding procession.

We could go by sea. Hachihime's first choice. But there was no way to know if we'd find a suitable vessel, nor could we be sure we could trust ourselves to any crew.

Besides that, as Mieko-*sensei* pointed out, late typhoons, fog, and other nasty surprises might make sailing to Pineshore a risky choice.

The route she and the other *kunoichi* recommended was through the mountain valleys where the Three Rivers, Dark Letter, and Serenity met. We would travel up the Boundary River to Luckfield Castle, then take to the trails that led to where Phoenix Temple hid among the peaks, cross over the ridge into Serenity, and finally ride down along the Weatherbank River to the castle in whose shadow I had spent my childhood.

Which was named, I was shocked to learn, Two Branch Castle.

"Why Two Branch?" Toumi's nose wrinkled.

"I have no idea," I answered truthfully. "I didn't know it was called that."

We all stared down at the squiggles in the dirt.

Hoshi said, "Barring any... surprises—" She nodded at the still-smoldering bridge. "—you should get to the castle around the same time we do. Maybe earlier."

Nodding, Mieko-*sensei* looked up at us. "We should leave before young Lord Oda can try to stop us."

Emi and I looked at each other. I spluttered, "Um, Kuniko-*sama*..."

"Yes, Risuko?"

Now they were all looking at me.

Emi jumped in. "We were thinking, Kuniko-*sama*, that you should travel with the honor guard."

"Why, Emi?"

Now, as Toumi had pointed out, the main reason was that we really weren't sure we could fully trust anyone but ourselves, but we couldn't tell Mieko-*sensei* that. My throat tight, I answered, "Two reasons, Kuniko-*sama*. The first is that, if we're going to be really unnoticeable, traveling with soldiers is only going to draw the wrong kind of attention to us."

"Soldiers?" Harē asked.

Masugu-*san* crossed his arms, eyes narrowed.

"I, uh..." I turned to the Takeda lieutenant, whose sword I carried, whom I thought of as a friend. "Masugu-*san*, would you allow your... uh... intended to travel without you on a dangerous mission?"

When he seemed ready to object, Hoshi snorted. "Oh, come on. You know you'd ride after her if she tried to go with them."

Mieko-*sensei* sighed. "Annoying, but true."

Ears bright red, Masugu-*san* shrugged. His second-in-command, Inuji, gave a snort of suppressed laughter.

"And the other thing is," Emi continued, "there were five of us in the procession to start with: Ladies Kuniko and Hachihime, Murasaki, Toumi, and me. Four *miko* joined us. If four girls in *miko* clothes leave and five ladies in kimono stay behind, most likely no one will notice."

"That is a very good point, Emi," conceded Mieko-*sensei*. Mitsuke and Sachi-*sensei* both nodded, while Shino stared at us blankly.

Masugu-*san* peered at my friend, then at me and Toumi. "You three make quite the team, don't you?"

Hachihime wasn't convinced. She scowled at me. "So, I am supposed to travel to my wedding over mountain paths with just the three of you for protection?"

Toumi bumped her shoulder against the tiny noblewoman's. "Come on. We've got your back."

"Besides," I pointed out, "think how happy Lord Nobutada and Lady Kichō will be not to see you for a few days!"

They all chuckled, Hachihime loudest of all. "Oh, it would have been such fun to torture them the rest of the way. But I suppose I'll just have to settle for teasing you three. And I get to disguise myself as a *miko*!"

And so it was agreed.

Hoshi rubbed out the maps with the butt of her staff.

———

n the back of the guard shed, Toumi, Emi, and I changed into our red-and-white *miko* garb and helped Hachihime into Mitsuke's.

Mitsuke dressed in Hachihime's most flamboyant kimono. White melon blossoms swarmed by her usual decorative bees over a field of sunset red. It shocked me that our youngest teacher was so short. Like everything else about her, Mitsuke's stature was unnoticeable. Yet as soon as she was dressed in the noblewoman's clothes, she seemed to *become* Hachihime, flicking her fan at the rest of us and making jokes at everyone's expense.

Once we'd all changed clothes and roles, Masugu-*san* said, "Toki sent a messenger across; the other side is secure. Lord Nobutada wants us all back on the road as soon as we can get across."

Mitsuke huffed, "Does Nobu-*kun* expect us to swim? I'm not going to ruin these robes!"

The real Hachihime tittered. "Absolutely not! That kimono is worth five gold pieces and fifteen silver!" She and her double nodded in agreement and then laughed. I'd never even seen Mitsuke smile before then.

Harē grinned. "There's a bridge an hour or so downstream. We'll let Commander Oda know we'll cross there and meet up with him."

Masugu-*san* called to Inuji, who was pulling an arrow out of his horse's hoof. "We need to let Commander Oda and Captain Tokugawa know that we'll make our way down to the next bridge, downstream. We'll meet up with them at Carp Pond. Think Arashi can make it across?"

Inuji tossed the arrow down and rubbed the stallion's snout. "No problem. He likes a nice swim after a battle, don't you, Arashi?"

Once Inuji was gone, Mitsuke handed Hachihime her glaive—disguised once more as a walking stick. The lady frowned and handed it to me in turn. Not having trained as much with the pole arm as my friends, I gave it to Emi.

My cousin chose two mismatched horses—one Takeda black, the other Oda grey. Neither, I was thankful, was the one who had thrown me onto the bridge. "These two aren't as big as my Haīro or Masugu-*san*'s Inazuma, so they aren't as likely to give you away, but they're both fast and easy tempered. My lady," he said, bowing his head to Hachihime, "who would you prefer to ride with?"

She pouted, peered at me side-eye, and then sniffed at my cousin. "I shall take the reins."

Between my friends and me, only Emi was truly comfortable on a horse. She sighed, "Toumi, would you rather ride behind me or Lady Oda?"

Toumi grinned darkly at me. "If I let you and Mouse-*sama* ride together, you'll be chattering and giggling the whole way. I'll ride with you."

I raised my eyebrow at Toumi, and she winked, though she looked anything but amused.

We mounted up.

"Stay together. If you lose your way," said Sachi-*sensei*, "just keep heading northeast. You'll hit the Weatherbank eventually. Then go down the river until you see the castle or Pineshore itself."

"Northeast?" Hachihime muttered. "How are we supposed to remember where that is?"

Emi, Toumi, and I all pointed in that direction.

"Good," Mieko-*sensei* said. "Good luck, ladies. Stay vigilant. Spend tonight at Phoenix Temple. The abbot is famous for his hospitality. See you in a few days."

Hachihime mounted the grey, and I clambered up behind her. Emi started in the direction of the black horse, but instead of mounting, she sprinted over to where Aimaru stood, watching us glumly. She threw her arms around his neck and pressed her lips to his.

After a moment of stunned silence, the rest of us all turned away.

The kiss felt as if it went on forever, though it was probably only a handful of heartbeats.

Finally, Emi strode back over to her and Toumi's charger. Her face was bright red, her eyes glistening, and her mouth set in what passed for as a grin. For her. Feeling our gazes, she took a breath and climbed up into the saddle. "Come on," she said. "Let's go."

I looked at Toumi. Even she was too stunned to tease our friend.

After murmured farewells, we headed in opposite directions along the riverbank. The other women and the two squadrons of guards rode downstream, while Hachihime and Emi turned our horses upstream.

"Horses again," muttered Toumi under her breath, her arms around Emi's waist. "Wonderful."

"You're always welcome to walk, Toumi-duckling," Hachihime said.

"Nah," Toumi sighed. "Wouldn't want to deprive you all of my company."

———

We rode a bit over an hour along the Boundary as far as the next bridge, where the river took a turn northward, into the mountains. The Oda side of the river had an even bigger garrison than the one we'd just left, while imposing castle Luckfield Castle glowered over the crossing from the Matsudaira side.

None of us said a word while we crossed the bridge, all holding our breath for fear of another attack. When we reached the far shore without incident, the Matsudaira guards waved us through without a second glance.

As we turned onto the narrow northbound road Sachi-*sensei* had drawn in her dirt map, Hachihime shook her head. "Really? We've been trying to invade this province for years. Three armed killers with their weapons on display, and they just let us in?"

"Well," chuckled Toumi. "We don't exactly look like killers."

Toumi nodded. "Which is precisely the point."

I added, "People see what they expect to see." It was a lesson that all of our teachers had drilled into us. *Look as they expect you to and they'll never question who you actually are.*

We rode on in relative silence through small villages and farmland. Talking or speed—we could only afford one. This plane was where we could make up the most time, since we would have to slow down once we climbed into the wooded mountains.

The road grew steeper, entering a narrow valley overshadowed with evergreens. Cypress, red pine, and cedar leaned over the path, with autumn-colored maples and hornbeam choking the spaces beneath. I desperately wanted to get off and climb, just to deal with the horror of the attack, the feeling of the bridge disappearing beneath my feet, the sound of the wood creaking as I snuck up on the three archers. I bit back the impulse and held onto Hachihime.

As towns and people disappeared behind us, the air around us darkened. The others began to chatter again.

Hachihime scoffed, "What a mess! Why doesn't someone clean this place up?"

Toumi laughed. "Yeah? Who? It's wilderness! Unless you're someone like Mouse, there, why'd anyone live *here*?"

"Because it's beautiful?" I sighed.

With a sniff, Emi looked around. "It is, isn't it? Different from the Full Moon."

"Yes," I agreed. "Completely different trees. And it's not really wilderness. You can see that the trees have been thinned by woodcutters." I nodded at stumps that had clearly been left after the trees had been chopped down, scattered among the living trees.

"I guess," Toumi granted grudgingly.

Trunks, sticking up like... teeth. Like the pilings of the ruined bridge. I closed my eyes and let the sway of the horse and Hachihime's steady breathing pull me back into my body.

Hachihime, scowling at me, Emi, and Toumi just after the battle: *It would also have been nice if our bodyguards hadn't wandered away from me and Lady...*

"Hachihime?"

She flapped at her hand at a dragonfly that had flitted up from the surface of the stream we kept crossing as we climbed. "Yes, Risuko?"

"Why did you call Kuniko-*sama* by the name Mieko?"

"What?" She turned in the saddle and gawked at me. "Why would...?"

On their horse next to us, Toumi and Emi both stared at her.

She blew a loose strand of hair out of her face. "Oh, fine."

"Fine?"

"You know Nobu had a spy at the Full Moon."

Fuyudori. "She tried to kill us all." *Eyes and mouth perfect circles, white hair flying as she fell backwards into the white night.*

"That wasn't her job. Nobu was curious about what Chiyome was up to. He sent that white-haired girl and some scouts to gather reports about the Full Moon and the troop strengths in the valley. One of the last reports she sent back told Nobu that Kuniko, one of Chiyome's chief assassins, had died in combat."

"She killed three Imagawa soldiers first," Toumi grunted, her eyes narrowing. "So you knew Mieko-*sensei* wasn't Kuniko the whole time?"

Hachihime shrugged. "Sure. But then the reports stopped coming, so we didn't know what happened afterwards. What happened to the girl?"

Toumi gave her least pleasant laugh. "Mouse killed her."

"Really?" Hachihime turned around again, eyes wide this time.

"No, I didn't."

Emi waggled her head from side to side. "Both of you went up, Murasaki. Both of you came down—"

"But Whitehead did it a *lot* faster and hit the ground a lot harder," said Toumi, top teeth gleaming over her lower lip.

"Huh." Hachihime peered at me, eyes half-lidded, reassessing. "Well, she was a very strange girl."

"That's definitely true," I agreed, trying to block out the memory of her face as she fell backwards.

Emi asked, "Why did your brother accept Mieko-*sensei* as Monogami Kuniko, then?"

"Well," Hachihime said, waving the dragonfly away again, "you saw Akita's an idiot and Uesugi isn't much of an asset as an ally anymore."

My mouth pursed. "But he's been one of Lord Oda's oldest friends."

"True," admitted Hachihime, "but if he can't play with the big kids, he should step aside as a power."

Toumi grunted. "Brutal."

Emi hummed. "Reality."

"Exactly," Hachihime said. "If Nobu's going to win and stop all of the fighting, he can't afford to be sentimental."

"And what about us?" I whispered.

"You?"

"Your brother's whole reason for reinstating our families' honor was regret for how he treated our fathers. That's pretty sentimental. What's to stop him from changing his mind?"

"Because, like Lady Kuniko, you're extremely useful to him. She's going to help him bring the north back under control. And you are keeping me alive."

Toumi spat. "And what if he decides he doesn't care about that? We just become useless trash?"

Hachihime sighed. "He'd never do that."

"Sentiment?" Emi asked, eyebrows knitted.

"No…" She craned her neck to look back at me, and then back at my friends. "Look. I understand why you'd be worried. Look what he did to your fathers, the old poop! And he does regret that, I know he does."

We all kept staring at her.

"Oh, fine." She closed her eyes. "You can trust him. You can trust me. I promise."

"Why?" Toumi asked.

"Why can you trust me? Why won't he ever think I'm not worth keeping around, and so you'll become expendable?"

"Sure," Toumi said. "Let's go with that."

Hachihime bit her lower lip, looking more anxious than I'd seen her. Aside from when we were under attack. "This is a secret, do you understand? This is something only a handful of people know. If I tell you this, you have to *swear* on pain of *death*, never to tell anyone. It would destroy *everything*."

"I swear," Toumi and both said immediately, but Emi simply nodded. "You're Oda-*sama*'s daughter, not his sister."

"I…!" Hachihime's eyes flew wide. "Why…? How…?"

"It makes so much sense!" I gasped. "That's why Nobutada and Kichō hate you so much!"

Toumi smacked her forehead with her palm. "And that's why he was calling you *Little Sister*."

"Yes." Hachihime faced forward, looking away from us all. Her shoulders rolled, bunched, rolled again, and then unclenched. "Nobu was even younger than I am now, and Nobuhide, his father, was off on campaign, and he… he was in love with… my mother. And she was with him."

Emi's eyes widened. "That is so romantic."

Hachihime nodded, tears spilling over her eyelids.

Toumi rolled her eyes.

I love a good love story as much as the next person. Except Toumi. And this was a very good one, I must admit. However, that wasn't the thought that sprang to my mind. "You aren't legitimate."

Now Hachihime's tears burst out like autumn rain. "No! And you can't tell anyone! If Lord Takeda found out…"

"We won't ever tell," I said. "We swear. Right?" I turned to Emi and Toumi. "Right?"

"Right," said Toumi.

Emi nodded. "We swear."

13 — Golden Light

Silence flowed over us for the next hour or so. Not an awkward silence. We hadn't passed a village for some time, and the climb was steep and steady, which gave us plenty of time to think.

The loudest thought in my head was whether or not we should warn Hachihime of the possibility that the man we were bringing her to marry might be behind the assassination attempts.

Without even talking with them, I knew Toumi and Emi would say we shouldn't. Emi because we couldn't be sure the Mountain had anything to do with the attacks, Toumi because she wouldn't be sure *the brat* was worth it.

The valley twisted westward as we climbed, so that the late afternoon sun shone from behind us, making the shadows of us and our horses impossibly long in front of us.

I was peering at the shadows over Hachihime's shoulder. Fresh hoof prints marked the path. I knew they were fresh because of how clean the edges were. It was almost certainly a warhorse—the prints were deep and showed a chip in the edge of the left front hoof.

The print spurred something in my memory, but it fluttered away like a butterfly, barely out of reach.

I whispered, loud enough for the others to hear, "I think we're being watched."

They all looked at me. Hachihime tensed, her eyes wide. Emi tilted her head to one side, curious.

Toumi, naturally, scowled. "Where? There's no one following us. I've been watching."

"No," I agreed, then pointed down at the hoof prints. "They're ahead of us. I've seen that horse's tracks before."

"You have?" Hachihime asked.

I shrugged. "Yes. But I don't know where. It can't have been too long ago, though."

Emi sat up straighter, alert. "If they're watching us from ahead, they must know where we're going."

"How could they possibly know that?" Toumi asked. "We aren't going at a gallop or anything, but we haven't stopped, and we haven't been passed by anyone."

Hachihime's back hardened, and her knuckles whitened as she gripped the reins harder. "Maybe one of the assassins from this morning overheard our plans and is getting ready to ambush us."

"None of them were on horseback," I pointed out. "And if they'd ridden off before us up the path on our side of the river, we'd have seen them, even if they went as fast as they could." The countryside around the bridge had been flat and open.

Emi nodded. "And that horse isn't galloping now, is it, Murasaki?"

I shook my head.

"Still," said Toumi, "I don't like this. If someone is watching us and knows where we're headed…"

I didn't like it either, but I didn't want us all to panic. "It could just be a coincidence?"

"Maybe," conceded Emi.

"Whatever," Toumi said with a sniff. "We should just keep our eyes open, right?"

"Right," we all answered.

———

We followed the winding road out of the valley. The ridge top above us glowed golden in the late afternoon light, and when we saw a group of buildings amidst the trees ahead, I thought it must be a small hamlet.

A blue silk banner fluttered in the breeze. It bore the Matsudaira ginger leaves.

Not a hamlet. A garrison. If I remembered the map Sachi-*sensei* and Mitsuke had drawn in the dust, this ridge marked the border between the provinces of Three Rivers and Serenity. These soldiers had originally been stationed there to defend against an Imagawa invasion.

Most of the soldiers—my training with Mieko-*sensei* told me there were probably sixty or so stationed there—mulled around a fire in the center of the camp. The smell of stewing meat and wild onions mixed with the wood smoke reminded me I hadn't eaten since morning.

Two Matsudaira sentries flanked the road. "Ladies," drawled the shorter one.

Before Hachihime could say something snooty or snarky that might cause trouble, I replied, "*Konnichiwa*, sirs."

The taller guard peered at us. "And a good afternoon to you. Where are you pretty young ladies off to, out here in the wilderness?"

"Oh," burbled Toumi, "we're headed from our village to the shrine, to perform the proper rites, you know." It sounded as if flirtatious Sachi-*sensei* had spoken through my prickly friend.

"The… shrine?" asked the smaller one, eyebrows arching.

We all nodded, even Hachihime, who added, "We've been preparing this for months."

Well done, I thought, fighting down a smile.

The taller guard snorted. "Aren't you all a bit… young to be praying at the shrine?"

"Young?" Emi asked. Her frown betrayed puzzlement rather than sadness.

The short one sniggered.

The tall one grinned up at us. "Usually only married ladies and such make it up here."

A feeling of dread washed over me like the river from a few days before. I suddenly had a pretty good idea what kind of shrine this was.

Bristling, Hachihime turned imperious. "Where is this shrine?" At least she didn't call the man a poop.

Grin spread to a leer, the tall guard said, "Just up the side track there, leads up to the temple. I'd be happy to escort you ladies there. I'd love to watch these… rites."

"Hey, Fujita!" growled he short one. "You can't—!"

"Oh, come on, Abe. Since we came on duty, the only other person by here was that courier. I'll be right back."

"But…!"

The tall guard ignored his fellow soldier, gesturing for us to follow him up the narrow path that led off the main route.

The short guard fumed but soon disappeared behind us.

"It's getting late," our self-appointed guide pointed out. "You lovely ladies planning to camp out tonight? All kinds of beasties in these woods, you know."

Emi answered, "Actually, we were told that the temple is famous for its hospitality."

"Oh, sure." He shrugged dismissively. "If you want to spend the night with a bunch of monks. Mind, they have some nice *sake*."

"Great!" Toumi chirped, sticking to the cheerful persona she'd put on that was as far from her as Hachihime was from Mitsuke.

The guard winked back at her.

I asked, "You mentioned a courier came through here? We haven't seen anyone since the last village."

"Oh, yeah, not too long ago. All dusty from riding hard, you know. He said he had a message for the abbot."

"Ah. Thank you, sir." I tried to think who would want to send an urgent message to the head of a Buddhist temple. It had to be the rider whose tracks we'd followed up from the base of the hills.

Before I could consider it too deeply, we rounded a corner and my fears were confirmed. Behind a small, weatherbeaten *torī* arch stood a *tanuki* statue, taller than a man and roughly carved from wood. It grinned down at us, an oversized bamboo hat perched on its head. From beneath its bulging belly, two round lumps projected.

A fertility shrine.

Hachihime tipped her head to the side and huffed. Emi's puzzlement deepened, and Toumi gawked.

"Here we are!" The guard chuckled. "So, what rites do you have in mind?"

"Consecration and thanksgiving," I sighed. Those were all-purpose rituals.

He winked at me. "Doesn't look like you have anything to be thankful for just yet."

"No, sir." I allowed the blush I'd been fighting to spread over my face like a wildfire. "But we are giving thanks for our village's good fortune this year and praying for healthy births in the year to come."

Hachihime still seemed to be trying to find the right angle to look at the statue, but recognition blossomed on Emi and Toumi's faces.

"Well," said the guard, "Don't let me stop you." Leer firmly in place, he gestured through the arch.

We dismounted and dug into our packs. The only musical instruments we had brought were Emi's flute and a couple of rhythm sticks, but they would do. I took out a small bag of salt and some leaf-wrapped traveling rations we'd brought from the capital just in case. These items I handed to Hachihime. "Just follow us," I whispered.

Lips pursed, she nodded.

Stepping to the *torī* arch, we bowed and clapped our hands. I gritted my teeth to hold in a gasp of pain. My palms were still raw.

We washed our hands in the water flowing from a small bamboo pipe into a bucket. I assumed it was fed by a nearby stream or spring.

Kneeling before the statue, we bowed again, and then Toumi and I began to tap our sticks together, and Emi played on her flute.

She wasn't the player Sachi-*sensei* was. Like me, she hadn't been playing long enough to have become a master of the instrument. Still, the simple, haunting tune of 'Cherry Blossoms' seemed to fill the shrine and echo through the pine woods around us.

Though he said nothing, I could feel the guard's presence behind us.

As I kept the beat, I whispered to Hachihime, "Do you know the Thanksgiving Prayer?"

She shook her head minutely.

"Don't worry about that. He can't see our mouths. Just try to move along with us. Can you do that?"

She nodded.

Hachihime generally responded to discomfort with either stiff formality or storming rage. Which one would prevail in this situation, I wondered?

After we had finished the song, I took the bag from Hachihime and sprinkled a small cone of salt in front of the *tanuki* to purify and sanctify the space.

Emi put down her flute and began the prayer, and Toumi and I joined her. Hachihime matched our swaying as we thanked the *kami*—the spirit of the shrine, as well as the other eight million gods.

It's a long prayer. I knew it the best, since I'd learned it from my father, but over the months, we'd all practised it.

I felt badly doing it under false pretences, as it were. But at least we were actually conducting the ritual.

Once or twice, Hachihime started to turn her head, to see if the guard was still there. Each time, I squeezed her knee. We had to assume he would be.

When the prayer finally wound to an end, I whispered, "Put the road cakes below its belly."

Hachihime, whom I had only ever seen kneel to her brother—*her father*, I corrected myself—shuffled over to the roughhewn statue on her knees and placed the packets of food on the *tanuki*'s... protrusions.

Once she had shuffled back, I took up the beat on my sticks again, and Emi played another round of 'Cherry Blossoms.' Toumi stood and did a simple dance. She was actually the best dancer of us, or so our teacher Rin had said. I think Toumi was more surprised than any of us.

Usually, we'd have used paper *shi-de* streamers to decorate the shrine, but we hadn't expected to have to perform an actual ritual on the road.

I hoped the *kami* wouldn't mind. I didn't think it would, trickster as it was. It was probably laughing at the absurdity of a bunch of maidens asking for its help getting pregnant.

The golden afternoon light had shifted to a scarlet sunset by the time we were done.

We stood and bowed to the statue once again and, to my chagrin, clapped our hands, bringing to ritual to a close. My palms sang with the sting.

The guard was still there, his smirk mostly gone, a mask of intense boredom on his face. "So, still want to head up to the abbey? I'm sure our lieutenant would be happy to find you a place to stay."

Toumi tittered again, a sound like a nightingale song pouring from a jay's beak. "Nice as that sounds, we promised our moms we'd spend the night up at the temple. They wouldn't want us having *too* much fun, you know!"

"Too bad," chuckled the guard. "Well, temple's up this track a little way. Not too far. You should get there before the sun's finished setting."

We thanked him and mounted our horses again.

He grunted and headed back toward the garrison.

"What a poop," growled Hachihime.

"Yeah," agreed Toumi. "Not sure why he stuck around. Seen one *baka* ritual, you've seen 'em all."

"Maybe he thought it would be funnier than it was."

"Poop," Hachihime grunted. "That wasn't funny at all. What was that carving of, a badger or something?"

"It's a raccoon dog. Remember what I said, that they're supposed to bring—"

"—prosperity, yes, Risuko, I remember."

"Also fertility," said Emi.

"Humph." For a woman on her way to be married, Hachihime didn't seem terribly excited about the prospect of getting pregnant. Not that I could blame her for that. "Anyway, why did you have me put that food on its feet?"

My head fell against her back. The blush flooded right back. "Those… weren't his feet."

She twisted around to stare at me. "What do you—?"

"They're his… um… *golden gems.*"

"His…?" Her mouth fell open. "*EWWWW!* Risuko! You poop!"

Toumi and Emi burst into laughter.

14 – God of Laughter

The path led through brilliant golden oaks and flaming red maples. At first, it paralleled the ridge top above, but the hilltop quickly climbed away and the slope we were on steepened. The beautiful autumn foliage gave way to soaring cedars and cypress. The distinctive *bu-po-so* call of Scops owls echoed among the enormous, ancient trunks.

"Want to get off and climb, Mouse?" asked Toumi.

I was sure she meant it as a tease, but I didn't care. I nodded.

"After making me touch that *disgusting* statue, Risuko," grumbled Hachihime, "I don't think you deserve to share a room with us. So you can climb to your heart's content and sleep up there with the bats and the owls."

My blush came back, but so did a smile. I hadn't *meant* to play a trick on Hachihime. But that didn't mean that it wasn't funny.

I could tell Emi was amused, though her face was downturned as ever, and Toumi had her knife-edged smirk firmly in place.

As the trail curved beneath a huge boulder, all smiles and frowns melted away.

To our left, a crystalline vista spread out beneath us: the entire valley we had just climbed out of, the plains where we'd nearly died, and even, in the distance, the glittering serpent scales of the sea.

It was a view fit for gods. It made me feel tiny and enormous, both at the same time.

Even Hachihime gaped silently.

Toumi whispered, "If that's the view, what in all the hells does the temple look like?"

———

The temple, in fact, turned out to be beautiful but small. Over the open red doors, a sign in gold leaf proclaimed: LANDING PHOENIX TEMPLE HALL. The interior was dark, but a statue of the Healing Buddha loomed in the shadows, its left hand holding out a medicine jar. A smaller version of the same figure presided over the kitchens at the Full Moon. And so, of course, I found myself thinking of Kee Sun. I hoped that he and the three girls who'd replaced us weren't torturing each other too much.

"The statue," said a prodigiously plump monk in rust-colored robes who rumbled toward us like a well-fed goose, "was a gift from the emperor himself, after our founder, my predecessor, cured his celestial highness of a terrible illness."

The man smiled, eyes closed and grin stretching wide across his round face, so that he resembled the statue of the God of Laughter in the Oda townhouse. "It is late, and you must be hungry, young ladies. We've just been sharing the most delightful meal. Come, and we will find you food for you and for your horses, and a place to sleep dry and warm. I hope you will tell me what has brought a quartet of lovely shrine maidens into these mountains."

We dismounted and followed him into a grove of flaming maples. Behind them rose a sheer cliff face that even I wouldn't have wanted to climb, and above it, shrouded in a scarf of clouds, rose a rocky peak. Phoenix Mountain, which had given the temple its name.

"You are fortunate not to have come up the usual route to our refuge." The monk nodded down the hill. A long stone staircase led all the way down into the small town in the valley below. "It's more direct than the road, but our horse brothers don't like the steps much."

Emi murmured, "We came up from our village in Rising Tail to give thanks for the healthy babies born this year."

"Rising Tail? Goodness!" The monk's thin eyebrows shot up. "How far have you come?"

"Not terribly far, your reverence," I said.

Hachihime joined in. "We left Seabell Station this morning."

"Still," chuckled the monk, "that's a long way to ride in one day! It's good that you chose to stop here. How lovely the autumn colors look." He gestured up at the gem-bright maples above our heads. Though the air was mountain cool with the approaching evening, his brow too was bright. With sweat.

"Very beautiful, your reverence," I agreed. "Our families told us this temple was renowned for its hospitality."

He smiled again. "How lovely to hear. And I hope that we shall live up to our reputation." He led us into a small collection of white-washed buildings:

a compact stable, what looked like a storeroom on pilings, and a low, wide building with numerous doors that reminded me of the Nunnery, the women's dormitory at the Full Moon.

"See to your mounts in the stable," said the monk with a nod toward the open door. "We just got some fresh hay in. There's one other horse in there. Hopefully they'll all get along!" He chuckled. As we brought the chargers into the shelter, the other horse let out a welcoming whicker. Toumi and Emi's horse answered it.

It was another black, with a notch in the front of its left hoof that looked to have been left by an arrow. The two horses exchanged friendly snuffles.

As we removed the saddles and packs and brushed the horses down, our friendly guide burbled on. "It's lovely that you visited the shrine. It hasn't seen much use of late. I haven't seen the priest who cared for it in nearly a year, since before the fighting last autumn. We used to play *go* together when he'd stay over after conducting rites over at the shrine. He lived.—lives—over on the Serenity side of the ridge. Such a lovely man. I pray he is well."

We mumbled agreement.

I said, "The shrine seemed well cared for."

"My monks and I have done our best to keep it from falling into disrepair. But of course, we aren't priests, so there is only so much we can do."

Again, we all nodded and said that we understood.

Hachihime, to our surprise, brought hay over for the horses. With the other black looking on—the courier's, perhaps—Toumi and Emi brushed out their stallion while I took care of mine. I tipped my head back toward the monk, who was humming and swaying as he stood in the doorway. I whispered, "He seems cheerful."

Toumi snorted. "He seems *drunk*."

Our guide chuckled at something. He was standing in the doorway and looking up into the trees.

Emi nodded. "He certainly seems to be enjoying himself."

Once we had cared for the horses and provided them with food and drink, the monk clapped his hands and rubbed them together. The pupils of his eyes, which should have grown with the gathering gloom, were black poppy seeds. "Now come. I shall see you are provided for!"

We followed him across a carefully raked courtyard to the dormitory. Smoke spilled upwards from the chimney. A delicious scent, more subtle than the stew at the Matsudaira camp, promised a meal worth waiting for. My stomach rumbled, and was answered by Hachihime's. She tittered. "I'm starving."

We entered the building, which was warm and filled with the scent of ginger and garlic. We passed through a narrow hallway and then turned into what seemed to be a combined prayer hall and dining room. An altar stood against the opposite wall with two large, golden oil lamps. Both lit. And a huge hanging of the white-skinned Sun Buddha, his right hand touching the ground, his right turning the Wheel of Truth.

A low black table took up the middle of the room, big enough for twenty. Only four figures sat at it, and one of them looked to be asleep.

Two saffron-robed monks were laughing with a soldier, whose back was to us. A third monk was passed out, his head in a bowl of what must have been the heavenly-smelling soup.

"Chigu-bō!" our guide said to the unconscious man. "What are you doing with your face in the soup?"

One of the monks looked up, putting down his porcelain cup of *sake* with a *thunk*. "We tried to get him back up, Lord Abbot, sir, but he's out cold."

The other monk sniggered. "Never could hold his drink." He went to take a sip from his cup, but then gave an exaggerated frown when he found it empty. He peered in with pin-prick eyes and shook it, as if it were hiding the *sake*.

"Here you go, my friend!" The soldier said, picking up one of the jars of wine and refilling the monk's cup. He turned to us and smiled. It was Inuji, Masugu-*san*'s right-hand man. "Ladies! Lovely to see you here. I wasn't sure when you'd arrive."

I kept my jaw from dropping. Barely. "And we didn't expect to see you here, Inuji-*san*."

Toumi's eyes narrowed. "Weren't you supposed to go across and tell the other commanders to wait for Masugu-*san* and others to cross the bridge?"

"Oh, sure," said the Takeda rider, his sword nonchalantly placed at his side. "But he also told me to keep an eye on you. I mean, you'd hardly think the Mountain would be happy to have his bride-to-be wandering through these woods without *any* protection!"

"That poop!" Hachihime fumed.

I looked to my friends. Emi's face was blank—not even a frown—and Toumi stared at the cavalryman as if expecting him either to attack or to shout 'Surprise!' and admit he was joking.

Though his smile was broad, he seemed to be serious.

"Come, ladies!" The abbot said, lowering his bulk into the cushion by Inuji's side. "There's plenty of the soup left, and this wine is positively enchanting." He poured a cup for himself. From the same black-and-gold jar from which Inuji had served the monk.

We sat. I next to Inuji, then Hachihime, Toumi, and Emi beside me.

One of the monks across from us filled lovely, large bowls with the soup, which was still steaming hot. There were noodles, bean curd, mushrooms, green onions, red beans and more in a rich golden vegetable broth that had filled the whole building with a mouth-watering scent.

We thanked him. At least, Emi and I did. And we were all soon slurping away at the perfectly made noodles and vegetables. Taste, texture, presentation—all were exactly as Kee Sun had taught us to prepare such a soup.

Toumi groaned, "So good!"

Across from us, the two monks still awake grinned and nodded.

On Inuji's other side, the abbot smacked his lips. "Colors! Such colors!"

Chuckling again, Inuji held up another jar of wine. Also black and gold. "Here you go, Risuko-*san*. It really is excellent. Join us!" He filled a cup for me and then handed me the jar.

Unsure, I poured for Hachihime, then passed the jar to Emi, who was, as always, frowning. She poured for Toumi and herself. "*Kampai*," she said, lifting her cup.

"*Kampai*," called Inuji, and the monks echoed him. We all lifted our cups.

The scent wafting up from the cup was unmistakable, one I could never forget. Under the tart, flowery rice wine, a sickly-sweet odor.

Poppy juice.

I caught Emi and Toumi's eyes. They both nodded minutely. We all pretended to sip from the cup, as Sachi-*sensei* had taught us to do.

Unfortunately, Hachihime had never learned that lesson. She drained her wine in one swallow and put the cup down. "Mmm. Sweet, but very good."

The monks all agreed.

So did Inuji. "Glad you like it, my lady." He winked at me. "Drink up, girls! You have some catching up to do."

Both of the men across the table seemed to be following their fellow into the land of dreams. The abbot drained his glass again and lay down, beginning to snore.

15 – Blood Diamonds

At the Full Moon, Sachi-*sensei* had taught us eight ways to make others believe we were drinking from a cup or eating from a bowl when we weren't. We learned these methods in case someone was trying to poison us. It also allowed us to pretend to drink or eat the same thing as someone else to get them to trust us—possibly so that we could poison *them*. It's what Toumi had done with the two Uesugi guards the previous summer, getting them drunk while not swallowing a drop herself.

In this case, we were convinced that the wine was drugged, so we couldn't even let it into our mouths. However, there were three of us. So we took turns very noticeably lifting our cup to our lips, which never opened to allow the liquid in. While one of us was doing that, another would smack her lips and comment on the flavor and potency of the wine, while the third would discreetly pour out the contents of her cup under the table or into her soup bowl. I was forced to do that since I was sitting immediately next to Inuji, who seemed clearly to have been the one who dosed the *sake* with poppy.

Another of Sachi-*sensei*'s lessons was how to pretend to be drunk. "The secret," she had told us, "is to work hard at trying to look sober. Drunk people don't *want* people to know they're drunk, after all!"

So, Emi was staring at her soup bowl, concentrating very hard on sitting up straight, which meant that she was swaying. Toumi was talking louder and louder at the drooping monks across the table.

I wasn't as good as my friends were at acting drunk. Or rather, trying to act sober. I just allowed my eyes to droop and my shoulders to slump as if I were getting sleepier and sleepier.

Next to me, Hachihime was doing the same thing, slumping against my shoulder, murmuring something about flying squirrels. Of course, she wasn't pretending.

"Hey, 'Nuji-*san!*" Toumi called down the table. "Wassit like f'your horse t'take 'n'arrow inna foot?"

Inuji laughed, placing his cup down on the table. "The hoof is mostly like a big toenail. The arrow didn't hurt him, fortunately!"

Toumi exclaimed surprise and started telling a story about trying to trim the thick toenails of her grandfather, who I knew she had no memory of.

Inuji chuckled, clearly enjoying the sight of his plan taking effect. Or so he thought. He poured himself another cupful—from a different, blue-and-white jar.

While Toumi chattered on more and more loudly and more and more incoherently, I felt Emi reach across Hachihime's lap and place a vial in my hand. A knock-out concoction devised by Kee Sun. Less potent than poppy juice but faster acting, it was made from the red-and-white mushrooms that grew in the woods around the Full Moon. A small dose would cause hallucinations and drowsiness. A large dose would cause waking nightmares and death.

Inuji leaned across me, chatting with Toumi.

Doing my best to appear almost asleep, I opened the small bottle and poured a single drop into his *sake* cup. I had just brought the vial back beneath the table when Inuji laughed, picked up the cup, and drained it.

If he tasted anything other than the wine, he showed no sign.

"Ah, Tarugu-*san,*" Inuji said, "I am sorry I have had to do this. I truly am."

"Do wha'?" Toumi slurred.

"I'm afraid I put something in the wine. I knew you were headed here, and I couldn't let you get through. The Mountain himself gave me orders that if you four separated from the main party, I was to make sure you never reached the wedding."

I made a show of trying to force my eyes open. "Orders?"

"Yes, Kano-*san.*" Sweat beaded on his forehead, his cheeks. One of the first symptoms showing the mushroom tincture was taking effect. "Takeda-*sama* handed them to me personally before we set out to escort you from the capital." He patted his chest, where a small letter case poked out from his armor. "Told me to open them only if you ladies split off from the main pack. Don't think he expected you to separate from Mieko-*san,* but I figured he meant me to follow Lady Oda here." He blinked, as if trying to rid a fleck of dust from his eyes.

"Why?" I asked, gazing up at him through my own half-lidded eyes.

"Well, don't think he means to marry the lady, begging your pardon." He swiped his hand across his face, attempting to clear his vision.

While he was distracted by the drug taking effect, I moved his sword behind me, passing it to Emi and out of his reach.

"Wha' ya gonna do wi' us?" Toumi asked.

Distracted as he was by whatever invisible things were clouding his sight, Inuji still managed to look abashed. "Um. Afraid Takeda ordered me to..." He shook his head, blinking wildly.

"Ordered you to do what?" Emi asked, no longer even trying to appear *not* drunk.

"To... to kill..." He shook his head again, then gaped as the realization of what we'd done hit. With a gasp, he grabbed for his sword.

"Looking for this?" Toumi asked, standing over my shoulder, the blade tip at his neck. "*We do not wish to harm you,*" she said, in a manner that made it clear that she'd actually be more than happy to do so.

"Don't frighten him, Toumi," I said, and then sat up and looked the soldier in the increasingly bleary eye. "We truly don't, Inuji-*san*. You were following orders. And the tincture we gave you isn't deadly, though you will probably feel very strange for the next few hours. We just want to protect Lady Hachihime. What did Takeda-*sama* want you to do to her?" I was pretty sure he'd already told us, but I needed to hear him say it.

"Told... you. Was to... kill her. And..."

"And?"

"And... Um... You." His head bobbled atop his neck like a snake that's looking for a place to bite you. Or like a drunken man trying to stay upright.

"Kill us?" Emi asked.

He tried to nod, but that was apparently too much. He tipped forward, face-first onto the table.

"So, was the Mountain behind all of the attacks on us?"

"Wha'?" Inuji was now the one slurring, and his uneven pupils told me he wasn't pretending. "Mountain... wou'n't..." His face fell slack as consciousness escaped him.

"Poop," muttered Hachihime against my shoulder.

"Are you all right?" I asked her.

"Feel funny."

"You would. He spiked your drink with poppy juice."

"Double poop."

Toumi flicked a finger against Inuji's slack cheek.

When that didn't stir a reaction, I pulled the letter case from his breast-plate. The broken seal showed the four diamonds. On the outside, a bold hand had written *Open only if targets leave party.*

Targets.

"Read it, Murasaki," Emi said.

The same strong, blocky script slashed across the fine paper.

> If the individuals you are detailed to convey separate from the party intended to guard them, you must pursue and eliminate them with extreme prejudice.
>
> Do it in such a way that no suspicion can be cast on me.
>
> Be sure to eliminate the attendants. That whole company have proven unreliable in the past months and will be discarded from our army for its greater security.
>
> This is a first-priority order. Failure to carry it out will be considered an act of treason.

The order wasn't signed, but it too bore a scarlet Takeda seal.

Once I'd finished reading, we all sat silently.

Toumi still held the tip of Inuji's sword against his throat. "So... What do we do now? Kill him?"

I moved the blade away from the unconscious soldier. "No. You heard the order. He had no choice."

"But we can't just leave him!" Toumi said through clenched teeth. "He'll just come after us or tell Takeda we got away."

Emi clicked her tongue. "I have an idea. We need to get out of here. Toumi, help me bind him. Murasaki, do you think you can find some ginseng in the kitchen for Hachihime?"

———

I walked back into the Matsudaira camp an hour later. The same guards stood back at their posts on either side of the main road.

"Decided to spend the night back here after all?" The short one asked with a leer.

"No, thank you very much, soldier-sirs," I said, head turned to the side and eyes downcast. "But something has happened, and we need your help."

"Help?" the taller guard asked.

I nodded. "We returned to the shrine after sunset to say a prayer to the rising moon." I nodded to where the bright lens-shape rose overhead. "While we were there, a gentleman stumbled in, talking rather strangely."

"Strangely?"

I raised my hand in front of my face to hide a blush that wasn't there. "I think he may have been drunk, sirs."

The short guard snorted. "Lucky him."

"He took out a sword and started to attack the big statue there, saying 'Me and my buddies will cut you down to size!'"

The tall one squinted at me. "Buddies?"

The other asked the question I'd been waiting for. "How was he dressed?"

"In armor, sirs, but his *mon* was different from yours." I nodded up at the ginger-leaf banner still fluttering overhead.

"What was it?" the tall one asked, now at full attention.

I drew the shape with my fingers. "A… a diamond, made up of four smaller diamonds."

The small guard gasped, "Takeda! What's he doing here?"

"Well," I said, looking back down at my feet, "that's what was the strangest. He, um, *passed out*, you see, right there in the shrine, muttering something about 'sneak attack.'"

Both guards hissed at this, understandably. The tall one barked at the other, "Go, tell the lieutenant. I'm going to go check on this Takeda *filth*."

They ran off, one into the camp, the other up the track that led to the shrine.

Job done, I sprinted up the main road and over the ridge to catch up with my friends and our horses, who'd snuck by while I'd distracted the guards.

16 — Nightwatch

I met up with the others on the road a stone's throw over the ridge into Serenity, the province where I'd spent much of my life. "Let's get off into the woods," I said.

"Why?" Hachihime grumbled. She was awake, but the *yin* poppy and *yang* ginseng warred in her system, leaving her more than a bit grumpy. It occurred to me that learning that her husband-to-be wanted to murder her might also have ruined her mood.

Emi nodded. "The Matsudaira are about to go on high alert. They'll send out messengers to warn other camps. Scouts will head out along all of the main routes, watching for an invasion."

"Fun," said Toumi with a smirk.

"Maybe," I conceded, "but it will also make it difficult for us to travel." I looked around at them. "And... where are we going now?"

Hachihime scowled at me. "What do you mean?"

Emi gave a huff. "Do we want to go to Two Branches Castle? Lord Oda will be there with guards, but so will Lord Takeda. It would be walking into a bear's den." She huffed again. "Or a tiger's."

We all turned that thought over. Would Hachihime be safe if Takeda Shingen were anywhere nearby? Would we?

"We could head back to Rising Tail," said Toumi. "Or the Capital. But that's a long way—and we've already been attacked on that route twice."

"*Three* times," said Hachihime.

Also, I still wasn't sure we could trust Lord Nobutada and Lady Kichō. "We could go back to the Full Moon."

Emi shook her head. "But we'd have to pass through Takeda territory to get there, and that doesn't seem safe, right now."

"True," I granted.

Hachihime stood up to her not-very-considerable full height. "I say we go to the wedding."

Toumi goggled at her. "But my… Hachihime! We already know Takeda-*baka* wants to kill us all!"

Did we really know that? I asked the others if we could tell that from the letter. Maybe someone else had written it?

"No," Toumi said, face set in a determined scowl. "That *baka* Inuji said the Mountain gave it to him himself."

Emi pondered. "I suppose someone else might have substituted a different scroll." She looked at Hachihime, then at me. "Would either of you recognize Lord Takeda's writing?"

I shook my head. So did Hachihime, looking even more annoyed than before.

I turned to her. "Then why do you want to go through with the wedding?"

Now Hachihime smiled—a vicious, nasty smile I had never seen on her pretty face. "So that I can slit the poop's throat on our wedding night."

———

Toumi, naturally, *loved* that idea. "Serve the *baka* right."

And Emi agreed after some consideration, pointing out that the Mountain clearly didn't expect us to arrive at the castle from this direction, if we arrived at all. Otherwise, why give Inuji orders for what to do if we left the honor guard?

I remained unconvinced. But between the fact that the others were right and there wasn't *anywhere* safe for us to go, and my desire to see my family again, I finally agreed to guide them cross-country.

In the morning.

I suggested we set up camp well off the road so that Matsudaira scouts couldn't find us and suspect us of being part of the supposed sneak attack.

"Is it safe in this jungle?" Toumi asked.

"Yes," I lied. "The woods here in Serenity aren't as thick as they are in Dark Letter, and most of the wildlife isn't a threat as long as you don't attack them. Deer, goats, *tanuki*. Pheasants and such. Other than owls and the *tanuki*, mostly they're active during the day." I chose not to mention the wild boar and bears that wandered these hills at night. They tended to stay closer to rivers and streams, and in any case, I figured they were less of a threat than any humans we might encounter.

So, we led the horses off the road. I picked up branches and we used them to erase the hoof prints. A determined tracker would still spot where we'd left the main way, but only if they were looking for us, which I hoped they wouldn't be.

We led our horses through the pines and cedar—three mounts now, with Inuji's stallion happily joining us. Once the moon reached its highest point, I looked for and found a clearing where a huge old cypress had fallen, taking out all the smaller trees. "Let's stop here."

It was a cool autumn night in the high Serenity hills, but we hadn't brought tents with us. Hachihime demanded we light a fire. Emi and I pointed out that unfortunately the light would reveal us to any Matsudaira or Takeda soldiers nearby. I didn't mention that a campfire would also attract any number of curious beasts.

Emi took the first watch, Toumi the second, and I the dawn. I figured that way, I might be able to see what direction to head in when we headed out in the morning. We all put on the heaviest clothing we could find, arranged our weapons so they would be close at hand, and wishing Emi an uneventful watch, climbed into our bedrolls, laying out of the night wind behind the rotting cypress trunk.

I fell asleep to the hunting calls of owls—Scops, Barn, and Greenleaf. I wished them good hunting, but hoped they didn't catch any squirrels.

———

When Toumi woke me and climbed groggily into the bedroll I had just vacated, the stars were still visible overhead. But faint pre-dawn showed hidden gold through the trunks and branches to the east.

As she began her rasping snore, I stretched and shivered.

The woods were quiet on this boundary between night and day. The night animals were heading off to their nests and burrows, having thankfully ignored us. The creatures of the day were just beginning to stir.

I clambered up onto the spongy cypress trunk with my sword and started some parry-riposte exercises to keep myself warm and alert.

As I was starting the third round, I turned to the west and saw five pairs of golden eyes moving toward me along the trunk. Startled, I took my guard.

They moved out of the deep shadows, furry brown creatures with black cheeks.

Tanuki.

They scowled at me.

I jumped off the fallen tree to where my friends slept and bowed up at them. "Apologies, Tanuki-*san*," I said to the big male at the front. "I hope we have not taken your den. We only wished to pass the night here. We will be gone soon, I promise."

The raccoon dog snuffled at me and waddled on down the wood highway. Its mate and their pups gazed down at me regally, curiously, as they passed. They went another five or ten paces toward the rising sun and then climbed down with surprising agility and hid themselves in a rotted-out section of the tree.

Smiling, I bowed again.

"What are you doing, duckling?" Behind me, Hachihime sat up in her bedroll, rubbing her eyes.

I went to squat beside her. "A family of *tanuki* just climbed into a hole in the trunk down there. I was wishing them a happy sleep."

"Ugh." She made a face. "I never want to see those things again. *Ever.* At the shrine, you made me touch its... *golden gems.*" She flicked her fingers as if to clear any lingering trace from the tips. "And before that, every time they've shown up, we've been attacked!"

"Hmm. I suppose another way to look at it is that every time an attack was about to happen, they've warned us."

Her eyes, still crusted with sleep, narrowed. "Are you always this disgustingly cheerful in the mornings?"

I shrugged and smiled. "Pretty much."

She pouted, then yawned, trying once more to clear her face. "I don't suppose there's any chance of a bath out here."

"No. I purposely didn't have us camp near water. And it would be very cold. But we do have field rations. Are you hungry?"

Neither of us had actually been able to enjoy much of the delicious soup at the temple.

"Yes. Starving." She pouted. "But field rations? Really? Do we have to eat like common soldiers?"

"Just for today, Hime." It was Lord Oda's nickname for her. *Princess.* I only used it when I wanted to tease her. "I'm confident we'll reach the castle by the afternoon. Once we're there, you can have fine food and take hot baths to your heart's delight."

She sighed longingly. "Wish we could just fly there like birds."

"Depends on the kind of bird. Warblers, finches, tits, robins. They don't fly very high or very fast. Falcons, on the other hand..."

She sighed again. "I *love* falcons. So beautiful. Nobu kept some for hunting when we were in Tranquility Castle. But nowhere to keep them in the city."

"No. I suppose not." I put a hand on her arm. "So, do you want some field rations? They'll at least fill your belly until the feasting at the castle."

"Oh, fine."

The rations made by the Oda cooks weren't, to my taste, as good as Kee Sun's. But though they were less flavorful, they were chewy, not hard, and they were definitely filling. Hachihime and I munched in silence.

"Murasaki?"

"Yes?"

"Did your mother really have to... sell you?"

I looked at her, still chewing on the baked cake of rice, barley, and mushroom. For once, her face was bent in an expression that I could only interpret as concern or compassion.

"Yes." I held up my own meal. "This would have been an absolute feast to us back then."

She sighed. "Your mother was such a wonderful storyteller—funny and elegant. It's hard to imagine you all starving. Poor."

I shrugged. "Many people are poor. Many are starving. It doesn't matter if you're witty or elegant... if you lose everything..."

She looked down, nodding. "I suppose." Her eyes flashed back up, and I could see that they were moist, as if rimmed with dew. "I'm sure they are all right."

Again, I shrugged, more anxious than accepting. "I hope so. There have been battles in these valleys. Soldiers might have wiped out the village. Or destroyed the crops."

She took my hand in hers. "They will be all right, Murasaki. I know it."

"I hope so." I blinked at her, tears now threatening my eyes. "Thank you. Thank you, Hachihime."

She nodded.

After a moment, she let go of my hand. "Now, if I'm going to cut my husband's throat, one of you is going to have to teach me. So? What are you waiting for?"

17 – A Reckoning

nce Toumi and Emi awoke as true dawn broke, Hachihime demanded they teach her how to kill "a big, fat, ugly man."

"With pleasure," laughed Toumi. She pulled out one of the many blades she had hidden beneath her miko tunic and handed it handle-first to Hachihime. "Now, this is one of my lightest and sharpest. It'll slit a throat or stab a man's heart just fine, but you have to know how to use it."

I watched as my friends taught Lady Oda first how to hold and handle a knife, then how to cut and stab, and finally where the best places were to kill easily and quickly. Slit throat. Stabbing at the heart from under the ribs. Slipping the thin blade under the back of the skull.

Hachihime's eyes glistened as she took all of this in. It occurred to me that, in fact, she would have made an excellent *kunoichi*, given the chance. And the motivation.

Once she had learned all the basics, I led us through the Sixty-four Changes. For the first time, Hachihime did the exercises with us not with empty hands, but armed.

By the time we had done the whole exercise four times, I told them to keep going and went to climb a tree to spy our way forward.

Climbing the rough-barked cedar, I thought of being tied up with Toumi on just such a tree a year before. So much had changed. So much had remained the same.

As I climbed up to the upper branches, golden sunlight warmed my already warm face. I looked out to see what was visible.

The view below me was a bit hazier than the astonishing vista we'd seen the evening before. In part, I supposed, that was due to the low angle of the sun shining up the valley. Even so, I could see all the way to Pineshore at the coast. Following the Weatherbank River's path up toward me, I soon found what I was looking for. The backlit castle in whose shadow I had grown up. I couldn't see any damage. Seeing it still standing somehow gave me hope that Otō-*san* and Usako were safe.

Silly. I knew the castle was standing. Why else hold the wedding there?

By the time I'd climbed back down, I was covered in sap and flakes of bark and even sweatier than my friends. Hachihime said I should be called Badger, not Squirrel, and that I needed a bath even more badly than she did. Toumi and Emi both laughed, and, giddy as I was feeling, I laughed along, trying to brush the mess off the front of my no-longer pristine red and white shrine maiden costume.

"Come on," I said, "let's get the horses ready." I pointed in the direction of the castle. "We're headed that way."

———

We rode along deer tracks and along streams. Always I knew exactly which we were headed.

Home.

"So, I get wanting to off the bastard," Toumi mused as cypress and cedar gave way to maple and oak. "But are we sure it makes sense to walk into this place? He might have another team set up right as we get there."

Emi shook her head. "He won't try to kill us in sight of the castle. The other lords would see what was happening, and Lord Oda would not be happy."

"I should hope not!" Hachihime said.

"Also," I added, "I don't think he expected us to come this way. That's why he gave Inuji the order to… um… eliminate us if we left the group. In case we did something unexpected." I turned back and looked at them. "What do you think happened to Inuji-*san*?"

"Don't care," Toumi grumbled.

Emi chewed on her lip. "Well, I'm guessing they questioned him all night. Of course, he still may not be exactly coherent. But their scouts won't have found anything."

Toumi pointed out, "Unless Takeda-baka actually was planning a sneak attack."

"True," admitted Emi. She shrugged. "As long as that wasn't the case, they may lock him up for a while, but I doubt they'll hurt him. Too badly."

"Shame," muttered Hachihime, and Toumi agreed.

Making our way out of the hills, we didn't encounter any assassins—or any tenuki, whether good omens or bad. Even so, we travelled not on the road but paralleling it in the woods. No point in making ourselves too easy to spot, after all.

Just past midday, I saw a bridge ahead of us. One that I'd climbed in and hidden under throughout my childhood. My pulse began to quicken. "We're almost there," I told the others.

Just as we were about to head out onto the road for the last stretch of our journey, however, I spotted another party approaching from down the valley to the east. A shiny black palanquin with a familiar blank-white disc *mon*, carried by two large men in blue. A dozen soldiers rode behind them. At their head, an armored man with a round face, a heavy mustache, and a shaved head.

Takeda Shingen.

———

As they approached the bridge, I stood there, alone.

Hachihime, Toumi, and Emi hid with the horses well back in the woods.

We had all assumed that I was the least likely of us for the Mountain to order an attack on, especially in front of Lady Chiyome and in sight of the castle.

I wasn't as scrawny as I had been the year before, and I had grown, though not as much as my friends. On foot, I was still unimposing and unarmed.

The Little Brother at the front gave two quick barks, a smile warming his ever-calm face, and the palanquin stopped. The general and his troops stopped as well, all staring at me.

The window to the palanquin banged open. "Why in all the forty-nine hells did you stop here," growled Lady Chiyome's voice from inside the box. She stuck her head out the window, a face promising typhoons and earth-quakes, but as soon as she saw me, she burst into what passed for a smile. "*Risuko!* What are you doing here? And just as dirty as the last time you and I were on this road!"

I tried to brush some of the bark and sap from the front of my tunic. Pointless. Taking a breath, I bowed deeply, first to her, then to the scowling commander. "My lady. My Lord Governor of Worth."

That respectful greeting, for some reason, caused a huge burst of laughter from the soldiers and from the man himself.

Chiyome-*sama* cackled. "That's not the Mountain, my silly Squirrel!"

I blinked up at him. Even from this distance, he certainly looked like Takeda-*sama*.

Smiling in a way I had never seen Lord Takeda do, the man riding beside the palanquin shook his head, chuckling. "Don't worry about it, young lady. I get that *all* the time. Probably related, but not on the *right* side of the bedroll, if you get my meaning."

The men behind him burst into laughter again.

Confused and relieved, I nodded.

Still smiling—a smile that warmed his eyes, unlike the Mountain's—he introduced himself, bowing in the saddle. "I'm Shirokage Akira, lieutenant in Lord Takeda's army. We are accompanying Lady Mochizuki here to the wedding."

I bowed again, though not quite as deeply as before. "Sir. My name is Kano Murasaki. It is a pleasure to meet you."

Before the lieutenant could begin the inevitable questioning about my family name, Lady Chiyome said, "So, my little bumpkin, what are you doing here? Where are your friends?"

Straightening up, I turned back to her. "They are fine, my lady. Actually... Would you mind getting out of the palanquin for a moment? I have something I need to discuss with you. In private." I gave a pained smile to the Takeda soldiers. "It's... a lady thing."

You would think I had just passed gas, the way the men all blinked and turned away, muttering that it was fine.

The Little Brothers lowered the palanquin, and Lady Chiyome rose stiffly from the box. "I certainly don't *mind* getting out of that prison, Risuko, but what's this all about?"

I stayed silent until we were out of earshot, well up the road.

When I stopped, Chiyome-*sama* gazed at me thoughtfully. "I'm sure this has nothing to do with any *lady thing*, Risuko. What's going on?"

What could I tell her? How much could I trust her?

I did trust Chiyome-*sama*. But she was fiercely loyal to Lord Takeda.

Still, as Emi had pointed out when we'd discussed this plan, if we couldn't trust her, we were as good as dead anyway.

"We were ambushed twice on the road from the capital. Once entering Rising Tail and again entering the Three Rivers."

Her eyes narrowed. "The Oda, perhaps. The wife and her son? Or Lord Matsudaira, though it's not exactly his style."

"We considered those possibilities, my lady. But we fear the person behind the attacks may be someone... closer to home."

Her brows drew together, and her lips pursed.

I told her about the quivers we'd found after the attack at the bridge.

"So… someone's hiring *ronin*. Difficult to know who, though."

"Yes, my lady. But it was clear that whoever of us was the target, it wasn't safe for Lady Oda to continue with the honor guard. Emi, Toumi, and I broke off yesterday, riding over the mountain road in disguise." I gestured at my filthy tunic and *hakama*.

"Excellent plan," she said, her eyes narrowing.

"But we were followed, my lady. Or rather, someone rode *ahead* of us and waited at Phoenix Temple. He tried to poison us there."

Now her eyes flew wide and her brows shot up. "And who was this man? I assume his identity is why you're playing this ridiculous game?"

"Partly, my lady." I gulped. "It was Inuji. Masugu-*san*'s second in command."

"What!" She gasped. "I have known that man for years! Who could possibly have suborned *him* into treachery? I can't believe it."

"It's true, my lady, and we were shocked too." Now was the moment when I would find out whether this had been a good idea or not. "I don't think it was an act of treachery. We are fairly certain he acted out of loyalty."

That took her aback. "You can't possibly mean Masugu-*san*?"

I shook my head and reached beneath my tunic to where I'd hidden the letter case. I wanted to tell her the rest. That he'd tried to drug us, kill us; that we'd turned the tables on him. But I found I couldn't speak.

She stared at me, and then at the letter case. At its Takeda seal, and at the label that told the reader to open it if the *targets* left the main party. With a sniff, she opened the case and tapped it out into her hand.

As soon as she'd unrolled it, her face went white and her jaw fell open.

Because we had all been desperate to know, I asked, "Do you know the writing, my lady?"

Still pale, her chin quivering, she nodded. "It is Takeda Shingen's."

"It couldn't be a forgery?"

"I don't think so, no." Color came back into her cheeks, and suddenly she looked angry, furious as I had only ever seen her twice. Once when she'd thought I had been the one who had drugged Masugu-*san* and once when she had confronted Lord Matsudaira and Lord Takeda about Mai's murder. She looked back down at the scroll, and her fury only increased. "'Be sure to eliminate the attendants'? 'The whole company has proven unreliable'?" She began to crush the order, but then got control of herself and looked at me, face still aflame, but eyes steady with deadly intent. "So. Takeda Shingen himself is behind all of the assassination attempts. I think I will have to show the Mountain just how *unreliable* my *kunoichi* are." She took a deep breath.

"Well done. I assume Toumi, Emi, and Lady Oda are up in the trees there somewhere?"

When I nodded, she gave a grunt and a nod, handing the incriminating document back to me. "Yes. Well done. Call them down. I think it's time for a reckoning."

18 – The Right-Hand Path

I gave the *all-clear* signal—a pair of loon cries. Toumi, Emi, and Hachihime led the horses down out of the woods. They weren't as dirty as me, but they were hardly the unspoiled shrine maidens they'd dressed up as the previous morning.

"Greetings, Lady Oda," said Chiyome-*sama* with a bow. "You certainly look ready for your wedding."

Eyebrow raised, Hachihime smoothed the front of her rumpled, travel- and sleep-stained tunic. "Delightful to see you, too, Lady Mochizuki. I take it, Risuko, we are welcome to join this party?"

I heard the underlying question. Were we safe traveling with Lord Takeda and his soldiers?

Chiyome-*sama* heard it as well. "We would be delighted for you to join us. Lieutenant Shirokage here and his troops would be happy to escort us all into the castle."

The lieutenant smiled and confirmed he and his men would be more than happy to serve as our guard of honor.

When my friends' eyes all shot wide, Lady Chiyome nodded grimly. "And are you going to ride those lovely horses, or lead them like a bunch of grooms?"

Mumbling, we mounted up—Hachihime on the gray, Emi and Toumi on one black, and me on the other.

We rode across the bridge with the palanquin. Shirokage and his squadron followed us.

"So," Emi whispered, "she believed you?"

I nodded.

Toumi leaned toward me, keeping hold of Emi's waist. "And did she recognize the handwriting? Was it *you-know-who's*?"

I nodded again.

They seemed to have no more idea what to do with that than I did.

On their other side, Hachihime was holding an equally terse conversation with Lady Chiyome.

The echoing sound of our horses' hooves dropped almost to silence as we passed from the wooden bridge back onto the dirt road I had walked a thousand times in my childhood. Without thinking about it, I turned my horse left, toward the path that would lead to the village and my old home.

Chiyome-*sama* cawed out, "This way, my Squirrel! You can visit the family manse later. We have business to attend to."

I wanted to argue. I was desperate to see my mother, my sister. To be sure they were all right.

But of course, Lady Chiyome was correct.

We had business to attend to.

———

I had seen the gate of the Imagawa castle—Two Branches Castle—many times. But I had never passed through it.

I had imagined my father walking through that gate. I had dreamed of it.

Looking up at the open oak doors studded with iron, at the stone and plaster wall around them, I realized that, while it was certainly a perfectly respectable castle, it was nowhere nearly as large as I remembered it being.

I have had that experience many times, returning to a place where I had spent time after a long absence. In my memory, my imagination, they are always more...

More impressive. Bigger. Brighter colors.

Suddenly, I was going into a place I had never entered, a place that had always terrified me, even as it fascinated me. Can you blame me?

And I found that I wasn't scared any more.

Some of the people who were likely to be inside frightened me. But I could handle that.

I had been shot at, had a bridge blown up beneath me, had been almost poisoned. All in the previous few days.

Expecting to encounter a group of lords and their retainers who might decide to attack me and my friends at any moment felt almost normal.

Even at the time, I knew that wasn't good. But I also knew that worrying about it wouldn't help.

We passed through the outer gate, a small walled space with guards staring down at us, then through the inner gate and into a courtyard.

At the entrance to the castle proper stood three *daimyo* surrounded by their samurai.

Lord Matsudaira and Lord Oda smiled in greeting. Lord Imagawa, whom I had not seen since the previous autumn, stood sullenly, looking like a bear in spring—his skin loose and gray, eyes rheumy, mouth set in a short-tempered scowl.

"NOBU!" Hachihime squealed, leaping from her horse and running to embrace her brother. Father.

"Hime!" He exclaimed as she barreled into him, burying her face in his chest. He blinked down at her and then looked at me, Emi, and Toumi—all dressed as *miko*, and all looking much less like the elegant bridal party we had been when we left the capital. His eyes narrowed, and it wasn't his clever look, but rather a dangerous one. To me, he said, "What has happened? Where is the rest of the company? I received a message this morning that Nobutada and my wife were accompanying you with a whole company of cavalry. Where are they?"

Looking at Hachihime's back—anywhere but at those frightened, angry eyes—I answered, "They were well when we were separated, my lord, after an ambush at the Boundary River bridge. We decided that the surest way to get Lady Hachihime here safely and quickly was to ride in disguise over the Redstone Mountains, just the four of us, rather than along the road."

"An ambush?" Lord Matsudaira asked. "Was my nephew there?"

Emi chimed in. "Yes, my lord. He and his troops helped Lord Nobutada fight off the attackers. I don't think the assassins expected us to have such a large escort."

"But the bridge got blown up," Toumi said. She managed to keep her tone almost respectful.

Oda Nobunaga rarely showed surprise, but that news shocked him. "Blown up?"

We all nodded. "By a boat full of gunpowder." I said, and Emi added, "It was the second ambush in as many days."

Lord Matsudaira too looked astonished, his eyes wide, his high forehead creased like the raised grain in a weathered board. "Who would attack your armed party, and in the middle of our domains?"

Lady Chiyome answered from beside me, "Someone who doesn't want the wedding to happen, my lords."

All three of the lords glanced at her. "Lady Mochizuki, welcome," said Lord Matsudaira. "Were you traveling with Lady Oda and her attendants?" Then he glanced back at me, and recognition widened his eyes. "You…?"

"Kano Murasaki, my lord." I bowed deeply. "We met this past spring at the Full Moon."

When I straightened up, I saw that Lord Imagawa's eyes too had widened. I wasn't sure whether it was a look of surprise or fear. Possibly both. As soon as I met his gaze, he looked away.

Hachihime finally unfolded herself from her father's chest. "She, Emi, and Toumi here have become my attendants. And we met Chiyome-*san* on the road just now."

"Well," said Lord Imagawa, "it's cold. And you've all got a lot to talk about, I'm sure. Let's head inside, shall we?"

————

He led us into the castle, and I had a strange sense of *déjà vu*. Though I had climbed the walls of the castle and looked in many times, it had been on the other side—the side overlooking the cliffs. I'd never seen this part of the castle. Yet the decorations all felt strangely familiar. White-washed stone walls and elegantly simple furnishings of cedar and pine, carved with the Imagawa comb-shaped *mon*. Some cushions on the floor, mostly marked with the *mon* as well. Few tapestries or statues. None of the martial grandeur of the Takeda townhouse, say, nor the colorful style of Lord Oda. Spare and open, but comfortable even so.

We were led into a large room overlooking the central courtyard. As the lords and Chiyome-*sama* settled themselves and servants brought tea and wine, I looked around for Lord Imagawa, but he was gone.

"What is it, Murasaki?" Lord Oda asked, startling me. "I'm not used to seeing you frown like your friend."

"Oh," I responded, trying to get my thoughts under control, "I was look-ing for Imagawa-*sama*. I had something I wanted to ask him."

"I see." His gaze bored into me, making me believe that he truly could see why I wanted to confront the former lord of this province. "I believe he has retreated to his chambers. Although this is his castle, I'm not sure he wants to be here."

"I suppose not, my lord."

A thin smile, like a cat's, twisted his lips. "I could speak to him for you. I *know* he would talk to me."

Ah, I thought, *another chance for you to rub the old man's defeat in his face*. "No, thank you, my lord. It is something… private. And I would not trouble you with it."

"My dear," he said, his smile warming, "I owe you a great deal. My little bumblebee has shared some of what you have been through in the past few days—what you, Toumi, and Emi have done—and I must say that I am even more deeply in your debt. She told me you traveled through Oak Leaf! I believe a decade's back rents and port fees are the very least I owe you."

The bones in my legs seemed to turn to rice porridge, and my middle to soup. It had been a long, eventful few days. I had almost forgotten the town that bore my family's crest. Almost. "Uh. Thank you, my lord."

"You are very welcome, Murasaki." He turned to Lord Matsudaira and Lady Chiyome. "Now, I think we would all like a full report of the events that have occurred in my Lord Governor of the Three Rivers' domain and in mine. Hachihime. Ladies. Please tell us everything."

And so we did. It didn't take as long as I would have thought. I laid out the bones of the story. The attack at the first river crossing, crossing the bay on the *Fukurukuju*, and the ambush at the bridge. Emi added details and Hachihime and Toumi kept up a running birdsong of commentary.

When we told them about Inuji's attempt to poison us at Phoenix Temple, the two lords got very quiet. I wasn't sure whether I should continue.

Chiyome-*sama* broke the silence, "Where is Lord Takeda, my lords? The wedding is two days away. I expected him to be here already."

Oda-*sama* seemed to be using all of his will to bite back a comment. Matsudaira-*sama* gave a grave, measured nod. "As did we. He sent word that he is dealing with Hōjō raiders but will be here tomorrow."

"Good," said Hachihime.

The door slid open, and an Imagawa guard I vaguely recognized bowed to us. "My lords. My Ladies. An Oda officer has just arrived in haste. May he enter?"

"Of course," Lord Oda and Lord Matsudaira echoed.

The guard nodded, began to turn back to the door, then saw me and nearly tripped. He shook his head as if to clear his vision. *What is the little orphan brat who was always climbing in the trees doing here?* He marched back out the door.

"It could be a scout," Lord Matsudaira said, "letting us know when my Lord Governor of Rising Tail's son and retinue will arrive, with the decoy bridal party."

"It could," Lord Oda agreed. "Let us hope so."

Through the door ran Harē, flanked by the Imagawa guard and Lieutenant Sakai, a Matsudaira officer. My cousin knelt in front of Lord Oda and touched his head to the floor. "My lord, we were attacked just after we passed Roughwell. They ambushed us from the trees as we were making our way along the lakeshore."

Where Oda Nobunaga had seemed moments before to be trying *not* to speak, now he appeared to have been struck speechless.

Lord Matsudaira grunted. "There's a garrison at Roughwell."

"Yes, my lord." Harē kept his head down. "We were out of sight of the village and the camp, but they must have heard the fighting, because they came toward the end of the battle and helped us drive the attackers off."

"Casualties?" Lord Oda found his voice. His eyes were fully closed.

"Mostly horses, my lord, though not all." Harē looked up. "Lord Nobutada and Lady Kichō were unharmed."

Oda-*sama* gave a quick snap of a nod, took a breath, and opened his eyes.

"A number of wounded men, a couple of the women, and three men dead. Two from Masugu-*san's* squadron, and one from the Tranquility company that joined us."

"The women were injured?" Lady Chiyome asked, though it was a question on my lips as well.

"Two, my lady." My cousin's face twisted. "I'm afraid I don't know all their names, my lady. But the funny one who plays the flute"

"Sachi," Chiyome-*sama* sighed, concern deepening the lines marking her face.

Harē nodded. "She got a slash across the face. Lots of blood, but it looked clean, and not too deep. And her long-faced friend…"

"Hoshi," we all groaned together.

"She got an arrow in the… um… *lower back*. Again, not a bad wound, though it definitely looked like it hurt."

"Shot in the butt?" Toumi whispered. "I bet it did!"

Emi was thinking along different lines. "They were attacking the ladies. Again."

Once more, my cousin nodded, mouth downturned.

"Again?" Lord Matsudaira's face looked as if he were waiting to hear the punchline to a joke—eyes quizzical, one side of his mouth upturned.

Oda-*sama* snorted, though his face didn't hold the slightest trace of amusement. "We can assume that the target of these many attacks was Hachihime here, since the attack at the monastery last night suggests it."

Harē blinked up at me and mouthed, "Last night?"

Before I could explain, Emi said, "Or they could have been after both your… uh… sister and Lady Monogami."

"Or they may have been aimed at *all* the ladies," added Lady Chiyome. "All *my* ladies, as well as yours, Oda-*sama*."

Lord Oda looked as if he might have been about to disagree with her. But before he said anything, he closed his mouth and shook his head. "No. No, you are right. Those are all possibilities." He leaned forward on his raised cushion. "Harē. Did we find any evidence to tell us who these men were, and who might have sent them?"

"No, my lord. None of the dead men showed any clan marks. As at the bridge yesterday morning, about half of them were dressed as monks—"

Lord Oda's brows shot back up. "Monks?"

"Yes, my lord, though we are pretty sure it was just a disguise. The other men seemed to have had their hair shorn recently. Like the assassin at the theater this summer."

"Ah. *Ronin*, then?" Lord Matsudaira asked.

"That's what Masugu-*san* suggested." Harē nodded at me and my friends. "And what we all thought as well."

"I see." Lord Matsudaira shot a hawk-like glare, first at my cousin, then at me, Emi, and Toumi.

Glancing up, Harē said, "As it happens, my lords, we did find clan insignia on the tack of two of the horses."

Both lords peered at him.

"The four diamonds." Harē gulped and looked down again. "And Lieutenant Masugu thought he recognized one of the riders as a former Takeda samurai."

"I see," said Lord Matsudaira, his face a mask. One whose neutrality suggested the anger boiling underneath.

Toumi walked forward, bowed, and showed Lady Chiyome and the lords the quiver I had brought her. "And Murasaki-*san* took this off the archers she disarmed."

The lords both peered at me. Even Lady Chiyome seemed curious and impressed.

"I just cut their bowstrings from behind," I muttered, not meeting their eyes.

Lady Chiyome mused, "Now, if they are *ronin*, someone else could have hired them."

Hachihime was having none of that. "Or my bridegroom could be trying to get me, Lady Kuniko, and the ladies of the Full Moon out of the way, all at once."

With a grunt, Chiyome-*sama* inclined her head, granting the point. One I'd already heard her come to herself.

"So," said Lord Matsudaira, "we suspect the Lord Governor of Worth Province of trying to assassinate his own bride, an heiress, and his own servants."

Lord Oda shot a fanged grin in his daughter's direction. "It would seem so, my Lord Governor of the Three Rivers." He turned toward me, Emi, and Toumi. "Don't you think so, ladies?"

We mumbled that it looked possible.

He laughed mirthlessly. "Then I think this *wedding* clearly should be canceled."

"No," said Hachihime with force. "The wedding must happen."

She smiled, but with even less mirth than her father. "Why, so I can kill him, of course."

"Ah." Oda-*sama* tipped his head.

Lord Matsudaira, eyes even wider, said, "As you wish, my lord. Nonetheless, I believe my Lord Governor of Rising Tail and I should confer with the lieutenant here. Perhaps you ladies would like to refresh yourselves after the long and arduous journey?"

Emi, however, had her mind on other things. "Please, my lord, may I...? Um, Harē-*san*, the men, the ones who were... casualties... Did...? Was...?" She frowned ferociously.

Harē had pity on my friend. "Aimaru-*san* wasn't injured, Emi-*san*. He fought like a demon." He turned to Lady Chiyome. "As did your women, Mochizuki-*sama*. Otherwise, things might have turned out much worse."

Lord Mochizuki raised an eyebrow about the mention of Mieko-*sensei* and the others fighting. Hachihime's father, on the other hand, didn't look at all surprised.

Harē reached into a bag and brought out two letter cases. "Young Lord Oda sent you a letter, Oda-*sama*, as did your wife."

Lord Oda scanned the letters and gave a satisfied grunt. "They've retreated to the town to treat the wounded. My son tells me they will spend the night in Roughwell and be here tomorrow morning." He turned to Lord Matsudaira. "He also tells me that your nephew, Tokugawa-*san*, has commandeered several platoons' worth of men from the company at Roughwell to serve as guards for tonight and as additional protection tomorrow."

"Good." Lord Matsudaira nodded, then glanced at Lord Oda, who nodded back.

Lord Oda turned to his lieutenant. "You can go, Harē. My Lord Governor of the Three Rivers' officer, Sakai, will help you find a place to rest." After my cousin had shuffled out, Oda-*sama* turned to us. "Ladies, pardon us. As my

Lord Governor of the Three Rivers suggested, we old men have some things to discuss concerning what we learned here today from you and from my soldier. Hachihime, I believe your chamber is on the top floor; your *attendants* have the chamber immediately outside yours. Mochizuki-*sama*, I believe your room is on the second floor, near ours. I believe there is a feast planned for this evening. We thought the guests and the groom would all be here by now. Please clear off the dust of the road and enjoy an unexpectedly quiet afternoon."

We bowed and began to leave, but before we reached the door, Lord Oda called out, "Oh, and Murasaki. If I have the chance, I will suggest to Lord Imagawa that he should speak with you."

"Thank you, my lord."

19 – No Place

We made our way toward the staircases, directed by Imagawa servants—several of whom looked thrown off balance when they saw me.

"Hey, Mouse-*sama*, how come the locals all keep looking at you like you're a ghost or something?"

Lady Chiyome gave a dry snicker. "Because they've all seen her before, but they can't figure out where that might have been."

I granted that was probably the case. That they had seen me, but never dressed anything near as well as I was now, and certainly not as an honored guest in the castle.

Hachihime giggled, gesturing to her muddy *hakama*. "These dirty rags are *better*?"

"Yeah, they are," said Toumi with a chuckle. "I remember what you were wearing when we met, Mouse. Stinky and more patches than not. *Those* were rags."

I agreed. There was no point not to… she was right.

"Ladies," said Chiyome-*sama*, "I agree with Lord Oda. You could all use a bath and some fresh clothes. So could I, for that matter."

We all agreed. However, I said, "And then, My Ladies, may I have your permission to leave the castle?" When Chiyome-*sama* smirked and Hachihime raised an eyebrow, I added, "To visit my family."

"We're going with you, Mouse," Toumi said, and Emi nodded.

"Oh!" I was touched, but also a bit overwhelmed. "But who will guard Hachihime?"

The lady herself huffed. "I don't need protection in a castle, for goodness' sake, and I would certainly like to see Risuko's mother."

Lady Chiyome gave her familiar sour grin. "I think perhaps you should let Risuko and her friends go first. We don't want to overwhelm the lady. Nor would your brother appreciate your leaving the relative safety of these walls so soon after arriving."

I agreed that she was probably correct. Oda-*sama* definitely wouldn't want Hachihime going anywhere for a while, and I wasn't sure *Okā-san* wouldn't be overwhelmed by my return, let alone meeting Toumi and Emi for the first time in over a decade.

Toumi laughed. "Don't know if Mouse's mom'll be overwhelmed or disgusted, us dressed like we've been rolling in pine sap and dirt."

Emi pouted. "And our change of clothes isn't any better." They were what we'd been wearing when the assassins had attacked at the bridge.

"Silly!" Hachihime tittered. "Nobu had our clothes sent ahead! What, did you think we were carrying all of that gorgeous silk in our saddle bags?"

Imagawa servants showed Lady Chiyome her room, and we were shown up the stairs to our private apartments. Two plain, elegant rooms with a spectacular view in all four directions.

In the slightly smaller outer room, which Emi, Toumi, and I would share, I peered out the window to the north, finding the village, and then the cherry tree and our small house. Still standing. That was good at least. And the *tatami* mats were leaned up against the outside wall. Someone was apparently cleaning.

———

In the other, larger room, servants had unpacked Hachihime's elaborate wedding kimono, as well as robes for each of us to wear over the next few days of feasts and rituals. Those clothes could only be called simple compared to the red-and-gold, many-layered silk wedding robes.

Hachihime said they made her feel like a sailing ship, but in it she reminded me of a pheasant, with its spectacular plumage and gorgeous trailing tail feathers.

I didn't share that image with her. She wouldn't have appreciated it. But I thought she looked beautiful.

The tailor had taken three days to train us to put the entire ensemble on, complete with the white headdress, the multiple layers beneath the outer *uchikake*, and the many hair ornaments. We would have to get up before dawn on the wedding day to get her ready.

Given how unwilling to leave her bed Hachihime generally was, we hadn't been looking forward to that.

Of course, she had been much more energetic the previous few mornings. So perhaps she would cooperate. Also, the fact that she now planned to murder her husband that night might keep her from sleeping too soundly.

In any case, once we had seen our rooms and picked out clothes that hadn't been stained and torn by battle, riding, and sleeping rough, we visited the baths and washed the road off us.

"What's wrong, Murasaki?" Emi asked as we dressed. "Aren't you excited to see your family?" Like me, she was tying the sash around a pale gold kimono decorated with exquisite, subtle yellow-and-scarlet oak leaves—the stem of each wrapped around an acorn, of course.

I ran my hands over the smooth, iridescent silk and sighed. "I am. It's just… I don't want to make them feel bad."

Hachihime tittered. "Silly! They'll be excited to see you. How could you make them feel bad?"

I looked to my friends. They would understand, surely?

Toumi favored me with a smirk. It was, for her, a soft, almost gentle one. "I think Mouse here is worried that if she shows up looking like a princess, her mom and sister'll feel like beggars."

I shrugged. That was close enough.

Hachihime's face wilted in a pout. "A princess? But these aren't…" Then a smile blossomed. "I know! You should bring them some clothes!"

I gawked at her. "What?"

"Clothes! And food! And… What else do poor people need, do you think?"

Now Toumi was the one gawking. "Really? Where are you going to find this food, huh? These clothes?" She narrowed her eyes. "You are such a brat."

Hachihime crossed her arms and scowled right back. "Oh, I know I am. It's funny sometimes. But there were supposed to be over a hundred people at dinner tonight, who won't be here. And you don't think there are some perfectly workable clothes that could use a new home, stuffed into the chests we've been walking past? I may be a brat, but I'm not a fool." She peered at me, her scowl softening. "Unless you think Chojo-*san* wouldn't want them."

"I…" I was more worried that us coming with castoffs would hurt her pride. But food, and new clothes… "I'm sure she'd want them."

———

An hour later, we were walking the road between the castle and the village, each holding a basket. Two of clothes, and mine with rice, cucumbers, radish, beans, and more. There was even a whole roasted duck and some smoked trout. It smelled amazing.

When we'd explained to the servants what we wanted and why, they'd been delighted to help. The food would have gone to waste otherwise, they told us. And, of course, when they realized who I was, several of them laughed. "I knew I had seen your face before!"

Toumi was still grumbling. "She probably won't take any of it. We'll just have to carry it back."

Emi asked, "When you were living on the streets, didn't you welcome it when someone offered you food?"

"Never took charity," Toumi fumed.

They had been having the same argument since Hachihime had made the suggestion. I couldn't listen anymore. "I can't let my family go hungry. And winter will be here soon. There are some warm outer robes in there. It's not charity. It's my family."

We turned into the village.

"Is this... the whole thing?" Toumi asked.

Along the narrow lane stood eight houses. Huts, really. There were a few outbuildings, like the one where Naru-*san* kept his pigs, and the hutch for Irochi-*san*'s chickens. A storehouse on stilts for the harvested rice. The now-dry paddy was on the other side, where the river took a wide bend.

When I'd left, it had been home to seventeen people, not including me, two dogs, some cats who refused to be counted, one rooster, a score or so of hens, and eight pigs.

I hadn't seen it in a year. In that time, I'd been in the Full Moon, the Takeda and Oda mansions, any number of inns, and a few temples. We had traveled through dozens of villages and hamlets that had been even more tattered and threadbare.

Yet seeing it again—the place that had been my home for the whole of my remembered life... I was once again overcome with that feeling of *smallness*. I would never have described the village as impressive or grand. But it barely seemed even to be there.

"Mouse?"

There was a reason no one had ever bothered to name it.

"Yes," I sighed. "That's the whole thing."

We walked up the dirt road toward the one house that had a tree in its yard—a cherry tree I had climbed and drawn and played under.

A young woman was using a broom made of twigs to sweep the dust off the *tatami*. Not my mother. For a moment, panic closed my throat.

Then she turned, and seeing three women in silk kimonos, dropped her broom and knelt, touching her head to the ground.

She was taller and looked less like a starved rabbit. But the large eyes that looked up at us, anxious not to offend...

"Usako?" I croaked.

Those eyes widened impossibly, and her mouth dropped open. "Risuko?"

My basket dropped to the dry grass. I ran to my sister and threw my arms around her.

"You're all right!" we both cried.

The chest I held tight was fleshed, not bony. She wasn't my height, but she had definitely grown.

There are feelings so big that you can't describe them. Like the place my father talked about reaching in meditation. The place that was no-place. There is no name for the feelings. You can only say what they make you want to do. And this rainbow of feeling—relief, joy, even a bit of anger and sorrow—made me want to hold on to my sister and never let her go.

Of course, I also wanted to know about our mother. Without loosening my grip, which wouldn't have made any difference, since she was squeezing me like a crimson glory vine smothering a pine, I peered down at her, ready to ask...

A figure stepped out of the open doorway, slight and small. "Usako?"

"*Okā-san*! Look who's here!" my sister squealed.

Again speechless, I looked up.

She approached, seeming to doubt her senses, a cat wary that a treat may be a trap. "Risuko?"

Still incapable of forming words, I nodded, my tears splashing over my sister's head.

Our mother joined the embrace, and there stood the Kano women. Weeping like infants, weeping like old people. Weeping like who we were.

Overcome as I was, I was surprised to find that I was my mother's height, if not a bit taller.

Like Usako, her ribs no longer seemed to be poking through her skin. Her face was lined, and a silver streak shot through the hair over her left ear. But she seemed healthier than I had seen her since *Otō-san*'s disappearance.

After some time, I heard a cough from behind me. Uncertain who that could be, I turned my head, and my sister and mother looked with me.

Toumi and Emi stood beneath the bare-branched cherry tree, looking as if... As if they were friends thrust into the middle of an emotional family reunion.

They bowed, the habitual expressions absent from their faces.

My mother gasped.

Emi murmured, "Kano *no okā-san*, it is a pleasure to meet you."

"Again," mumbled Toumi.

Usako looked at my friends with curiosity.

My mother, however, expelled a huff of air as if they'd punched her in the stomach. "You?"

Seeing the chasm opening behind her eyes, I held her tight. "Mother, I believe you remember Hanichi Emi and Tarugu Toumi."

Again, they bowed, their politely blank looks now melting into discomfort.

"Know them?" my mother cried. "Of course I know them! I changed their diapers! I told them stories!" She ran to them and embraced them as tightly as she had me. "Oh! I never thought I would see you again! You're both so tall!"

I ran over and threw my arms around them all. Usako, caught up in the sheer waterfall of the moment, joined us.

Soon, we were all weeping. Even Toumi, though she tried to hide it by glowering. Then we were laughing. Then giggling, crying again, sighing—all in turn.

Eventually, Okā-*san* let out a long, even breath. She squeezed my friends, me, and my sister. "Usako, get the water boiling for some tea. I have a feeling we're about to hear quite a story."

20 — Teller of Tales

Okā-san peered over her shoulder at the baskets we carried with us as she led us into the house. "You've brought us gifts?"

"Um… clothes and food. From the castle." I felt even worse than I had before, looking at their clothes, which certainly weren't as exquisite as ours, but were well-made, clean, and unpatched. And their cheeks showed that they had been eating. *Why did you sell me, Okā-san?* I wondered. If it had been for food and new clothes—and what looked like new brushes and ink sticks on the writing table—I couldn't blame her, but it was hard not to feel stung. *They're alive. And so am I. That's all that matters,* I told myself.

She continued into the front room. "Your kimonos are quite lovely."

Toumi answered, "Thanks, Mouse Mom."

"Mouse…?" My mother stopped and gawked at her, then shook her head and gave a dry laugh. "I can see that you got your snark from your father." She walked around the fire, not waiting to see Toumi's stunned reaction. "In any case, yes. Lovely robes."

I nodded, gazing at the small room—fireplace, writing desk, a few cushions, just one bedroll now instead of two. A full sack of rice and some smoked pork. "They're part of the story."

"I assumed." She sat.

Usako asked, "How come you called *Okā-san* Mouse Mom, Tarugu-*san*?"

Toumi smirked at her. "'Cause I love mice so much."

I rolled my eyes. "*Mouse* is her nickname for me."

My sister looked back and forth between us, trying to work out the joke. To be fair, I'd been trying to do that for a year. "But…"

"Usako," my mother said, "start the kettle. Ladies, please have a seat. I can't wait to hear everything."

And so, I told her. The whole tale, though not in quite as much detail, or we would have missed the wedding.

I left out some parts just because they didn't seem as important. And, in any case, they weren't things I wanted to tell my mother.

At least not yet.

I didn't tell her about Jolalo. I didn't tell her about my friends going through their first moon time. You'll notice I haven't told you about mine, because it didn't affect how events played out as theirs did.

But I told them all about the journey to the Full Moon and learning the school's true purpose. Mieko-*sensei* and Masugu-*san*. The Mt. Fuji Inn. Bandits on the mountain. Fuyudori's death. The cursed map. Invasion by the Takeda and Matsudaira, the espionage and subsequent murders, our role in uncovering the truth. Lord Takeda's mission for the three of us—to *avenge our fathers' dishonor*.

Emi and Toumi helped, adding details and commentary, and answering questions from my mother and sister. But mostly, sitting there by the fire where I had heard my mother tell me and Usako stories of gods and monsters, heroes and villains and lovers and tyrants, I wove the story of the long, strange trip we had been on.

I told them about Mieko-*sensei* teaching me to use a sword, about feeling as if I were holding a shard of frozen lightning in my hand, but also feeling that I was somehow more complete in wielding it.

Usako listened, eyes wide, refilling the teapot and topping up our cups, but otherwise remaining unusually silent.

Mother listened too, head cocked. When I talked about the sword, her eyes narrowed, but she gave a grunt, shook her head at herself, and went back to listening with rapt attention.

When I told them about the mission, they both gasped.

I told them the story of Tiptown, how we had helped deliver the fortified town to the Takeda and nearly fought Brother Gyohiro's rebel farmers.

I said nothing about my torment, trying to reconcile *Otō-san*'s final words to me with the fact that I didn't see a way to do *anything* without doing some *harm*. It was my struggle. One I didn't want to burden anyone else with.

Both my sister and my mother were excited as I described our entry into the capital. Usako bounced on her cushion, taking it in like what it was—a traveler's tale of exotic, distant lands.

Okā-san's excitement, on the other hand, looked bittersweet, tinged with nostalgia, sadness, and perhaps a bit of anger. Well, more than a bit. I was, after all, describing the city from which my father's disgrace had banished her.

When I described meeting Hachihime, the anger intensified, though I could see she was trying to bank it, as if keeping the fire for future use.

I told them about the second trip to the theater, the assassin's attack, and how the three of us—plus, of course, Mieko-*sensei*, had killed the attacker, but Mieko-*sensei* had been wounded, and so we had been taken to, of all places, the Oda townhouse. Where we were born.

My mother looked down at her feet, but I could see her shoulders shaking.

I told them about meeting Lord Oda, and that brought *Okā-san*'s burning gaze back up to meet and hold mine.

I paused, expecting her to say or ask something, but once more she shook her head. "This is quite the story, Risuko. I can't wait to see how it turns out."

I told them how I had snuck into Lord Oda's chamber, intending to kill him. How he had woken, how we had talked, my sword at his throat, and struck a strange bargain to cement the alliance with the Takeda by marrying Hachihime to Lord Takeda and bring Japan closer to peace.

How Oda-*sama* had expressed deep regret for what he had done to our fathers.

How he had returned our families' honor.

Even my mother's eyes were wide, hearing that. Not as wide as Usako's, but no one's eyes are as wide as Usako's when she's caught up in a story.

I told them about the trip back to Serenity for the wedding. The three attacks and how we had escaped them.

"And now we're here," I said. "*Owari*."

My mother shook her head in amusement. "But it isn't the end yet, is it?"

I smiled, sipping tea to wet my dry throat. "Well, you were the one who always said that life isn't like stories. It just keeps going."

She chuckled. "I suppose I did say that." With the tip of a finger, she traced a circle around one of the oak leaves decorating the silk draped over my knee. "And I suppose you have explained how you come to be wearing a version of your father's *mon*."

I nodded.

"But I am not sure that I can forgive Oda Nobunaga so easily." The fire flared back in her eyes. "He destroyed our families, our lives. Can you girls truly *trust* a man who would do such a thing to his most trusted servants and closest friends?"

"Kano *no Okā-san*," Emi said, voice low. "We know he isn't trustworthy. But his grief for what he did seems real. And he seems to have kept every part of the bargain. And Hachihime… he cares for her a lot. He's trusted her life to us."

My mother touched her finger to her lips, usually a sign that she was trying to decide whether or not to tell us something.

I assumed I knew what she was pondering, so I said, "We know his true relationship to her."

Usako looked between our mother and me, clearly bewildered. But this wasn't a secret I could share, even with her.

My mother clearly already knew it, or at least suspected. She nodded and sighed. "Yes. She was always very dear to him. Is she still a little brat?"

Toumi laughed. "Absolutely! Still spoiled, and still a shrimp. But she's not so bad once you get to know her. Kind of like Mouse, here." She nudged me with her elbow.

"Thanks, Toumi," I said.

"Any time."

My mother frowned. I thought it might be about our serving as Hachihime's bodyguards, but her mind had wandered elsewhere. "Toumi-*chan*, I know your mother died when you were born, and she was so looking forward to holding you. And we heard what happened to your father and yours, Emi-*chan*. We were devastated that they had made that choice, rather than joining us in exile." She faded for a moment into her own sad memories. "But Emi-*chan*, your mother, Azami, what has happened to her? Is she well?"

Emi looked for a moment as if my mother had slapped her. She quickly composed herself. "I am afraid not, Kano *no Okā-san*. My mother died about four years ago."

"Oh." My mother covered her mouth. "Oh, I am so sorry, Emi. Your mother was my closest friend, aside from my own sister. I can't imagine what it must have been like to lose her."

"Thank you," Emi said, then shrugged. "We were living in an alley for the last two years. She just sort of… gave up."

"Ah."

My friend gave her almost-smile. "I remember you, Kano *no okā-san*. I've told Murasaki. I remember you laughing and telling stories."

My mother smiled, though her eyes were once more wet. "You were such a happy child." She turned to Toumi. "You both were."

I forced myself to smile. "They still are. They just hide it better."

Toumi did me the favor of chuckling.

I turned back to my mother and sister. I meant simply to invite them to tell us what had happened to them over the past year. But another question forced its way out. "*Okā-san,* why did you sell me to Lady Chiyome?"

She blinked at me. "Sell? I... I didn't *sell* you, Murasaki-*chan*! Why would you think that?"

Usako's wide eyes began to flick back and forth between us.

I tamped down hurt and impatience. "Lady Chiyome told me you did."

"Why?" She shook her head again, sorrow welling up in her eyes. "I suppose it doesn't matter. She gave me money, and I let her take you away. But we never discussed *selling* you."

A year had taught me patience. I waited.

Okā-san sighed. "The day she came..." She closed her eyes. "After your father's... disappearance, you know I took some work as a scribe, as a seamstress, but no one wanted a woman scribe, not to mention one in increasingly threadbare robes, and so the money was never enough. Lord Imagawa stopped using us, and he had been your father's main client. I had been forced to sell off everything, bit by bit. Both my silk kimonos. The last bits of jewelry. A few weeks before, I had sold the box with what was left of my cosmetics for a few coppers. But those coins had run out, and last year's rice harvest wasn't good, and so the rice I gave you and Usako the night before Mochizuki-*sama* came was the last our neighbors had been able to spare from their own pantries. If nothing had changed, we wouldn't have made it through to the new year.

"When she came and talked about her school, about offering you an apprenticeship of sorts, all I could think was that at least one of us would live. But I told her I had nothing to pay her for your apprenticeship, as is the custom. She said that she had met your father and owed him a debt. That she felt that, rather than me paying her for your place, she should pay me!"

She shook her head as if in disbelief. "*Three gold coins!* And another thirty of silver! Enough for me and Usako to live on for years, and even get some new clothes and writing implements, so that I've been able to take in work as a scribe again. And she promised that you would be well fed and cared for, and that you would learn a trade. I never imagined it would be waving a sword around. Risuko, I was so happy that, just when things looked darkest, this strange woman had come and offered a way to save *both* of you, I would have done anything."

She took both of my hands in hers. "I swear to you, Murasaki, if there had been any other way, I would never have let you go. But what Lady Mochizuki promised was too good a chance to pass up."

I squeezed her fingers and tried to smile. "I understand." It still burned in my chest, but I understood.

Toumi cleared her throat. "Um, Kano *no okā-san*, we didn't mean any offense with the clothes and food or anything. Just thought they might be really helpful."

Emi added. "We lived on the capital's streets for many years. We know what it means to starve. And be cold."

"And if it was rude," Toumi said, "it was Hachihime's idea."

"Hachihime-*sama*?" Shock froze my mother's face. "How unexpected!"

"As Toumi said, she's not as bad as she looks." I smiled, and Usako laughed, still not getting the joke but not caring. When I became serious again, her mouth closed tight. I said, "*Okā-san*, you said you had to sell everything. I'm so sorry. I didn't know."

She shrugged.

"Did you… were you able to sell *Otō-san*'s swords?"

"Oh!" She leapt up. "Usako, tell them about Irochi's daughter Miku and Karoku, the castle guard! I'll be right back."

Usako giggled and told us how the guard had seen Miku, who was closer to Hachihime's age than mine, and was far from a delicate flower, cleaning her family's clothes under the bridge, slamming the wet fabric against one of the rocks.

Apparently, Karoku had been so taken with Miku's sturdy frame and strong hands that he had gone right then to ask her father, the pig-keeper, for his permission to court her. How, once that permission had been given, and Miku was finally convinced that it wasn't some kind of joke, they had begun to *step out* together, as we put it in that part of the world. Going for walks in the hills. Him helping her slop out the pigs.

And how just the previous week the happy couple had come by to ask if they could get married under the cherry tree in our yard the following spring, while it was in full blossom. Which my mother had of course said they were very welcome to do.

"Aw," said Toumi, bumping her shoulder against Emi's. "Isn't that romantic?"

"Yes," answered our friend, her ears and the back of her neck turning the color of those very *sakura* blossoms.

My mother came back holding a long bundle wrapped in grease-stained linen. Her face was washed with tears, but she was smiling.

I stood without realizing it. "Are those…?"

She nodded. "Your father's swords. I could never sell these, though I was offered bags of silver more than once. They were my last piece of *him*."

I ran over to her, embracing her and the swords as well.

The scent of clove oil filled my nostrils.

Our mother sniffled. "I think your father would want you to have these. I don't know that he would have imagined you as a swordswoman, or that he would have been comfortable with the idea. I am not at all sure I am, but I know he would have been *so* proud of you, Murasaki." She pulled back and held my face in her hands. "As am I, my brave squirrel. You have brought honor back to the Kano clan. You humble me."

I embraced her, and Usako bolted to join us.

My mother lifted her arm, and like chicks running under a hen's wing to get out of the rain, Emi and Toumi joined us as well.

And then we were all weeping again.

———

When it came time to go, I asked, "Would you like us to bring the food and clothes back up to the castle? We truly didn't mean to embarrass you."

My mother shook her head. "No. There are some in the village who could truly use the clothes with winter soon closing in. And I was thinking that perhaps we might share the food with our neighbors, since they were always so kind to share with us."

"And that duck smells so good!" my sister gasped.

And so we left the baskets there.

I asked my mother if she would come up to the castle, that Hachihime very much wanted to see her again, as did my cousin Harē.

Both she and Usako seemed overwhelmed that Harē was so close, and an officer in the Oda guard, no less. *Okā-san* said she would try, but that the idea of walking through those gates...

I understood, and so simply hugged her again.

Usako proclaimed Emi and Toumi her *new sisters*, and made us promise that we would come and visit again, which we all solemnly swore we would do without fail.

As we walked back up the road toward the castle, I felt the rainbow of emotion shifting toward the brighter, light colors. It felt as if the only things anchoring me to the ground were my father's *katana* and *wakizashi* clutched to my chest

Toumi started chuckling again. "And you didn't even tell her about your town, Mouse-*sama!*"

"*Our* town," I said, adding a fake growl.

She laughed, and Emi and I joined her.

21 – Mobilization

When we reached the castle, a large company of Matsudaira soldiers were setting up camp on the bare hill just outside the yawning gate. Captain Hattori, one of the Matsudaira commanders who had accompanied his lord to the Full Moon the previous spring, was barking at the men, speeding them along in erecting not just tents but also barriers that could serve as low fortifications and barricades.

Not wishing to distract the commander or his men, we walked by quietly, but all of us were curious. "What's *that* all about?" Toumi asked.

Emi pursed her lips. "It looks like they're preparing for an attack."

"From?" I asked.

Emi shrugged, and we passed back through the gate.

Once we were inside again, the reason for the Matsudaira forces' sudden alertness became clear. Two Matsudaira soldiers—one of them the tall one from the garrison near Phoenix Temple—were standing in front of their lord and Oda-*sama*. Between them knelt a battered, bruised Inuji.

The tall guard described finding Inuji passed out in the fertility shrine. He'd been wearing his Takeda armor.

Matsudaira-*sama* scowled down at Masugu-*san*'s second in command, then at the tall guard. "And what were *you* doing at the fertility shrine, Fujita? Weren't you meant to be guarding the road over the pass?"

The tall one, Fujita, glanced at the other, who seemed to be an officer. Fujita then bowed to Lord Matsudaira. "Yes, my lord! But this *miko* we'd met earlier last night came running up, saying a drunk samurai had attacked the shrine while they were in the middle of conducting a ritual. That he'd been muttering about a *sneak attack*, my lord, and that the man wore the four diamonds. So Abe and I split up, him to get the lieutenant here and sound the alarm, and I to check on what the girl had said. And there he was, my lord, drunk as a plover, begging my lord's pardon, and wearing Takeda armor!"

Over Lord Matsudaira's shoulder, Lord Oda raised an eyebrow and peered at me, eyes half-closed. "A *miko*, you say?"

Again, Fujita checked, first with his lieutenant, and then with his lord. Both nodded at him to answer the question. "Um. Yes, my lord." He gave an awkward, deep bow.

"Was it one of those girls behind you?" Lord Oda nodded at the three of us.

The man whirled around, confusion on his face. When he saw us, his eyes nearly exploded from his head. "Yes, my lords! The short one in the center, there!"

Not knowing what else to do, I bowed, though my father's swords made that awkward.

Emi and Toumi mirrored me on either side.

Oda-*sama* stepped forward. Nodding down at Inuji, who was swaying on his knees, he asked, "Ladies, was this the gentleman you told us about earlier today—the one who drugged the monks and attempted to kill you?"

"Yes, my lord," we murmured together.

"And did he say anything about a Takeda invasion?"

Emi and Toumi both looked at me.

Great.

I kept my head bowed and held onto *Otō-san's* blades for support. "No, my lord. All that we learned was in the letter that we showed you. Inuji-*san* had been ordered to kill Lady Hachihime and her attendants. Us. I told Fujita-*san* there about the *sneak attack* because we needed to get our lady away safely and quickly."

Lord Matsudaira's hawklike glare lanced me, holding me in place. "Are you telling me, Kano Murasaki, that you launched two whole provinces of my troops into full mobilization in order to sneak Lady Oda over the border between the Three Rivers and Serenity?"

I gulped but did my best to stand tall. "Yes, my lord."

Toumi jumped to my aid. "In our defense, my lord, Inuji-*san's* trying to poison us was the third attack in three days."

Nodding, Emi added, "The... um... *misdirection* seemed like the only way to keep Hachihime-*sama* safe, which was our duty and our mission, my lords."

Lord Oda nodded. "And I think you will find, my Lord Governor of the Three Rivers, that having your troops on heightened alert just now is not a bad thing. Though the attack Risuko warned your soldiers of may have been a fabrication, that doesn't mean that there isn't one aimed at your territories at this very moment."

Lord Matsudaira took a deep breath, closing his eyes. When he opened them again, his glare was merely annoyed, not raptor sharp. "True, my Lord Governor of Rising Tail. Nonetheless, ladies, may I ask that you not use my armies as your playthings in future?"

We all knelt and bowed. "Yes, my lord."

"Hmm." Matsudaira-*sama* stared at us for a while, shook his head, and then nodded down at Inuji. "And what did this lout have to say for himself? I can see that you… interrogated him."

Fujita's lieutenant stood up straight. "Nothing that he told us made any sense at all, my lord."

Emi cleared her throat. When the men all stared at her, she looked down at her feet and said, "When we discovered he was trying to poison and kill us all, we turned the tables and gave him a concoction brewed from forest mushrooms. It was a small dose, enough to confuse him for a while."

Lord Oda gave a snort of laughter. "You mean he's been hallucinating this whole time?"

Together again, we all said, "Yes, my lord."

To Lord Matsudaira, I added, "Apologies, my lord."

Now the tall *daimyo* smiled. Not exactly in amusement but at least appreciating the irony. "No need to be sorry, ladies. As my Lord Governor of Rising Tail says, it's all for the best."

"Yes, my lord," I repeated.

Lord Oda glanced down at Inuji and then back at us. "In any case, perhaps you ladies should head back upstairs. Although our bridegroom and many of our guests have not yet arrived, you need to get my Lady Bee and yourselves ready for this evening's feast."

"Yes, my lord!"

———

Dinner was a strangely festive affair. Even though one group of the missing guests had been attacked and even though we believed the bridegroom to be behind that attack, everyone seemed in high spirits. Musicians played. Toumi noted that they might not have been *much* better than us, but also that she was glad to let them have the stage. Dancers danced.

The meal itself consisted of at least fifteen separate courses, mixing the five colors and the five flavors with extraordinary variety.

The roasted duck had been shredded and served stuffed in delicate, delightful dumplings with a tangy red sauce flavored with garlic, ginger, and wineberries.

Again, Toumi enjoyed pointing out that we neither had to serve, nor cook, nor clean.

We hadn't really had to do that since we left the Full Moon. But I had to admit, it was still nice to be one of the diners, rather than one of the people preparing and serving the feast.

We also all enjoyed the meal, which was as good as anything we had pre-pared at the Full Moon, but much more elaborate.

Beside stone-faced Lord Imagawa sat Hachihime and her father. Lord Matsudaira and his captains were next to Imagawa-*sama* on the far side of the table. One of Oda-*sama*'s most trusted commanders, Toyotomi Hideyoshi, the common-born samurai Hachihime had told us about, sat beside his lord.

And I sat beside him, with Emi and Toumi next to me, and then Lady Chiyome at the end.

I had met Captain Toyotomi. We had spoken a few words to each other, and I had always found him interesting. Clever as his lord, though less polished.

That night, however, his was only interested in Lord Imagawa. Toyotomi-*san* had been responsible for the victory that had assured Oda independence from their traditional Imagawa lords, and had begun the collapse of Imagawa power and prestige.

And Captain Toyotomi seemed pleased not to let Lord Imagawa forget it.

Hachihime laughed, clapped, and giggled, throwing jokes and comments in our direction that, to be honest, were actually funny.

Lord Imagawa never smiled, however. And he never looked my way.

———

The manic mood followed us up to our rooms after the feast.

Harē, who had been seated with other Oda and Matsudaira officers, seemed to have had just as good a time. When he heard where we had gone while he had been resting, however, my cousin wanted to know how his aunt and cousin were.

Hachihime wanted to hear the whole story in detail as well, and so we sat in the antechamber—Emi, Toumi, and my room—answering their questions. We drank more *sake* and Hachihime declared this the best night of her life.

I smiled, having drunk more wine than I should have, and said that I hoped her wedding night would be even better.

That sobered us all up—even Harē, who didn't know her plans for Lord Takeda. My cousin wished us all a good night and went back down the stairs, leaving us alone.

"Now we go to sleep," yawned Hachihime. "Tomorrow, Takeda-poop shows up. The next day we marry. And that night…" She mimed a knife thrust we had taught her in the woods that morning. She laughed, not her usual birdsong titter, but a throaty chortle that sounded positively blood-thirsty coming from the delicate noblewoman.

"Yes, Hachihime," we all said.

She turned toward her chamber. "Now, come sleep with me, ducklings. We could all use it."

That was certainly true, after the long, emotional day—and all the *sake*.

We all looked at each other and sighed.

Emi said, "As much as we'd like to, Hachihime, someone needs to stand watch. We'll stay out here. And take turns on guard."

"Me first," Toumi muttered.

Emi nodded. "Midnight watch for me."

"And dawn for me," I said.

Hachihime pouted, but she saw the logic. And was too tired to make a fuss.

———

I didn't think I'd be able to sleep, tipsy and anxious as I was.

At first, I fidgeted in my comfortable bedroll—much nicer than the forest floor we'd slept on the night before. I stared out the open window at the moonlit night.

And then Emi was jostling me gently, yawning and saying my name. The east-facing window showed the faint glow of approaching dawn.

"Thanks, Emi," I croaked, and got out of the bedroll. Emi got into hers and was asleep before I'd stood.

I slid open the door to Hachihime's room. She too was sound asleep, burrowed into the bedroll so that her face was only visible from the nose up. It always shocked me how peaceful she could look when she was sleeping, and how young. Usually, Hachihime banished peace wherever she went.

There, in the big bed where her husband would be joining her—for one night at least—she looked like a baby bird in an enormous heron's nest.

She looked no older than Usako.

I sat beside her, tracing the soft, smooth lines of her face with my eyes. *I won't let him harm you*, I found myself promising silently.

Then I smiled at myself for imagining that somehow I could do such a thing. I walked back out the door and closed it.

On a chest beneath the window, my father's swords lay, still wrapped in their oil-stained shroud.

I sat on the chest and carefully unwrapped them, revealing the sleek black sheaths, the burnished leather handles. The hilts were undecorated, but I would have known them anywhere. I had seen *Otō-san* clean them and practice with them every day before he disappeared into the very castle where I now sat.

Before I could think about it, I drew the *katana* and stood in the Two Fields, sword in front of me, stance balanced.

It was longer and heavier than Masugu-*san*'s short sword, but even more exquisitely balanced, and so as I quietly moved through the Sixty-four Changes, it didn't feel as if it took any effort at all to move the sword through the lethal cuts, thrusts, parries and ripostes of the forms. It was as natural as breathing.

It was as if my father were standing behind me and moving through the dance with me.

By the time I'd finished the exercise once, my heart was pounding in my chest like a woodpecker's beak against a trunk. It wasn't because it was hard. If anything, it was because of how *easy* it felt to wield my father's sword.

As soon as I reached the Two Fields again, I drew the *wakizashi* as well and started over, now wielding both swords at once.

Mieko-*sensei* and Hoshi had done exercises with me on fighting with two blades at the same time. It had always felt awkward. I'd worried about the blades banging into each other—about the challenge of controlling each with just one hand, rather than grasping a single handle with both.

This felt like flying. Like having my arms, my wings, slicing through the air as I moved from cuts to blocks to slashes and back.

The feeling of freedom was so complete that even the awareness that Lord Oda was watching from our doorway didn't stop or slow me.

When at last I came to the Two Fields again, both my swords aimed at his heart, I slid them into my sash and bowed. "*Ohayō-gozaimasu*, Oda-*sama*."

He nodded back and whispered, "A good morning to you, too, Murasaki. I remember watching your father do those exercises. It's extraordinary to see you moving with the same freedom and authority."

"Thank you, my lord."

"Are those his blades?"

"Yes, my lord."

"I thought they looked familiar." He looked at Emi and Toumi, snoring in their beds. "Come and talk to me on the stairs. I have something to show you."

"Show me?" I wasn't sure why, but that statement swept away the sense of release I had felt only moments before. My swords still in my sash, I joined him on the stairs and slid the door to our room closed behind me.

22 – Red and Gold

"I talked to Imagawa after the feast," Lord Oda murmured. "I asked him why you might wish to speak with him, and why he seemed to be trying so hard to avoid you."

He was two steps down from me, and so we stood eye to eye.

I cocked my head.

"He said in no uncertain terms that it was none of my business. I told him that, since I had rescinded my mistaken action in stripping your family of its rank, you and your father were very much my business. That I suspected you wished to ask him what happened to Kano Kazuo after Imagawa ordered him to come to the castle." Lord Oda sniffed. "I assume that was what you wanted to discuss with him, Murasaki?"

Mouth dry, I looked down. "It was, my lord."

"I can see why." Now Oda-*sama* frowned, the same sorrowful expression he had worn the night he had told me why he had banished my father and condemned Emi and Toumi's. "He did tell me, though not at first. Would you like me to share it with you? I would understand if you chose not to hear it."

Still avoiding his gaze, I nodded. Of course, I didn't *want* to know the truth, but if I was being honest, I had felt for some time that he must be dead—must have died not long after he entered the castle. It was like having a splinter in your foot. You know that removing it will hurt, but leaving it will allow it to fester. I forced myself to meet his eyes. "Yes, my lord. I need to know. So do my mother and sister. Not knowing has frozen us and we cannot move on until we know the truth."

"Very well." Now he looked down. "First, I must tell you that Kazuo died the day after leaving your home. Imagawa didn't want to tell me this, didn't want to talk about any of it. But finally, he confirmed that he had called your father to conscript him into fighting against me and the Matsudaira. That he could already see the doom of the Imagawa clan rushing down at him and, in desperation, turned to the legendary swordsman who served as his scribe and occasional *go* partner."

Lord Oda took a deep breath and grasped my shoulders. "Murasaki, your father refused. Absolutely and unconditionally. He said that when I destroyed his honor, he had put down his swords" He nodded down at my sash. "—those swords at your waist, and would not take them up again for or against anyone. That he would rather die than do harm to any man."

It felt as if he had slammed his knee into my gut, but I managed to remain standing and still.

Oda Nobunaga nodded, mouth downturned. "And so, Imagawa condemned him. He was beheaded at dawn." Tears began to stream from the usually wry eyes of my late father's former friend and lord. "Imagawa immediately regretted what he had done in a fit of panic and temper. And yet it couldn't be undone. He was wracked with guilt, and that was why he felt he could not speak to you. It was why he refused to continue to use your family's services as scribes. He was and is ashamed. And to such men as Imagawa and me, Murasaki, shame is neither a familiar nor a welcome visitor. We are bred to look forward, never to look back. And yet I know his shame. It is my own. Your father's death stems directly from my own actions, my own… mistakes. Because of my choices, your father, Emi, and Toumi's are all dead. My three most trusted samurai and closest friends. I am so sorry."

I felt my pulse flow through me, strong and steady. "Oda-*sama*. I can't take the guilt away for you, but you at least acknowledged it, which my friends and I appreciate, and which we feel reflects honor on you. Lord Imagawa can't even do that."

"Well," he said, some of the dark humor coming back to his eyes, "the old man has lost everything. It's easier to be magnanimous and admit one's faults when one has *won*."

"True, my lord." I smiled, and it wasn't entirely forced. "But, you said you had something to show me?"

"Ah!" He nodded again. "Indeed. Come with me."

I followed him down the stairs to where his chambers were. He nodded at Kuroi, who was standing guard outside his door.

The pock-marked, grumpy Oda guard commander grunted and bowed slightly. "Kano-*san*."

"*Ohayō-gozaimasu,* Kuroi-*san.*" I bowed back as the other guard opened the door for us. I followed Lord Oda into the room.

Oda-*sama* simply stood in the middle of his own antechamber, smiling his foxish, droop-eyed smile.

I was curious what he might have to show me, but as soon as I began to look around the room, I saw it. On one of the walls hung a scroll. The paper wasn't particularly fine, nor the ink, but I would have recognized the brush-work anywhere.

It was my father's hand.

> Even in springtime
> I remember autumn leaves
> Our start is our end

Around it, picked out in quick slashes of ink, a swarm of oak and maple leaves floated down. Although the ink was black and the paper off-white, I *felt* the vibrant reds and golds, the movement of the leaves.

And hidden amongst the autumn foliage, three tiny, beautifully rendered animals: a squirrel and a rabbit, each with large, inquisitive eyes, and a mother tanuki, glaring fiercely at the viewer as if daring anyone to harm the other two.

Tears now flowed from my eyes, leaving me blind, and I stood there, blinking, unable to see, but not wanting to look away.

After some time, Lord Oda spoke, his voice low. "When your father was in the cells below, he asked the guard for paper and ink, which the man supplied, knowing and respecting Kazuo. When the guard went to clear the cell after the execution, he found this. He brought it to Lord Imagawa and asked if he could send it to your family, but the old man, already bitten by shame, refused and told him to burn it. The guard, however, a man named Karoku, couldn't destroy it. He brought it up to the guest rooms. Where it has waited for you." He removed the scroll from the wall and presented it to me.

⎯⎯⎯

Still weeping sometime later, I reentered our chambers.

"What you got there, Mouse?" Toumi asked. She and Emi were finishing rolling away our beds.

I showed them and told them what Lord Oda had found out about my father. Emi threw her arms around me and, after a moment's hesitation, so did Toumi.

"So," said Hachihime from the doorway, voice sleep-rough, "Kano *no otō-san* is dead?"

When I nodded, she too came over and joined the embrace, and once again we were all crying.

Tears and friendship. I hadn't had the luxury of either for many years. Neither had Emi nor Toumi, nor, for her own reasons, had Hachihime.

Yet there we were. All crying. All together.

In my head, I said a prayer for the safe passage of my father's soul. It was a prayer he had taught me, so it felt appropriate.

When we had cried our fill, we armed ourselves and, dawn light streaming through the open window, we danced the Sixty-four Changes.

We were just finishing up our breakfast when the door to the dining hall opened and Masugu-*san*, Mieko-*sensei*, and Lord Matsudaira's nephew Tokimatsu strode in, windblown and dusty from the road, and knelt in front of the high table.

Lord Matsudaira welcomed them. "We are very glad to see you all unharmed. Were there any further difficulties?"

"No, uncle," said Toki. "But then, in addition to Lord Nobutada's cavalry, we were accompanied by another hundred infantry, thirty archers, and a dozen musketeers drawn from Roughwell and several other garrisons. It would have taken a battalion to launch an effective attack!"

Lord Oda grunted, nodded, and asked, "My wife and son?"

Mieko-*sensei* answered, "They are making their way up to their rooms, my lord. I believe they both felt in need of a visit to the baths."

"I can't blame them," said Lady Chiyome. "And how are Hoshi, Sachi, and my other girls?"

"Well, Chiyome-*sama*," said Masugu-*san*. "Sachi-*san* needed to be carried in a sedan chair because of her injuries, while Hoshi-*san* needed to be carried in a litter on her belly. Neither wanted to be left behind."

"I should hope not!" The mistress of the Full Moon exclaimed. "Where are they all?"

"Out with the troops, expanding the camp outside the gate." Masugu-*san* looked around. "Um... Has my lord uncle not arrived yet?"

Lord Matsudaira shared a look with Lord Oda. "No. He sent word that he was held up by raiders on his northern frontier but would be here this afternoon. Now, nephew, Lady Monogami, if you haven't eaten yet, would you join us for a meal?"

After the meal, Lady Chiyome led us out of the castle to check on the *kunoichi*. They had set up camp between the Matsudaira and Oda tents.

"It was Sachi-*san*'s idea," sighed Mitsuke, no longer dressing or acting like Hachihime, "She says that having all the pretty boys around takes her mind off her troubles."

Our music teacher sat, surrounded by cushions, the right side of her face covered in bandages.

"It's not as bad as it looks," said Hoshi, who lay glumly on her belly by her friend's side. "The garrison surgeon applied salve by the bucketful to keep infection away, so we needed ridiculous amounts of bandages." She waved her hand at her own backside, which looked like a small hill.

"I'm surprised you took that lying down, Ho-*chan*," said Sachi-*sensei*, a sly grin showing on the visible part of her face.

Hoshi groaned. "How long are you going to keep that up?"

In a stage whisper, Sachi-*sensei* said, "Hoshi doesn't like being the butt of jokes. It backs her up completely."

Hoshi groaned again, letting her face fall into the bedroll.

Chiyome-*sama* chuckled. "You're both fine, I see."

"They've been impossible," grumbled Shino.

Just then, Aimaru ran up to Emi, eyes wide. Clearly, he had intended to embrace her, and yet the presence of so many spectators stopped him short.

They stood a handbreadth apart. Too close to bow, too shy to hug or kiss.

After staring at each other for enough time that we all leaned forward to see what they would choose to do, Emi turned to Chiyome-*sama*. "My lady, may Aimaru and I take a walk around the castle?"

Smirking, the noblewoman waved them off.

"Have fun, kiddies!" Sachi-*sensei* called.

"Not too much fun!" Hoshi-*sensei* added, and then they both laughed, which set the rest of us off as well.

We talked with the ladies of the Full Moon until midday, listening to their exploits and sharing our own.

At some point, Aimaru escorted Emi back to the open tent where we were gathered. They both looked a bit bright-faced and disheveled, and were smiling. Even Emi.

Aimaru bowed to her, then to us, and made his way back to Masugu-*san*'s squadron.

Once the older women got tired of teasing Emi, we continued discussing the ambushes.

Mitsuke mused, "So whoever it was behind the attacks, they didn't care who they took out."

"Actually," said Toumi, leaning forward. "We have a theory about that—"

Lady Chiyome harrumphed. "A theory that needs to be verified before we start bandying it about."

"Er, sorry, my lady." After Lady Chiyome moved on, discussing the tactics the other *kunoichi* had used in defending themselves during the attacks, Toumi looked over at me and Emi.

We both shrugged.

I wasn't sure how much more verification we needed to be sure that Takeda-*sama* was behind the attacks, possibly as far back as the assassin at the theater. But I could understand why Lady Chiyome felt we had to be absolutely certain.

"Of course," Sachi-*sensei* was tittering, "the attacks actually weren't the biggest news of the journey." She managed to flutter just the visible eyelashes, which was disconcerting.

"What do you mean?" Lady Chiyome asked.

Before Sachi could say anything, Hoshi jumped in, or rather, interjected from her prone position, "Lady Monogami and Lieutenant Masugu are apparently *engaged*."

"Engaged?" Lady Chiyome said, her plucked brows shooting up toward her hairline.

"To be married," Shino said.

"Yes, yes," growled Chiyome-*sama*. "I understood that. I meant how did that happen?"

Emi, Toumi, and I explained how Lord Oda's son had been flirting outrageously with Mieko-*sensei*, but Hachihime had informed Nobutada-*sama* that Lady Monogami was Masugu-*san*'s intended. And that they had both been glad to confirm that announcement.

"I bet Masugu-*san* was happy," said Mitsuke-*sensei*, face set in a mild pout.

"Oh, I bet Lady Monogami was happy!" Sachi-*sensei* laughed.

"I see," muttered Lady Chiyome. "Well, I look forward to discussing this with the little chit. *Engaged*. Hmph."

———

Though no one was talking about it, everyone was wondering whether Lord Takeda would come to the castle that afternoon as he had promised.

Clouds over the Redstone Mountains were glowing scarlet and gold when a call went up from the castle walls that a body of troops bearing Takeda banners was approaching.

The not-so-small army outside the castle walls immediately formed up into what my cousin referred to as parade formation—standing at attention in units, weapons on display, banners flapping in the gentle evening breeze.

Emi pointed out that it also looked a lot like a defensive formation, flanking either side of the gate.

She, Toumi, and I watched with Hachihime from the window in her room high above.

At the front of a line of soldiers that looked, from our vantage point, to be just about as large a contingent as the Oda and Matsudaira combined, Lord Takeda rode up to the gate. He was easily identifiable by the long tuft of white hair and golden demon horns decorating his helmet. To either side rode officers with equally fearsome decorations.

In the courtyard, Lords Matsudaira and Oda greeted the newcomers. As had become his custom, Lord Imagawa stood beside them, pretending that he didn't exist.

"Ready, Hachihime?" I asked as the *daimyo* entered the castle's inner gate.

She took a breath, then looked at me and our friends. "Ready."

23 - A Feast

We whisked Hachihime down the stairs so that we were standing there, breathless but decorous, waiting for the *daimyo* to arrive. We had spent the afternoon dressing in our second finest attire, putting our hair up, and doing our makeup. We looked like a bride and her bridesmaids, visions of silk, ribbons, and flowers. Hachihime's kimono was bridal red and gold; ours were exquisite gold, with red oak leaves in startling contrast.

Naturally, we were also heavily armed. Emi and Toumi had knives up their sleeves and garrote wire in their hair. I had caltrops and one of Mieko-*sensei*'s poisoned fans. Hachihime had Toumi's thin dagger tucked beneath one of the inner robes, just where she could reach it if she needed it, held in place by her wide *obi*.

In front of us, servants parted, shuffling backwards, revealing Lord Imagawa—managing to be invisible though standing in the front—followed by Lord Matsudaira and Lord Oda.

And between them, the Mountain. Gleaming black armor, fearsome helmet, swords at the ready.

Lord Oda grinned and gave a half-bow, presenting us. "My Lord Governor of Worth," he called, his voice echoing through the hall, "here as promised, your bride!"

If I had any questions about whether or not the Mountain was behind the many attacks we had fended off, they were completely answered by the momentary expression of shock on the general's face—eyes wide, lips tight, ears red, cheeks white.

He covered it well, bending in a stiff, deep bow. "Lady Hachihime. Your beauty and your grace far exceed all report."

Over his head, Lord Oda caught my eye. The fox's smile was back. He, too, had seen it.

Takeda-*sama* had not expected his intended to make it as far as Two Branches Castle.

Hachihime bowed even lower, and we bowed with her. "My lord Takeda, your wisdom and your might are known throughout the empire, and yet your courtesy outshines them both."

"Come," said Lord Matsudaira, nodding through the doorway into the dining hall, "we have a feast prepared to celebrate tomorrow's nuptials."

———

Servants and soldiers had spent the day transforming the dining hall into a wonderland of silk, golden lanterns, and flowers. If there were a late-blooming blossom left in Serenity, I would have been shocked.

There were even cages of lacquer and gold distributed around the room, each containing a live golden pheasant, spectacular in their autumn plumage.

Where the previous evening's meal had displayed giddy excitement, however, the only word that could describe that evening's was *tense*. The smiles were bright, as were the eyes. The toasts were elaborate and flamboyant. The food was extraordinary. Nine separate courses, each presenting two or three different dishes, any one of which I would have been proud to present.

Everyone remained festive and boisterous.

But beneath all of the smiles and under the laughter, like rancid oil, lay a thin layer of fear.

Where the Oda and Matsudaira troops had intermingled the previous night, this night each clan's soldiers sat at separate tables.

At the head table, Lord Imagawa sat in the middle, looking blank-faced at the opposite wall. To his left, on our side, sat Hachihime, Lord Oda, Nobutada-*sama*, Lady Kichō, and we three attendants.

On Imagawa-*sama*'s far side sat Lord Takeda, Captain Baba and Captain Hara. Beyond them, Lord Matsudaira sat between his nephew Toki and Captain Hattori.

I had asked Toki if his uncle minded being off to one side, less prominent than the other lords. I had offered for Emi, Toumi, and me to seat ourselves with Lady Chiyome, Mieko-*sensei*, and some of the lesser dignitaries.

Toki had laughed and said, "As a matter of fact, my uncle is delighted to sit off to the side and watch tonight. Between old Imagawa's discomfort and the sparks likely to fly between my Lord Governor of Worth and his new lady, he wouldn't want to miss it." He leaned in and whispered, "And it's a good thing you and your friends will be seated close to Lady Oda, Kano-*san*. I doubt things will get *too* exciting, but I wouldn't want her bodyguards to be too far away." As I turned away, he added, "Oh, and I enjoyed getting to know your cousin Harē-*san*. Good in a fight, great rider. A bit serious, though, don't you find? You should tell him to loosen up a bit."

I smiled, trying to imagine saying that, or anything *like* that, to Harē. My cousin did, it is true, take himself *very* seriously.

Someone was reciting a lovely old Chinese poem about a virtuous young woman who lived on a small river island, and how a prince saw her, fell in love with her, and courted her, while the river hawks cried, the river flowed by, and the duckweed floated, all in harmony. It had been a favorite of my father's.

My breath caught as I realized. My *late* father's.

The musicians from the previous evening played a number of songs, among them 'The Deer's Call.' I peered out to where the *kunoichi* sat. All but Hoshi-*sensei*, who couldn't sit. Sachi-*sensei* smiled, but her visible eye tightened every time the flute player tried and failed to hit one of the high, mournful notes that gave the tune its power.

I heard Takeda-*sama* chuckling to my right—an odd reaction to the sad song. He was leaning across Captain Baba and sharing a joke with Toki, who seemed to be enjoying it as he always did. The Mountain chuckled and slapped the young Matsudaira captain on the thigh, then sat back up and schooled his features when Captain Baba cleared his throat.

As we ate a delightful soup made with daikon and mushrooms—not the red and white ones—in a pork stock, a group of actors came out and performed *High Dune*.

A priest comes along an old couple cleaning the needles beneath an ancient pine—he with a rake, she with a broom. The priest asks what makes the twisted pine so special, and they proceed to tell how this tree, in the town of High Dune, on the south end of the Inland Sea, was paired with one in Bayhome at the other, northern end of the sea. That the *kami* of the two trees have been harmoniously mated through all eternity, despite their separation, and so the couple cares for the pine to honor their commitment. Then, of course, the old couple reveal that they themselves are the spirits of the two trees.

Not exactly a thrilling love story of the type Emi has always adored, but a sweet play for a wedding, I thought.

———

As the banquet wound down, more *sake* was poured, and the guests proceeded to offer toasts and blessings to the couple.

Happy couple.

Takeda-*sama* and Hachihime sat with almost identical frozen smiles.

"You know," Emi whispered in my ear, "you might almost think they were well suited to each other, age aside."

I nodded, but said, "Perhaps. But only in that each wants the other dead."

Toumi, who had been lifting a cup to her lips, coughed, splattering her drink everywhere.

Lady Chiyome rose, proposing a toast to the two soon-to-be-married nobles. She spoke of her own marriage—something she rarely did—and said that she hoped that this couple would be as fortunate in their marriage as she had been.

Then, as the hall was lowering their cups, Chiyome-*sama* held her cup high again and said, "I believe that there is another couple on whom we should all wish the gods' blessings." She turned to Mieko-*sensei* and Masugu-*san*, who were seated next to her. "A little bird, named Sachi, told me that my ward, Lady Monogami Kuniko, and this dashing cavalry officer, Takeda Masugu, have decided at long last to tie the knot eternal."

I was used to seeing Masugu-*san* looking embarrassed. As usual, he took it in good humor.

Mieko-*sensei*, on the other hand, sat with a smile frozen on her face that looked so brittle it might shatter like frozen reeds.

Lady Chiyome continued, "I was astonished that I had not heard of this until today. However, anyone who knows these two knows that any ritual binding them together will be only an outward show, for those around them. They have known they were meant for each other since they first met. May they continue to walk the road together, far, far into the future."

Masugu-*san*'s men cheered, as did the women of the Full Moon, me and my friends included. The rest of the guests took up their cups and wished the couple luck.

Masugu-*san* was laughing.

Mieko-*sensei* was crying.

But they both looked very, very happy.

———

Soon thereafter, Lord Takeda recited a poem, praising Hachihime's virtue and her beauty.

Hachihime, swaying slightly, thanked him and said that it was time for her to wish him a good night. That the next time they would see each other would be at the wedding ceremony.

He bowed to her.

She bowed to him.

And then she sailed out of the hall, her three ducklings in her wake.

All of us trying very hard to look *sober*.

When we reached our rooms on the top floor and Emi had slid the door closed, Hachihime collapsed onto her bed, fully dressed. "Thank the *gods* that is over. I felt as if that poop was going to try to grind me up into his bowl and eat me."

"Yeah," said Toumi, "but you looked as if you were ready to slice him into strips and eat him raw."

"Ew!" Hachihime laughed, and it was the kind of laughter that comes out after you've been trying to hold in screams.

Of course, we all laughed with her. The previous hours had been difficult for us as well.

Toumi snorted. "Wish we could actually have had some wine. Could have used it tonight."

Emi stared at her. "You didn't, though, did you?"

Toumi shook her head dismissively, then looked over at me and at Hachihime, who was collapsed face down into the huge bed. "Mouse? Brat?"

I shook my head as well, and Hachihime groaned. "I think Imagawa would have poisoned my wine just by *sitting* there. Old poop." She sighed. "I could have used some, too."

I sat beside her and put my hand on her back. "After. We can all celebrate after."

"Oh, fine," she sighed, and flopped over onto her back. Her pout was severe. "Don't want to sleep alone."

Emi and Toumi sat on her other side. Emi said, "We'll be right here, Hachihime. We won't let anything happen to you."

"Promise?"

We all looked at each other. "Promise."

24 — The Mountain & the Bee

The assassin made no sound as he slid open the door to Lady Hachihime's chamber. Careful not to wake the attendants sound asleep in the bedrolls in the outer room, he entered what would never be the Oda child's bridal chamber.

The little girls had been beyond drunk when they'd stumbled up the stairs. Neither the spoilt Oda *princess* nor her puny bodyguards were likely to wake from their stupor. But it was still best to be careful.

The moon had set, and so it was dark, which suited him. After taking a moment to listen for any unexpected sounds, he slid the door closed again and approached the tiny figure in the enormous bed.

From his belt, he drew a long dagger, a knife with the crest of three wild ginger leaves on the end of the hilt. He knelt on the bed and pulled the bedclothes down, revealing the sleeper's childlike face.

Oda Hachihime. His target.

He lifted the knife, preparing to slash the little brat's throat.

"Please, stop. We do not wish to harm you." Emi stepped from the shadows in the corner of the room, her staff, once again revealing its lethal, bright blade, aimed at the murderer's throat.

Though clearly surprised, the assassin was prepared. He sprang to his feet, stepping over the sleeping girl to get inside the glaive's blade and kill the frowning girl.

But before he reached her, he heard the sound of a short bow being drawn. "I wouldn't if I were you," Toumi drawled.

His head flicked back and forth between them, but before he could act, I dropped from the rafters above him and touched the tip of my father's *katana* to the back of his neck. "Please, my lord. Don't make this worse."

He growled, whipping off the black cloth he had wrapped around his head. "You!" Takeda Shingen spat at me over his shoulder. "This is all your fault, Kano-girl. Marriage? After my Jofū? And to this little insect?"

"Poop!" Hachihime shouted from the bed between his feet and then punched him where his legs met.

With a mighty *oof*, the Mountain doubled over.

We all winced. We may not have known what it felt like, but it definitely looked painful.

The wince, involuntary as it may have been, was a mistake.

The lord grabbed the collar of Hachihime's sleeping robe and pulled her to him, setting the stolen Matsudaira blade to her throat. Still bent at the waist, he pulled her off the bed until he could see all three of us and pulled Hachihime in front of him as a shield. "Drop your weapons," he snarled, voice high and ragged.

"No," Emi said. "If we disarm, you'll kill her and then us. And you'll leave that dagger you stole from Tokimatsu-*san* to make it look like the Matsudaira were behind it."

He chuckled, still winded. "Not as stupid as you look, Hanichi-girl." He glared at me. "Then why would you not want me to dispose of this little… girl? Her brother is the reason you all grew up fatherless!"

"True, my lord," I said, both blades raised. "Oda-*sama* has admitted his mistake and sought to make things right. He has dealt honorably with us. You, on the other hand, sent *ronin* and assassins after Lady Hachihime and after Lady Chiyome's servants."

"After *your* servants, you *baka* bastard!" Toumi said, lips curled back to bare her teeth. "After *us*. And Mieko-*sensei* and the rest. *Che!* You didn't care what happened to us as long as we were *out of the way*."

His eyes widened but then narrowed. Held between him and my swords, Hachihime looked furious. She also looked humiliated, pulling her robes closed, even as the knife stayed at her throat.

Emi nodded. "We took your order from Inuji-*san*. We saw that you intend to dispose of the *kunoichi* with as little consideration as you meant to dispose of your bride."

"Bride." He gave a completely humorless laugh. "Fine. Yes. The *miko* thing worked well for a long time, but the other lords' soldiers had begun to figure it out, and what use were you to me then? So yes, I wanted to get rid of you all, replace you with a proper army of assassins—*ronin* and cutthroats and bandits who would do anything for a few pieces of silver."

Emi hummed and tilted her head to one side. "And yet we defeated all of your *proper* assassins. Every single one. Are you so sure it made sense to discard us?"

Clearly running out of patience, Lord Takeda slapped at my *katana* with his knife, intending to beat it into the *wakizashi*, leaving me vulnerable despite my longer weapons.

I had anticipated such an attack, however, and dropped the tips of my swords, letting his dagger pass over both, and then slashing up across his forearm with my *katana*.

A thin line of blood, black in the dark, erupted in my blade's wake, and Lord Takeda gasped in pain, dropping his blade. He glared at me, eyes wide... and then his eyes flew wider still.

Hachihime had retrieved Toumi's dagger from inside her robes, turned, and thrust the vicious blade up under his ribs and into his heart.

Just as we had taught her.

"You?" he gasped, letting her loose at last and falling to his knees.

"Yes, me!" she shouted in his face. "Me, you nasty... poop!"

With a groan of pain, and disbelief, Takeda Shingen sank to what had been meant to be his marriage bed and let out the sigh that only the dying give.

We approached carefully, watching to make sure that the Mountain wouldn't rise again. When he only deflated and bled out, eyes unfocussed and rapidly glazing over, we dropped our weapons from their guard and looked at Hachihime.

"Did you see me?" she crowed. "Boom! Pow! Just like you showed me!" She was breathing as if she'd run all of the way up from the courtyard, then back down and up again. Her hair and eyes were wild, and a thin line of blood showing where he had scored her throat with Toki's stolen knife.

I nodded. "Just like we showed you."

"Good job, Brat," chuckled Toumi, reaching out and taking back her blade from Hachihime's shaking hand.

"Yes, well done," said Emi, face set in a pensive scowl. "Now, what are we to do? How do we take care of the fact that the Lord Governor of Worth is dead in our rooms?"

"And how do we admit that we killed him without starting a full-scale battle?" I closed my eyes, thinking about two lessons I had learned.

First, as my mother had told me, in life, unlike in adventure tales, one never gets simply to say *owari* and let the story end. Second, as Mieko-*sensei* and the other teachers had drilled into us at the Full Moon, the most difficult part of a mission ending in death is the question of what to do with the body.

"Ew!" Hachihime shouted, looking down at her blood-soaked silks. "Look what that poop did to my clothes!"

———

Aimaru and Harē were on night watch in the corridor downstairs, thankfully, and so when I asked them to bring Lady Chiyome and Lord Oda up to our rooms, they didn't ask too many questions.

Neither did the lord and the lady when they reached Hachihime's gore-splattered bridal chamber.

Lady Chiyome looked down at Lord Takeda's dead body with profound disappointment. We told her what he had said. That he had admitted to wanting to rid himself of her and the *kunoichi*. Her only response was to glare down at the Mountain's stunned, slack face and mutter, "Ruffian."

Lord Oda embraced his daughter fiercely, not caring that Takeda Shingen's blood was now all over him as well. Both of them cried, which seemed like a reasonable thing to do.

After a while, Chiyome-*sama* cleared her throat. "Well, Oda-*sama*. How do you suppose we should deal with this? It is clear to me, as I am sure it is to you, that the ladies here were fully justified in acting in their own defense. That this... *man* had been willing to use deadly force on them, and so they had every right to use it on him. But I know how this story will play out, my lord," she continued. "Rumors will spread that Lady Oda here invited her groom-to-be up to this room under the pretext that they *get to know one another better* the night before the wedding. Not a virtuous act perhaps, but not at all uncommon. And that she and her attendants set on him while he was... *unprepared*, killing him, and planting the Matsudaira dagger to make it look as if there were another attacker entirely."

Without letting go of Hachihime, Lord Oda took a breath and nodded. "You are right, of course. And, as the old saying goes, *a lie will fly across the empire before the truth gets out of bed.* We must make sure that the lie that flies is ours." He looked down at the body, which now lay in a pool of its own gore. "If only he hadn't died here. Hadn't died tonight. His death will stain the reputation of my little bumblebee and that of these brave young women. But it will also scuttle the peace that Murasaki here so cleverly brokered. It will set the Takeda on a war path toward the capital, when my troops are elsewhere." He kissed the top of Hachihime's head. "It was not your choice, Hime, but I wish he had waited until *after* the wedding to try to kill you."

"Me too!" She sniffled into his chest.

I found myself saying, "I don't think he ever intended to marry Lady Hachihime, my lord."

"No?" Lord Oda asked.

Emi nodded. "He said as much. And I don't think he meant the alliance to hold either. I believe he was trying to set you and Lord Matsudaira at each other's throats and put himself in a position to dispose of both of you."

Lord Oda peered at Emi appraisingly, then back down at the corpse. "Yes. Yes, that does sound like something he'd do." He gave a humorless laugh. "Or something I'd do, for that matter. Even so, this timing is... unfortunate."

Lady Chiyome clicked her tongue "Are you suggesting, Oda-*sama*, that we somehow hide the fact of this man's death?"

He shrugged. "I'm not *suggesting* anything. Merely trying to think how best to deal with this situation." Again, he laughed, this time with a bit more of his humor to it. "I have been dreaming of ways of defeating this brilliant, annoying man for years. I truly didn't expect to see him die in a virtuous young lady's bedroom."

"No," Lady Chiyome agreed with a dry chuckle.

"My lord," said my cousin from the doorway, "I don't see how we could possibly keep everyone from finding out about the death immediately. They all expect him to marry my lord tomorrow."

"Yes," sighed Lord Oda. "That's why I am not sure how best to turn this—" He flicked his head at the dead body "—to our best advantage."

"Um, if I may, my lord, my lady?" Aimaru said, staring down at his boots.

Lady Chiyome looked at him in surprise. "Yes, Aimaru? What is it?"

"Well," he said, now shifting from foot to foot, "if what my lord is worried about is everyone finding out when Lord... the lord there died, then I might have an idea."

Oda-*sama* peered at him, tapping his nose with a finger on the hand not clutching Hachihime. "Yes, soldier? You've whetted my curiosity. What is this idea?"

Aimaru gulped and then looked up at Emi, and then at me. "You see, my lord, there's this Takeda officer. He's a dead ringer for the dead lord here. One of the men in his squadron was telling me, he's from a bastard branch of the Takeda line."

Lady Chiyome gave a huff of recognition. "Lieutenant Shirokage. He and his men accompanied me here."

Lord Oda's eyes shot wide. "If I understand the young man—Aimaru-*san*, I believe?—we could substitute this Shirokage as a double for the late

Lord Takeda." He sniffed. "But how would we convince him to play along with the ruse?"

Chiyome-*sama* gave a soft chuckle. "Oh, I believe I can convince the good lieutenant. Aimaru, go, wake him, and bring him here. Tell him it is a matter of the utmost urgency and the utmost secrecy." As he bowed and ran down the stairs, she gave nother chuckle, this one not so soft. "Oh, and Risuko, do you still have Masugu's short sword, by any chance?"

25 — Shadow Warrior

While Aimaru fetched our accomplice, we set the scene for the play that needed to be performed.

We took Toki's dagger and hid it to be cleaned later. Into the dead man's hands we placed Masugu-*san*'s Takeda *wakizashi*.

Then Lord Oda and my cousin pushed the sword into the wound that had killed him. They folded his legs so that it looked as if he had been kneeling when he committed *seppuku*, but had fallen over when he died.

"Why's this going to work when it didn't at the Full Moon?" Toumi whispered to me and Emi.

Before I could answer, Emi said, "Because this man actually died of a stab wound to his middle, not a broken neck. And because his face looks shocked from pain, rather than surprise."

Toumi nodded. "Fair enough." She chuckled. "Serves him right. *Baka*."

Lord Oda and his daughter changed into clean clothes so that none of us had any blood on us.

Shirokage was wiping sleep from his eyes when Aimaru showed him into Hachihime's room. Seeing the body and our concerned faces, he gasped and fell to his knees beside the bed. "My lord!" Blinking, he looked around. "What happened here?"

As we had agreed, Hachihime stood up, eyes still red and full of tears— no pretense involved. In a shaky voice, she said, "Shirokage-*san*, it was a tragedy. My lord came to my rooms tonight, full of passion and… desire." She looked down modestly. "He said that seeing me tonight, he realized that he could not wait until tomorrow to… to… consummate our marriage, that he could not live if we did not, um, share a pillow tonight."

"Oh," mouthed Shirokage.

"My attendants tried to dissuade him, to tell him he had only to wait one more night and we would be wed, but he could not live if we did not taste connubial bliss immediately." She sniffled, hiding her face. "When I told him that while I would accede to his every wish once we were married, I am a maid and have always attempted to be a virtuous one and could not give him what he so wished without destroying what we both wanted—a happy marriage. Then... Oh!" She covered her face and buried it in her father's chest.

Emi and Toumi both nodded at me.

My turn. "At that moment, the lord seemed to realize what he had done. He drew his *wakizashi*." I nodded at the sword he was holding. "At first I feared that he meant to attack Lady Hachihime, but no..." I turned to Emi, who continued, "He said that he was ashamed—ashamed to have dishonored himself in Lady Oda's eyes, ashamed to have brought dishonor onto the Takeda clan, and even on his marriage to his beloved late wife."

Toumi leaned in. "Then he knelt down, and he stabbed himself. Real fast. We had no idea what he was going to do, or we'd have stopped him!" Her face was pale and drawn. Really, she was very good at this whole spy thing.

Shirokage continued to stare down at the cooling corpse.

Somber and solemn, Lord Oda said, "Shirokage-*san*, we turn to you as the one person able to preserve the honor of both the dead man and of his clan. To preserve the alliance that will guarantee us power and peace. Will you do this, lieutenant? Will you help us?"

"What do I need to do?" The poor man looked as if he were preparing to have a tooth pulled.

Lady Chiyome whispered, "We know that you have served as the general's shadow when the need arose."

Her tone was as soft and gentle as I'd ever heard it, but you would have thought she had slapped him. "My lady!" He glanced over at Lord Oda.

Oda-*sama* waved the objection away. "Do not blame Chiyome-*sama*. I was already aware that Lord Takeda did this—too many reports of him appearing at more than one place at a time. And we hope to use your unique talents for one last important mission." He let go of Hachihime and stepped close to Shirokage. "What we ask is that you... represent the late lord at the wedding tomorrow. By doing this, not only will you make it unnecessary for the story of how this honored lord actually died, but you will save the Takeda clan from implosion, discovering that their rock, their... Mountain... is gone."

Shirokage stared at Oda-*sama*, and then at Hachihime. "You want me to... marry her?"

Lord Oda nodded. "It is essential. Otherwise, your late commander's shame must be known."

"But... But...?" Shirokage's forehead was suddenly dripping sweat. Then his eyes widened in terror. "What do I say to the captains? To his family?"

Oda-*sama* nodded at this completely reasonable question. "Of course, you may tell them. They will recognize that you are not your late lord. After. Wait until the ceremony is complete. When they question you, you may send them to me or Lady Mochizuki here, and we will explain why this is essential. But they must agree to keep this a secret for as long as possible for the sake of the Takeda, for the sake of our alliance, and for the sake of the empire. Do you understand, Lieutenant?"

The look-alike nodded, his face frozen in a grimace of horror.

"Come, Shirokage-*san*," said Aimaru. "I will bring you to the dead man's rooms. We have a few hours before dawn. I will help prepare you."

Thank you, the poor man said without emitting a sound.

Aimaru walked him back out the doorway, giving us a wink as he slid the door closed.

"So... why did he go along with that?" Hachihime asked, her smooth forehead wrinkled in a rare frown.

Lord Oda looked at Lady Chiyome, who gave him a smile of spiderweb and lightning. She said, "Lady Hachihime, I believe it was as your father said. The one thing holding the Takeda clan together is the Mountain. He has been the rock on which the other three diamonds rest. If the armies, his vassals, and his allies were to learn of this too soon, chaos would follow. A civil war within a civil war. As for his close family and captains, giving them time to sort things out is also for the best for everyone." She flicked her chin at the dead man. "This ruffian's son and heir, Katsuyori-*sama*, is rash and unliked by the soldiers under his command. Once again, if the Takeda mantle passes too quickly, it would inevitably result in mutiny and revolt. Lieutenant Shirokage is a good man and a fine officer, though by no means a master of the grand game of *go* played by lords such as Oda-*sama* and the dead lout, here."

"All very true, Lady Mochizuki." Lord Oda bowed his head. "I always felt you were a clever and astute lady."

"Thank you, my lord. Of course, you also placed a spy at my school."

"A mark of my respect for you! Would you have done any differently?"

She returned his crafty smile with one that came as close to warmth as hers ever did. "No, my lord. I suppose not."

He quirked an eyebrow at her. "And... 'as her father said'?"

Now Lady Chiyome's smile broadened, though the warmth diminished. "Yes, my lord, her father. As you say, I would not have done any differently." When he glanced at us, she continued, "And no, I did not learn of the nature of my lord and my lady's true relationship from these young women. I have my own sources. My lord."

When they stared at each other appraisingly, I asked the question that had been worrying me since Shirokage's departure. "Pardon, my lord, my lady, but what is likely to happen to the lieutenant after the wedding? Will they punish him?"

Lord Oda shook his head. "I think not. The captains and clan will see that he offers too much of an opportunity to be wasted."

"I see," I said. "Thank you, my lord."

"He seems a lot nicer than the dead man," Hachihime sniffed. "But Nobu, this marriage will *not* be consummated, understood?"

Lord Oda embraced her once more. "Understood, my little bumblebee."

———

I t turns out that being the most powerful lord in the empire has advantages: disposing of the body becomes a lot easier. Even when the body happens to be the second most powerful lord in the empire.

And you don't even have to get your own clothes dirty.

While we moved to the antechamber, six of Oda-*sama*'s most trusted servants took away the body and the blood-soaked bed. What they did with them, I never learned, and I never wanted to.

Once they were gone, there was a brief conference about what to do next. Who needed to be informed about what had happened, and what version of the events did they need to know?

Emi asked if Lord Matsudaira's support wouldn't be useful, since the castle was in his domain. Lord Oda and Lady Chiyome argued both sides of that question before deciding that, yes, the Lord Governor of the Three Rivers ought to be brought in.

After clicking her tongue for a moment, Lady Chiyome said, "I think Lady Kuniko and her intended might be useful as well. Risuko, Aimaru."

We bowed. "Yes, my lady?"

"Risuko, Captain Tokimatsu seems fond of you. Bring him his dagger and ask him to fetch his lord uncle, quickly and quietly."

Lord Oda chuckled. "Tell the young man his knife was found someplace compromising, and I would like to speak to him and his lord to ensure that no embarrassment ensues."

"Yes, my lord." That presentation of the facts seemed less than entirely straightforward, though it was all true, and I could see how both Toki and his uncle would want to come up to prevent any scandal.

"Aimaru," Lady Chiyome barked, "I assume that Lieutenant Masugu and his new fiancée are together in her chamber on the first floor. Tell the two turtle doves we require them immediately to help us create a diversion."

"Yes, my lady!"

Emi handed me the dagger, and Aimaru and I both sprinted out of the room and down the stairs.

Aimaru continued down to where Mieko-*sensei* and Masugu-*san* had spent the night, while I headed down the back corridor on the second floor toward where the Matsudaira were housed.

The guard at Toki's door wore a familiar snow-monkey, sunken-cheeked face. "Good morning, Kobayashi-*san*!" I called.

"Risuko-*san*!" he answered, smiling. "Good to see you. What brings you here so early in the morning?"

"I urgently need to speak to Captain Tokimatsu."

The guard scratched his ear under his helmet. "Well... Are you sure it can't wait? Tokugawa-*san* and Lieutenant Sakai were up... um... celebrating until just after I came on watch at the hour of the Ox."

"I'm afraid it is urgent, Kobayashi-*san*."

The guard knocked on the door, which was opened, not by Toki, but by a bleary-eyed, disheveled Sakai. "What is it, Kobayashi?"

When we explained that we needed to speak to Captain Tokugawa, he stumbled, grumbling, back into the dark room. We heard water being poured—on Toki's head, presumably—and a shout of surprise, then Sakai's low voice.

After a moment, Toki appeared at the door, hair dripping, light robe soaked from the waist up. He blinked when he saw me, covering his chest with his arms. "Kano-*san*! What brings you here?"

I delivered his dagger and Lord Oda's message, and he was suddenly wide awake. Snapping of crisp bow, he said, "I will fetch my uncle and meet you upstairs, Kano-*san*. Thank you."

On the way up the stairs, I met Aimaru, Mieko-*sensei*, and Masugu-*san*. The couple looked almost as disheveled as Toki and Sakai had, but nowhere nearly as hungover.

Back up in the room on the top floor, Hachihime, Emi, and Toumi had retreated behind a screen and started ritually bathing the bride for her wedding. I joined them.

On the other side of the screen, I heard Oda-*sama* say, "Lieutenant, Yuri-*san*. We have a favor to ask of you. As young Aimaru there no doubt told you, we need your help in creating a diversion."

I had expected them to want to know what kind of diversion, but Masugu-*san* asked, "Yuri, Oda-*sama*?"

"Yes," said Lord Oda, a smile in his voice. "Yuri Mieko. The real Monogami Kuniko died around this time last year while defending Lady Mochizuki here when a band of retreating Imagawa tried to loot their own village."

Lady Chiyome gave a disgusted snort, then muttered, "How would you lovebirds like to get married today?"

They both gasped. "Today?"

"Yes," said Lord Oda. "We have a... situation."

And he proceeded to explain what had happened. The full story.

When he was done, Mieko-*sensei* said, "And so, my lord, you wish our wedding to delay the conversation about Lady Hachihime's bridegroom for as long as possible?"

"Yes, that. Also, I must admit, I have need of Lady Kuniko."

"My lord?"

"Akita has proven very weak, both as an ally and as a *daimyo*. Much of Wingtip Province is in revolt—*Ikko-ikki*, clans still loyal to the Monogami, minor lords playing their own games. I believe that having the lost heir of the rightful clan returning would create a much more stable situation. And I think the two of you would make an excellent lord and lady of that province, whether or not either of you was born a Monogami."

Lady Chiyome huffed. "So, my Lord Governor of Rising Tail, are we to understand that you saying you knew the chit's actual name was just showing off?"

"As I asked before, my lady of the Full Moon, would you have done any differently?"

After a moment, she huffed again, this time in amusement. "No, my lord."

Pouring the third bowl of cold water over Hachihime's head, Toumi whispered, "You know, Brat, your dad and old Spiderface seem to be enjoying each other's company way too much."

We all agreed with that thought. Hachihime's teeth were chattering too hard to speak, but she nodded.

Lord Matsudaira came in with Toki, and Lady Chiyome and Lord Oda once again recounted what had happened. This time, they told the version of the story we had shared with Shirokage—that Takeda-*sama* had killed himself out of shame after trying to force himself on his virtuous bride.

Lady Chiyome finished by saying, "Since the late lord had intended to plant your dagger on the scene, Tokugawa-*san*, we felt it essential to inform you and Tokugawa-*sama*—"

"Tokugawa?" Lord Oda asked.

"Yes," said the lord of the Three Rivers. "I have returned my clan's name to its noble roots. Like my nephew here, I now bear the name Tokugawa. Please, call me Tokugawa Ieyasu."

"My lord Tokugawa," Lady Chiyome said, and the rustle of her robes told me that she had bowed.

"So," Toki said, clapping his hands together, "we're not going to have just one wedding, but two?"

26 – Owari

Although it was midday, the hall was dark as midnight. A fitting setting for a wedding.

Lanterns glowed from the rafters around the *tatami*-covered section of floor where the weddings would take place. Around the space hung banners with symbols of longevity, prosperity, and fertility—a turtle, a crane, an ancient pine, and, naturally, a *tanuki*—to bless the unions.

The spectators, who included representatives of many of the important clans, sat silently on the floor around the ceremonial stage.

We stood in the shadows behind them, me in front of Hachihime and Emi and Toumi flanking her.

Just because the Mountain was dead didn't mean there weren't any more potential assassins waiting for their opportunity.

The priest from the shrine to the *kami* of the Weatherbank River stepped into the sacred space, purifying it by waving a *harai-gushi*, a wand streaming strips of white paper. The gray-bearded man turned toward the crowd, who stood and bowed, and the purification ritual was repeated.

Now it was time for the bride, the groom, and their attendants.

I watched from the back as Mieko-*sensei* glided forward, attended by Mitsuke-*sensei* and Shino in their best *miko* attire. Sachi-*sensei* and Hoshi-*sensei* had both expressed dismay at not being able to participate, but they were both in attendance, albeit bandaged.

Mieko-*sensei* entered in the red-and-gold kimono Hachihime had worn to dinner two evenings before. Her head was covered with a folded length of white silk that had originally served as an Oda banner.

A murmur of surprise rippled through the crowd and grew as Masugu-*san* marched onto the *tatami*, followed by the Matsudaira—or rather Tokugawa—captain, Tokimatsu, and the Oda lieutenant, my cousin Harē.

Masugu-*san* had first thought to ask Inuji to serve as his groomsman—but once we told him about his subordinate's attempt to kill us, his face settled into a mask that did little to hide his anger.

The lieutenant wore dark *hakama* and a small, black kimono jacket. On either shoulder was a *mon*—not the Takeda diamonds, but the three stripes of the Monogami. Mieko had embroidered them on earlier that day.

The white-robed priest waved the *harai-gushi* over the bowing couple, and the mutters died down. He turned away, chanting in a loud, gravelly voice toward the small altar to the gods. He asked the blessings of all the *kami*, thanking them for bringing the couple to that place on that day. He asked their blessing on the union of the couple who had approached the altar. Then he turned back to them and nodded.

Mieko-*sensei* spoke in a thinner voice than I'd ever heard from her. "I am Monogami Kuniko, daughter of Monogami Yoshiuri, son of Monogami Yoshihiro. I am come to pledge myself to Takeda Masugu, and to take his clan as my own."

Masugu-*san*'s voice wasn't as strong as I was used to either. "I am Takeda Masugu, son of Takeda Minoru, son of Minuri Hirojime. I am come to pledge myself to Monogami Kuniko, and to take her clan as my own."

Mitsuke stepped up with three cups, placed one inside the other, forming a tower. From what looked like a clay teapot, she poured *sake* into the smallest, central cup. Once it was full, the wine spilled into the middle cup, and then into the largest, bottom one.

Once they were all full, Shino handed the smallest cup to Masugu-*san*, who took three sips, and then passed the cup to his bride. Once she too had sipped three times, Shino handed Masugu-*san* the middle bowl and they repeated the process before completing it with the largest, lower bowl.

Each cup represented a different part of their lives together—the smallest cup the past, the middle the present, the largest the future. The nine sips were the heart of the wedding ritual, mingling their lives together like the wine they shared.

Then they approached the small, gilded altar and knelt. Masugu-*san* had surreptitiously grabbed onto Mieko-*sensei*'s hand.

In a much louder voice, he proclaimed, "On this auspicious day, before the honored *kami* and in the presence of these witnesses, I, Masugu, son of the Takeda clan, take—"

She intoned, "Kuniko, last daughter of the Monogami clan."

"—as my wife. Her clan shall be my clan, and her name my name. From this moment forward, I shall be Monogami Masugu. I pledge to protect and honor her in times of peace and of war, to provide for her in times of prosperity and in times of hardship, to remain faithful to her throughout this life. I accept the sacred duty of husband, and together we shall serve our ancestors, honor our families, and walk the path of righteousness side by side. Before the *kami* and these witnesses, I make this solemn oath."

I've always found it strange that only the groom pronounces a vow. But then, her promise would be to be quiet and obedient, so perhaps silence is the perfect vow.

Shino and Mitsuke removed the white headdress, revealing that Mieko-*sensei* was crying, but smiling.

I found that I was doing both as well. Why do we cry at weddings? To this day, I don't quite know.

Harē and Toki stepped forward, each carrying a *sakaki* branch. Harē handed his to Mieko-*sensei*, while Toki handed his to Masugu-*san*. They placed the branches on the altar and stood. The couple, their attendants, and the priest all clapped their hands twice.

And with that, they were married. Lord and Lady Monogami.

Lord Oda, seated close to the *tatami*, stood, gave a slight but respectful bow, and said, "May this union bring ten thousand years of peace and prosperity!"

Lady Chiyome and Lady Kichō joined him. "*Banzai!*"

The rest of the spectators stood and repeated, "Ten thousand years!"

The two newly married, newly renamed lovers stepped off the *tatami*, and well-wishers encircled them. Most were Oda and Tokugawa. Of the Takeda, only Masugu-*san*'s own riders were among the first to congratulate the former lieutenant. Even Inuji joined, however timidly.

Finally, Captain Baba and Captain Hara offered their well wishes, along with the other senior members of the clan.

And then it was time for the match that everyone had actually come for.

Hachihime was in her spectacular robes and headdress. Emi, Toumi, and I were dressed as *miko*, the white tunics and red *hakama* made of silk rather than linen. And of course, we all carried weapons hidden beneath the silk. I even had Mieko-*sensei*'s steel parrying dagger in my hair.

Lieutenant Shirokage's face was set in a fierce scowl, giving him a remarkable likeness to the late Lord Takeda. His groomsmen were not officers or Takeda family members, but riders from Shirokage's own squadron.

The ceremony was basically the same. There was a lot of exchanging gifts between the clans, and my friends and I poured wine for each of the guests.

Where Mieko-*sensei* and Masugu-*san* had radiated warmth and love, this bride and groom were muted. Even standing just a pace or so away, I could barely hear Shirokage as he spoke his vows, stumbling when saying "I, Sh-shingen…"

My friends and I were at full attention, senses straining to detect the slightest hint of a threat. None came. Instead, most of the spectators seemed confused, as if they knew *something* was off but couldn't put their finger on just what that might be.

Even the priest kept looking around, eyes narrowed, searching for clues in our faces.

Once we all clapped our hands to mark the end of the ritual and Lord Oda offered his blessing on the marriage, his wife and son, as well as the other Oda and Tokugawa guests, joined in the cheer. It took some time before the Takeda joined in.

When we walked off the *tatami* into the crowd, I stayed close to Hachihime's back, and Emi and Toumi guarded her shoulders. Again, the Takeda were among the last to offer their congratulations.

Like many of the guests, Captain Hara approached Hachihime holding a gilded lacquer box bearing interlinked Takeda and Oda crests. The box itself was a precious gift, and no doubt contained a wedding present that was equally lovely and valuable, if not more so.

No blades or needles. No smoke, so not a bomb. His hands were bare, so unlikely to be painted with a contact poison.

"Welcome to the Takeda clan, Lady Hachihime," he mumbled.

Hachihime handed the box to Emi and bowed deeply to the captain. "Thank you so very much for your gracious welcome, Hara-*san*."

"Hmm." He looked over at Shirokage, who was whispering intently with Captain Baba. Not to be overheard, Hara leaned forward and asked, "My lady. What's going on?"

We had known this question was coming. I was mostly happy that Hara-*san* seemed more confused than furious.

In her sweetest, least bratty voice, Hachihime answered, "A most understandable question, Captain. May I suggest that you ask Lord Oda, my brother. Something *has* happened, something of grave import to all of us present today. I know that Oda-*sama* and Lady Mochizuki wished to discuss these matters with you, as well as Captain Baba and the rest of the Takeda here today."

He glanced at Shirokage and then back at Hachihime and us. "I see. Well, then, Hachihime-*sama*. As I said, welcome to the clan. I think."

"And again," she said with a bow, "thank you, Hara-*san*."

As each of the other guests approached, my friends and I remained alert to whether any of them posed a threat. At the same time, we couldn't not notice a subdued but heated conversation among the Odas, Lady Chiyome, and the Takeda officers. The Tokugawa watched the conference from a safe distance.

I heard later from my cousin and Lady Chiyome that the Takeda started outraged, then, when they saw the order written in the late lord's hand condemning Hachihime and us to death, they surrendered to shock. At that point, they accepted the story that Lord Takeda had been overcome with lust and had committed *seppuku*.

After the guests had left the hall for the feast in the courtyard, Hachihime's father, Lord Tokugawa, Lady Chiyome, and the Takeda captains approached Hachihime and Shirokage, who fidgeted, looking down at the floor.

Oda-*sama* looked around. "We have all agreed that it is to all our benefit not to make known what actually happened here today. And yet it is clear that this marriage cannot serve the purpose for which it was originally conceived." He nodded to me. "We will ask the priest to perform a rite of annulment, and that will be that. I hope that we shall continue to work together, but this marriage should not be our alliance's lynchpin. Do our newlyweds agree?"

Shirokage, whose face was slick with sweat, gasped, "Please. Yes."

Hachihime bowed demurely. "If it please Shirokage-*san* and Oda-*sama*, this humble woman will abide by your wise decisions."

Next to me, Toumi coughed. When I turned to her, she mouthed, "Humble?"

And with that, their marriage—the marriage that I had hoped would lead to a lasting peace—was over.

And even I had to agree that was probably a good thing.

———

The Takeda left before the feast was over, spreading word among the guests of another border incursion. At the head of the column rode poor Lieutenant Shirokage, who would play the part of Lord Takeda for the good of the clan.

Of course, he wasn't the Mountain.

I asked Lord Oda how he thought it would all turn out. Whether the alliance would continue.

He smiled and turned to Emi. "Hanichi-*san*, what do you think?"

Emi frowned. "Well… I don't think so, my lord. I think that if the dead lord wasn't willing to commit to an alliance in which they would be equal partners, then one in which they are junior partners will almost certainly hold no interest to them."

He nodded. "Well put, Emi-*san*. Does that answer your question, Murasaki?"

"Yes, my lord."

Mieko-*sensei* and Masugu-*san* became the guests of honor, much to their shock and our delight.

The only remaining Takeda troops were his lancers. Inuji led the others, helmets in hand, up to the head table to congratulate their commander.

"Um… My lord, my lady," Inuji said as the others pressed up behind him. "I hope you will both accept our well wishes. And also… Um…" He looked back, and the other riders all nodded. "Um. We would like to offer ourselves for your service. We would like to serve the Monogami."

Masugu-*san* sat back, stunned. Putting her hand on his, Mieko-*sensei* smiled up at the lancers. "We are honored to accept your service, gentlemen." She glanced over at me, seeing my frown. "Although, Inuji-*san*, I believe that you owe an apology to Hachihime-*sama*, Murasaki-*san*, Emi-*san*, and Toumi-*san*."

"Of course, M— Monogami-*sama*." Stiff-legged, he walked over to where we were seated, knelt, and touched his bare head to the stone. "Ladies. Please accept my most sincere apologies for my actions at Phoenix Temple. I was doing my best to fulfil my duty in following my lord. I hope you can forgive me."

Emi, Toumi, and I looked at Hachihime. She pursed her lips but then rolled her eyes and shrugged. "Oh, fine. But may I suggest, Inuji-*san*, that you stop obeying orders without thinking about them? Because a samurai's duty is to obey his lord, but not without question."

"Yes, my lady. Of course, you are right, my lady."

All four of us forgave him, though I could tell Toumi was doing it under protest.

———

As the feast continued, the sun sank halfway to the horizon, and the crowd began to get giddier, I let the other women know I wanted to leave for a bit but would be back before it got too late.

I expected them to ask why, but the three of them looked at each other and tipped their heads in acknowledgement. Toumi said, "Get out of here, Mouse. Say hi to your mom and our new sister for us, will you?"

I grinned. "I will. Thanks. I'll be back before dark."

Hachihime wagged a finger at me. "See you do, young lady!"

Still smiling, I stood and bowed. "I will, my lady."

In my silk *miko* outfit, I followed the path I'd walked a thousand times from the gate, through the pine woods, and down the lane into the collection of houses where I had grown up.

Broad-shouldered Miku was carrying a dog-sized pig up the lane. "Hey, Miku!" I called.

She nodded, as if we had seen each other that morning, and not a year before. "Risuko."

I was still giggling when I walked under the bare-branched cherry tree and into my old home.

My mother and sister were sitting next to the fire, getting ready to eat dinner. It felt as if they had been waiting for me.

I knelt, touching my head to the *tatami*. "*Okā-san. Imōto-san.*"

My sister goggled at me.

My mother narrowed her eyes. "Yes, *Musume-san?*"

"I am going to be leaving soon. Perhaps tomorrow. As I told you when I last visited, Lord Oda has returned our rank, and with it the town of Oak Leaf. I was hoping that you would join me, Emi, and Toumi in making our home there."

They weren't at all excited about the idea at first. But when I pointed out that we would be able to have a home that was relatively safe and *ours*, and that we would have money, they agreed.

And then I showed them *Otō-san*'s poem.

It won't surprise you to know that we all cried for some time.

———

As the sun began to turn the western sky eight million shades of red and gold, I was up in the same pine I had been in when Lady Chiyome had found me the year before.

Climbing it had been easier than I remembered. On the other hand, I couldn't climb quite as high since I was no longer starving.

Looking toward the castle, I saw smoke from the bonfires in the courtyard. The party was still going strong. Tokugawa and Oda banners floated above the highest tower—the room where my friends and I had slept. Where Lord Takeda had died.

My eyes were red from the tears that I had cried with my mother and sister, but I had to admit, there above the forest, no one near me, I had never felt so *not* alone.

Epilogue – Murasaki

urasaki means purple. *Murasaki* means a small plant whose roots are used in medicine and for making purple dye. *Murasaki* means the author of one of the greatest love tales, and also one of the characters in her tale.

Murasaki means me.

A year ago, I left the shadow of Lord Imagawa's castle. Ragged, starving, lost, and alone—aside from the strange old noblewoman and her enormous carriers who were dragging me down the road and into the unknown. Purchased away from my family. A family stripped of its birthright.

I ride away now knowing who I am, and who I am with. Well-fed and strong, in elegant clothes that bear my own restored clan's *mon*, I find I couldn't care less about those things. I am more concerned with my sister, riding behind me, her arms tight around my waist. With my mother, who is laughing—laughing!—with her nephew on the horse next to ours. Toumi and Hachihime are laughing too, though it sounds as if their joke is less polite than Harē's. Beside them, Emi sits behind Aimaru, her head resting on his armored shoulder.

His armor, too, now bears the Kano crest.

With the fingers not holding the reins, I trace the lines of my father's swords where they rest in front of my saddle.

I will use these swords to defend, not to attack. If I do harm, I trust it will be to prevent even greater harm.

I will face the consequences of those actions, both in this life and in those to come.

And I know that I will face them with my friends and family—these people who are riding with me.

I pity anyone who tries to attack us on the road.

There are many others I now know I can trust.

Lady Chiyome, who rides behind me, carried by the Little Brothers in her palanquin, will leave us at Pineshore and return to the Full Moon. She must decide what to do with her school and her *kunoichi*. I know we will always be welcome there.

Lord and Lady Monogami—Masugu-*san* and Mieko-*sensei*—rode off at dawn with what was left of his squadron of lancers to begin the process of winning back Wingtip Province from the traitorous Akita.

Lord Matsudaira stayed at the castle, conferring with his captains to prepare for the coming war with the Takeda. Lord Oda stayed to plan their strategy together.

Can we trust them? Perhaps. For today.

The air is sour with the scent of approaching snow.

We are headed to Oak Leaf. My town. *Our* town. I don't know what it holds for us, whether the people will accept long-vanished samurai clans represented by three heavily armed young women. But I know we will make it work.

Can one small girl win a war? I didn't think so this summer.

And no. I don't think so now.

But together?

Together we can do *anything*.

My name is Kano Murasaki. But most people call me Squirrel.

Risuko.

Thanks so much for travelling with RISUKO!

R isuko and I appreciate you joining us on this journey. We'd love to know what you thought, as always.

Feel free to email me at **david@risuko.net** or reach out on the website, **SeasonsoftheSword.com**. Send me your thoughts, your questions. And when you post a review of the book, I'd love it if you'd share that with me too!

And no—this is not the end of the voyage! I'm planning to explore this world in short stories, a video game, a television series (!), and possibly more novels. Stay tuned!

———

N ot ready to leave Risuko and her friends behind?

Get exclusive stories available only on **SeasonsoftheSword.com** —prequels, sequels, crossovers and more! By signing up, you'll also be the first to get news about new books, giveaways, information about Risuko's world, all for free.

Plus, I personally reply to every email because this community means everything to me.

Want a feel for what it's like? Check out on of the prequel stories on the next page!

Join us at **SeasonsoftheSword.com/sign-up** or use the QR code below. Your inbox is about to get way more interesting.

DAVID KUDLER

david@risuko.net

Kunoichi Companion Tales

MEET THE *KUNOICHI* BEFORE RISUKO DOES!
Kunoichi Companion Tales introduce characters and themes from
the Seasons of the Sword novels, and are currently available free
exclusively to Risuko subscribers, along with news, blog posts,
and other exclusive gifts!

Find out more on
SeasonsoftheSword.com
Follow on:

twitter.com/RisukoKunoichi • risuko-*chan*.tumblr.com
facebook.com/risuko.books • instagram.com/RisukoKunoichi
risuko.livejournal.com • tiktok.com/@kanomurasaki

White Robes

The first of the **Kunoichi Companion Tales***, this story shows Lady Chiyome's fateful meeting with Mieko and Kuniko, and the birth of the Full Moon.*

White snow. White robes.

White is the color of grief.

This isn't a new thought to Chiyome. At this point it isn't even a very interesting thought.

Grief is not terribly interesting.

As her carriers lug her, squashed in her palanquin, up the switchbacks to Rice Paddy Pass, Chiyome considers the snow covering the slopes above and below, all around.

Not terribly interesting.

And yet as the garrison that guards the pass finally appears at the top of the mountainside, it strikes Chiyome as appropriate that the whole landscape is covered in white. The whole nation is wrapped in grief. A hundred years of war have left no province, no family free from more than its natural share of sorrow.

Even so, Chiyome feels her own losses like physical wounds. Two daughters and a son, taken by disease and Uesugi raids — years later and yet these still swath her in blank, white grief. And of course, her husband. That loss is the hardest of all, as unforgiving as these mountains.

Not terribly interesting.

A crimson Takeda flag adds a startling flash of color over the wooden palisade wall that marks the very top of Rice Paddy Pass — why it's called that, no one has ever been ever been able to explain to Chiyome. She doesn't particularly want to spend the night among her husband's old soldiers, but the Little Brothers have had a long, miserable walk up from the valley and they won't make their way down to a safe shelter until well after dark, and so as her palanquin reaches the brief moment of equilibrium there at the frozen, white top of the world, she leans out the small window of her cramped box and barks, "In. We're spending the night. Bugano had better have heated the baths."

The carriers grunt in acknowledgment and turn toward the palisade gates. Steam streams from their bald heads like snow from the top of these mountains.

White.

The baths are in fact hot — the garrison has little to do here but gather wood and watch for enemy invasion, and so the hot tub is in fact blessedly hot, returning a small semblance of humanity to Chiyome. The Littler Brothers have set up her traveling tent inside the garrison's storeroom — better than the stables, at least, and private. The days when she might have enjoyed a night trapped in the company of a hundred young men are long gone.

When Lieutenant Bugano shows up with a serving of the garrison's rations, steaming if greasy, Chiyome waves her carriers away to take their own turn in the baths. They've more than earned it.

"Chiyome-*sama*," murmurs the dog-faced officer, placing her bowl on the traveling table. "You honor us, as always."

"Liar," Chiyome says, and then laughs when the lieutenant has the good grace to look uncomfortable. Chiyome can't remember the last time she laughed. "I'm a soldier's wife — was a soldier's wife. I know you're not running an inn. But where else are we to stop?"

"Indeed." Bugano laughs along, but it's still uncomfortable, and that makes Chiyome laugh some more. He raises an eyebrow, and she does her best to try to be moderately polite.

Bugano was there at Midriver Island, after all. He fought with her husband, was there when he fell. Bugano deserves some respect, even if his face is unfortunate.

Nodding, he says, "Actually, we have a couple more travelers who begged our hospitality tonight. That's what I was going to ask you about."

"Ask?"

"It…" He scratches the top of his balding head. "It's a couple of young ladies. Shrine maidens, trying to get away from the fighting."

"There's nowhere away from the fighting."

Now Bugano's eyes meet Chiyome's, and she can see that his eyes too are filled with white grief. All he says is, "No. Not really." Then he shakes his head, causing his jowls to quiver. "But away from where it's worst right now."

"Shrine maidens?" Chiyome can't imagine why a pair of *miko* would be trekking through the mountains in mid-winter, but she supposes everyone has something to get away from.

"Yes. And see…" Again Bugano scratches his head. "See, one of 'em's real pretty, but even the other one is getting more attention from my men than's good. I was wondering if they could spend the night in here. Not in your tent!" he adds. "Just, you know, in the storeroom. Away from the men."

"Ah." Chiyome knows that there are women who earn a meager living providing soldiers with feminine companionship, but it is not an easy life, and clearly these young women would prefer not to walk that particular path. "Certainly. They are welcome to sleep in the storeroom."

With a nod and a grim smile, Bugano leaves Chiyome to her barely edible meal.

By the time she has eaten all that she can stomach, there is a knock on the rough wooden door. Again, Chiyome gives a snort of laughter, caught by the incongruity of the whole affair. "Come in."

Two figures in red and white shuffle through the door, carrying bedrolls. One looks like a man in a dress — broad-shouldered, square-faced, and sullen. The other couldn't be more different. *Pretty*, the lieutenant called her, and yes, she certainly is that. Fine features and smooth skin. But there's something about the way she moves….

"My lady," the two girls in shrine maidens' dress murmur, kneeling on the dirty wooden floor.

"Oh, for goodness sake," Chiyome clucks, "close the door. It's cold."

The bigger one slides the big door shut with one hand, turns around, and they both kneel and touch their heads to the dirty floor. Without looking up, the pretty one says, "Thank you, my lady, for letting your humble servants share your quarters."

"Well, they're hardly mine," answers Chiyome. "It's a spare storeroom the lieutenant is kind enough to let me have when I'm stuck here. Now, what are your names?"

"Mieko is this humble servant's name," says the pretty one.

"Kuniko, lady," says the other.

"Somehow, I don't get the feeling that either of you is at all humble, or much of a servant for that matter. Are you even *miko*?"

"Oh, yes, my lady," both girls murmur into the boards.

"Mph." She finds herself staring at them. Chiyome knows liars, knows she's being lied to, but can't spot the lie. And she isn't sure she cares. "Fine. You're sleeping out here." She points at the bags of rice against one wall. Then she points to her tent. "I'm sleeping in there. My men are sleeping in the barracks. If you so much as open the flap of my tent, they will happily break your fingers, do you understand?"

"Yes, my lady," they repeat, heads still down.

"Mmph.

—

Chiyome wakes with a start, the tendrils of dream streaming behind her. *A girl with white hair flying through the snowy night....*

Shaking her head, she shivers, though her thick bedroll is comparatively comfortable and warm.

From outside of her tent comes a click, the slow creak of a hinge. *What are those two—?* Chiyome stands, wrapping her silks around her, and peers through the entrance to her tent.

At first she sees nothing; all seems still. But then she notices the open storeroom door and watches as two bulky shadows sneak through—not out into the snow, but in toward where the two girls are curled up like cats on the floor.

Chiyome is about to shout, to call for the Little Brothers, when the larger of the girls, the one with the square face—Kuniko—leaps to her feet as if she hasn't been sleeping. As if she was waiting for just such an invasion. Knees bent, she balls her fists and grunts, "Get out."

One of the shadows chuckles and steps toward Kuniko. "Like this one," he laughs. "She's got fight."

The other one—Bugano's soldiers, they must be—says, "That leaves the pretty one for me." He steps toward Mieko, who Chiyome is shocked to see standing, motionless. Unflinching. *When did she stand?*

"Please," the smaller girl whispers. "Please don't make me hurt you."

Chiyome, who has been frozen between rage and terror at what she was watching, gawks at Mieko, even as the soldier laughs. *Don't make me HURT you? What can the idiot girl be thinking?*

The first soldier reaches out to grab Kuniko, but the girl slaps his hand away with the knuckles of one hand. "I do like 'em feisty," he says with a grunt, and steps toward her again.

She punches at his face; he grabs her hand, but doesn't anticipate the swift knee to his crotch that bends him forward. Before he can howl and push her down, Kuniko slams her free fist into his throat, then as he begins to crumple, grabs his hair and slams his face against her still-raised knee.

He drops to the floor as if shot.

Chiyome's eyes flick to Mieko, standing statue-still over the other soldier, who lies motionless on his back. The man's eyes are open. A dark stain that must be blood spills from his ear onto the floor.

In the doorway, Chiyome sees two more large shadows. The Little Brothers. Her carriers stand wide-eyed, gawking at the scene.

It reassures Chiyome that her carriers are as shocked by what they've just seen as she is. Otherwise, she would be tempted to believe it never happened. Trying to sound as if she is in control, she barks, "Take these two ruffians out of here. Drop them with Bugano."

The carriers bow and drag the two men—the one flailing, gasping man and the slack body—out of the storeroom.

Chiyome considers the two girls, still dressed in their oh-so-innocent *miko* garb. They are standing now, no pretense of humility. Kuniko's face is dark, her nostrils flaring. Mieko looks as if she's been enjoying a lovely nighttime stroll, except for the dark circles in the middle of her cheeks and the splash of dark red across her white sleeve.

"Well, well, well," Chiyome laughs. "Aren't you two entertaining."

"Yes, my lady," Kuniko grunts through clenched teeth. Mieko says nothing.

Two homeless girls, Chiyome thinks. *Harmless. And yet they took down two Takeda soldiers in less time than it would have taken me to tie my robe shut.* "You two have done this before. You've had training."

This time Mieko joins Kuniko in mumbling a polite assent.

"Weapons? Or just your hands and feet?" Not that their hands and feet weren't lethally effective.

The girls stare at each other for a moment; even the ridiculously calm Mieko has the good grace to look nervous when she says, "Glaives, my lady."

Ah. Chiyome smiles at them. It is clear now: these are no village girls. They must be from a samurai family or possibly even nobility to have received training in the long-bladed spears. *Who would think it?*

An image: a beautiful screen Chiyome saw at the imperial palace, when her father brought her there to observe some ceremony or other. The screen seemed to her child's imagination to have shown the whole of Japan, peopled by thousands of figures: armed samurai, elegant nobles, monks, merchants, and, scattered throughout, young girls in red and white.

An army.

An anonymous army. Invisible. Able to go everywhere. Able to gather information. Able to strike.

With her toe Chiyome writes on the dusty floorboards: *ku* (く), then *no* (ノ), and then finally ichi (一). "Can you two read?"

Kuniko scowls down at the marks. "Nine... in... one?"

Mieko's peers at Chiyome. She murmurs, "Kunoichi."

Kuniko blinks at her companion. "Kuno... What's a *kunoichi*?"

Mieko's eyes remain on Chiyome. She knows.

"Ah," says Chiyome, grinning to herself, "it is... a very special kind of woman. Tell me, ladies. Would you like to end this ridiculous war? Would you like to be kunoichi?"

"Yes, my lady," the girls answer. Kuniko's eyes are dark, but Mieko's glisten.

———

White snow. White robes.

White robes over red skirts.

White is the color of grief.

Red is the color of blood, the color of luck—the color of weddings.

A *miko* marries herself to that which cannot die. A *kunoichi* marries herself to duty, and to Death.

Watching the two *special* girls walking alongside her palanquin, Chiyome considers that, perhaps, the time for mourning has come to a close.

An anonymous army.

Much more interesting.

Author Note + Acknowledgements

I have to say, it's more than a bit hard to write *owari* (The End) on the Seasons of the Sword.

I first thought of the story almost twenty years ago, and so Risuko and her friends (and enemies) have been part of my life for a long, long time.

But every year comes to an end, and so does this one. I hope you have enjoyed the trip as much as I have.

I do want to discuss this book on two fronts.

First, the original idea that I had all of those years ago was for what I thought was a single book. I wrote and outline that started with Risuko up the tree, spying on the castle, brought her up into the mountains, then the capital, then back to the castle, where she confronted the ghosts of her past.

Of course, in the course of fleshing out that outline, I discovered that I had written almost two-thirds as many words as you'll find in this volume, but I hadn't even gotten a quarter of the way into my story!

It took me a while, but eventually I figured out that I had to split the outline up into four books—and so Seasons of the Sword was born.

The actual storylines for *Bright Eyes* and *Kano* both ended up changing quite a bit from that early outline, as did the last few chapters of *Risuko* and the first half of this book.

But the last half is pretty close to what I planned all those years ago. Actually writing out scenes that I'd been imagining for decades was a strange and humbling experience. It was also very nice to feel as if the story that I'd been trying to set up all seemed to fit.

I hope you felt the same way!

I also want to discuss these books as historical fiction.

I've tried my best throughout the series to stay as historically accurate as I could. Ironically, *Murasaki* is the book in the series most crammed with historical events and characters.

It's also the one where, in order to tell the best possible story, I'm afraid I had to fudge things a bit. For example, by the beginning 1571, the Lord Governor of the Three Rivers had already changed his name to Tokugawa Ieyasu, a name that rings quite loudly in Japanese history books. However, Takeda Shingen was already a major character, and I didn't want to confuse my readers with too many *T* names, so I had him keep the Matsudaira clan name until the end of this book.

Likewise, if you look at most scholarly books and articles, they'll tell you that Lord Takeda died in 1573 (by a sniper's bullet or possibly illness, not be a bratty bride's blade), almost two full years after the events of this book. The Takeda clan *did* try to keep his death a secret, since the Tiger of Kai was literally the foundation of their army's success. I simply extended the ruse. A lot.

If you are interested in the story of the Mountain's death and the subsequent coverup, check out Akira Kurasawa's amazing movie *Kagemusha* ("Shadow Warrior"). It's a a fictionalized telling, told from the point of view of the dead lord's double, and it really is wonderful. It obviously inspired me enormously in writing this book.

In any case, as I've said before, the tightrope a historical novelist has to write is making the most out of both halves of the job title. A historian must present facts as accurately as possible (although complete accuracy can be impossible—trying to track down the movements of the various historical figures in autumn, 1571 made me pull out some of my hair, since any one of the lords might have been said to have been in locations all over Japan at any one time). A novelist tries to tell a compelling, moving, interesting story.

It's not always possible to do both. Where I've had to compromise, I hope you will forgive me. I hope, at least, that the story is worth it!

———

When *Risuko* first came out, I joked that if it takes a village to raise a child, it takes an army to publish a novel. That army has continued to grow, and it is a pleasure to be able to thank them once again.

First, I'd like to thank my middle school English teacher—who happens also to be my mother and a published poet in her own right. As I mentioned in the dedication for *Kano*, she was my first audience as a writer, and one of the first to read and comment on each of my novels—until this one. Although

ALS took her from us last summer, what I learned to her about the power of words to pain pictures and tell stories informs every page of this book.

Also, once again, I'd like to thank Brenda and Donal Brown, who read the manuscript for *Risuko* long before it was finished and provided both their wisdom and their apparently bottomless enthusiasm, which sustained me through many of the darkest passages in my journey to bring Risuko's to print. They also introduced my book to Danielle Svetcov (see below), for which alone they deserve literary Elysium—if they hadn't already earned it in a thousand other ways. The dedication for this volume is the least that they deserve.

Danielle Svetcov of Levine|Greenberg|Rostan Literary Agency continues to represent these books as they seek out new audiences. Alexis Boozer Sterling and Maury Sterling of small idea media are currently working to bring Risuko's world to one of those audiences, the world of video, which excites me enormously, and I hope excites you.

Sugandha Gupta once again provided a sensitive, thoughtful, thorough, *quick* copyedit that improved this book in many ways. She provided a wonderful answer to the question, *Quis editorem edit?* ("Who edits the editor?")

The Risuko Beta Team provided incredible feedback as I was completing the book. A heartfelt *dōmo arigatō* to Hazel Levinson and Ania Mieszkowska, as well as One Anjana, Stephanie Curtner, Azalea Dabill, Stephen Gerringer, Suzanne Hartog, Rob Henn, R. Mar, Michael Lambert, Shannon, Carson Smith, Cherrie Walker, and a small army of anonymice for helping me see where I'd gone wrong (and right).

Without the Kickstarter backers who backed the campaigns that supported the launches of *Risuko* and *Bright Eyes*, this third and fourth books literally would not have been published. Margot Avery, Kendra Arimoto, Roger Beckett, Isaac "Will It Work" Dansicker, Sylvia-Michelle Hostetter, Alithea Howes, John Idlor, Ania Mieszkowska, Empress Diana and Imperial Princess Amara of the Most Illustrious Lee Dynasty, Lenhoff Family, magycmyste@gmail.com, mywayhoff11@aol.com, Ripley Patton, Roman Pauer, Cara Melia Pico, Jason Png, Ritske Rensma, Jeremy Reppy, Kalilah Robinson, Roy Romasanta, Rachel S., Riccardo Sartori, Ken Schneyer, Robert Walter, Susan R. Woodward, Eron Wyngarde, Heesung Yang, and yet more anonymice—you are angels in every sense of the word.

I dedicated *Murasaki* to my wife Maura Vaughn for many reasons. First of all, she has read this book more than anyone other than me. Also, she has put up with Risuko and all of her friends monopolizing my focus for so many years. Having been fortunate enough to be her husband for over three decades, I am daily thankful for her Chiyome-level insight, Masugu-level support, and Mieko-level patience.

Last and greatest as always is my debt to my own two daughters, Sasha and Julia. When I began writing *Risuko,* they were young—in Julia's case, too young to read the book on her own. As I publish *Murasaki,* it stuns me to realize that they are now both older than Mieko or Masugu. Regardless, they are wonders in their own rights. I continue to hope that I have captured half of their spirit in Murasaki and her friends.

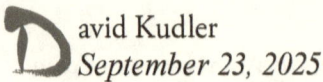avid Kudler
September 23, 2025

Also from Stillpoint/Atalanta

Kunoichi Companion Tales

Seasons of the Sword prequel stories

Meet the characters before Risuko does!
Sign up now and get these stories FREE!
SEASONSOFTHESWORD.COM/SIGN-UP

Winter Tales

David Kudler & Maura Vaughn

Holiday stories from around the world!
STILLPOINTDIGITAL.COM/ATALANTA

DAVID KUDLER is not afraid of heights. He just has a healthy respect for depths. "I'm as surprised as anyone," he says, "that I've written a series of books featuring a young woman who loves to be as high up in the air as possible."

His multi-award-winning Seasons of the Sword historical adventure novels (*Risuko, Bright Eyes, Kano,* and *Murasaki*) have been featured in *Foreword Magazine, Kirkus,* and others. *Risuko* graced the cover of *Publisher's Weekly.*

Also an editor and publisher, he's overseen the publication of more than two hundred titles including Joseph Campbell's best-selling *Hero with a Thousand Faces,* an exploration of hero stories from across the ages and around the world.

He lives just north of the Golden Gate Bridge with his wife, actor/teacher/author Maura Vaughn, their wordsmith daughters, and their (apparently) non-literary cat.

For more information about David Kudler and his writing, visit

SeasonsoftheSword.com

You can also follow him on social media:
twitter.com/dkudler • davidkudler.tumblr.com
facebook.com/davidkudlerauthor • davidkudler.pinterest.com

www.ingramcontent.com/pod-product-compliance
Lightning Source LLC
Chambersburg PA
CBHW022045240626
47154CB00007B/2567